C000092957

CRASH

ISOBEL ROSS

BLOODHOUND
— B O O K S —

Copyright © 2024 Isobel Ross

The right of Isobel Ross to be identified as the Author of the Work has been
asserted by her in accordance with the Copyright, Designs and Patents Act 1988.

First published in 2024 by Bloodhound Books.

Apart from any use permitted under UK copyright law, this publication may only
be reproduced, stored, or transmitted, in any form, or by any means, with prior
permission in writing of the publisher or, in the case of reprographic production,
in accordance with the terms of licences issued by the Copyright Licensing
Agency.
All characters in this publication are fictitious and any resemblance to real
persons, living or dead, is purely coincidental.

www.bloodhoundbooks.com

Print ISBN: 978-1-916978-84-3

ONE

MONDAY 8TH SEPTEMBER, 2008

My brain felt fractured, my mind a mess of images as I drove too fast through the narrow country lanes, noticing oncoming cars too late, relying on other drivers to save themselves. Hedgerows reared and swerved, the road surface shimmered, a pheasant ran for cover, briefly iridescent. Car horns sounded, loud at first, then faded behind me.

I parked several streets from the school, ashamed that I'd arrived safely because of the skill of other drivers. In the driving mirror, I wiped away mascara from my cheeks and brushed my hair. I was calmer, but fear dragged at the corners of my eyes and mouth. I felt unfairly angry with Dan. Had he been there, I might have hit him. Yet the frustration of our awkward meeting, the one that had almost made me late for Tom, was my fault. I had planned to tell him about the medical investigations ahead of me but I'd lost courage to say the words. There was too much to explain. Of course, he hadn't noticed my distraction until it was almost time to part and by then, it was too late. I had no idea when we would risk meeting again. His absence felt like a hole, a hollow emptiness more powerful than his presence.

I stayed in the car, sliding down in my seat and closing my

eyes. Tom would find me. A moment later, he tapped on the window, and I sat up to unlock the door. Each day his appearance seemed to change as adolescence grappled with his childlike body. Today, in the shadows of the car's interior, his nose seemed larger on his face, as if borrowed from someone else, like the false noses sold in gift shops, the ones that catch your hair in the elastic.

Tom looked at me, his eyes narrowed. 'You look like shit. Are you okay?' His voice cracked on the upward cadence of the question. 'Been talking to the school?'

I turned the key in the ignition as he threw his bag onto the back seat. 'No, should I have been?'

He stared straight ahead. 'No worries, it's nothing. I'll tell you later. Let's drive.'

I inched the car through groups of parents and children at the pedestrian crossing outside the school gates.

'Your voice is breaking,' I said. 'I hadn't noticed.'

'Yeah, it happens. Mum, I'm fifteen. Come on, let's get home.'

Our journey out of the city was slow. Almost stationary traffic inched towards each junction, only a few cars forcing their way through at each turn of the lights. I blew out heavily, exasperated at the infuriating congestion. Had every parent of every child in Leicester chosen this very day to collect them by car? Sweat trickled between my shoulder blades but the roar of the air conditioning felt like torture. I released the soft top of the car.

'That's cool. Dad doesn't allow the top down in the city.' Tom reached for a CD. 'Can we put this on, really loud.'

'No,' I snapped. 'It will attract attention. What is everyone doing? Why don't they walk their kids home from school? Why aren't they all at work?'

'Like you?' Tom stared at me.

'We live miles away; I have to pick you up. All these other people,' I waved a hand airily to encompass all the white vans, buses and cars that crowded us, 'they have a choice.'

'That's so unfair,' Tom argued. 'Anyway, if you'd let me go to the local school, I could go by bus. It's your decision to destroy the planet for my education. My school is rubbish, by the way. I hate it there.'

I glanced at Tom, stung by this rebuke, but seeing him smile I reached out to touch his face. His skin felt rough, where part-healed spots and stubble had replaced the child's soft cheeks. I felt the frustration drain from me.

'Tom,' I said, with exaggerated patience. 'I know what you think of The Mount, but there wasn't a choice, not once you'd been asked to leave Ashridge Grange. The school has to be secure; your dad is clear about that.'

Tom grunted. 'That says more about Dad than me, don't you think?'

'It doesn't matter what I think.' I sighed.

We crawled past Victorian parks and churches, framed by elegant Edwardian terraces. These prosperous streets were followed by rows of redbrick terraces and small shops selling Asian sweets and jewellery.

'Dad and I lived here when we were students, just up that street there. Did I ever tell you?'

'You've mentioned it once or twice.'

'That Co-op, it used to be a proper greengrocer.'

'Yeah, you've said that too.'

We inched through more traffic in silence until, at last, a flyover led to a ring road, which I'd read had ripped out the city's medieval heart. I decided not to mention this to Tom. The traffic began to flow, and we reached the last fifteen minutes of our journey home, turning off a dual carriageway through the mirrored glass and steel of a new business park, promising more shopping and housing to claim a wasteland that had once been farms. The city stuttered and fell away into narrow lanes, heavy with hawthorn berries. Through the open top, I caught the spicy scent of yarrow, which crowded the verges, and slowed the car to turn into our village. The cottages that lined the main street were almost all built of honey-coloured stone, but the village pub was rendered and whitewashed, standing out from its neighbours like one good tooth. The pub's hanging baskets were beginning to fade, and the cottages looked rested and expectant, on the edge of summer's end.

Outside a high brick wall, built to match the colour of the village, we waited for the electronic gates to recognise us. They trembled, then hesitated, as if unsure, before inching open. I circled the car around the barren fountain, a little too fast, tyres dragging in the gravel, and parked below the threshold of our newly built Queen Anne style house. The electronic gates would deter anyone who was after Carl's ideas, since industrial espionage was a more gentlemanly affair, I now understood, than rough old burglary. Was this really true or were our fancy gates an early sign of Carl's paranoia, when such arguments still lay on the right side of normal?

Tom tossed his schoolbag under the hall table and ran upstairs to his bedroom, calling out, 'What's to eat?' from the landing.

The slam of his bedroom door left no room for a reply. I held myself in the cool hall and smelt furniture polish underlaid by freesias. The gilt mirror reflected the flowers and above them, my face, dark shadows under the eyes and deep lines around my mouth. I pulled my cheeks up towards my ears, which stretched my lips, making me look even more canine than usual. A tight, angry feeling returned, crouching like a weight on my forehead. Blood throbbed in my ears.

To the mirror, I repeated the words I'd just said to Dan. 'Do you think we'll ever be together?'

Why had I bothered to ask him? We'd had this conversation before. It never led anywhere. Today, with my world about to change, I had forced him to say it again.

'Alice, you know I can't leave Sarah and the children. You said you felt the same about Carl and your family. Things might be different one day... you know how much I want to be with you.'

I had pushed him again, challenging. 'What we have only works if things go on the same, but they won't, they can't.'

Dan had frowned at me, puzzled, and brushed his lips across mine, disregarding that we might be observed. 'Then we'll cross that bridge together.'

In the kitchen, Honey slowly became aware that she might not be alone. She scented the air and listened, her head on one side, then stood up in her basket and shook herself, stretching her legs and wagging her tail in a half-hearted greeting, not quite certain whether anyone was with her. I knelt down and took her ears in my hands and breathed in her dog sweat.

'Poor Honey,' I said aloud, and she yawned in recognition. 'Let's go for a walk.'

'I'm taking Honey out,' I shouted, from the hall. There was no response from Tom. I climbed the stairs and pushed open the door to Tom's bedroom, dangling Honey's lead. He didn't look up but waved at me without taking his eyes from his PlayStation. His shoes lay on the floor and the room already smelt of unwashed boy.

Honey staggered, stiff-legged, towards the back door, shaking her collar. We crossed the lawns where I had left a pair of gardening gloves on the grass beside the rose garden. I picked them up and pushed them into my trouser pockets, keying open the gate in the wall before putting Honey on a long lead. It was a slow walk through the woods as she stopped and examined every smell. I waited on a warm, rotting log at the edge of a glade and watched Honey circle away from me, hesitating every few yards to check the air for my presence. A few remnants of bluebell flowers hung listlessly, etiolated in the shadows of the trees.

I dug into the bark with a stick and watched a woodlouse scuttle away, determined to find a safe haven in the woodland litter and save his tiny life. This time, things had worked out for him, but I already felt certain that this medical problem of mine wasn't going to come right. If that was the case, everything would have to change. Dan had no idea because I had chosen not to share it with him, or anything else about my car crash of a life. There were no bridges we would cross together.

I felt my mood lift. Blaming Dan was unfair. Whatever else was happening, there was still the company of an old dog, this wood and the sun falling across us in shadows that were just beginning to lengthen. If I can have a bit more life, I bargained, I'll make my days count.

Honey snuffled her way back and sat down, panting. 'Sadly,' I spoke aloud, scratching behind her ears, 'you have no choice and that's okay for you. But I haven't had the life I want. I'm still waiting for it to start.'

'Mum, is Dad at home?' Tom called from the landing as I crouched down to remove Honey's lead.

'No, he's in London,' I said. 'Can you come down now and give Honey some water while I check to see if there are any phone messages.'

Tom descended the stairs head forwards, gripping the banister with both hands and swinging one leg over, as he had done ever since he became tall enough to manage such a feat. At the bottom, he struck his forehead with the palm of his hand as if he had just remembered something. 'It's nothing serious but the head teacher wants to see you and Dad.' Tom dug deep into his schoolbag and brought out an envelope that already looked days old.

I held the letter between two fingers. 'How long have you had this?'

Tom reddened. 'Just today, Mum, I promise.'

He followed me into the kitchen, where we sat across from each other, on opposite sides of the table. I searched for my new glasses in my handbag and peered at the words. Tom had been found with a small amount of cannabis in his possession. Normally this would result in immediate expulsion, but he had denied any knowledge, insisting it had been planted. To give Tom the benefit of the doubt, he would have two days at home to think about his story, with a meeting on Thursday to discuss his future at the school. There followed some placatory words about the long and positive relationship the school had enjoyed with our family. The letter was signed by the head teacher's secretary.

I threw the letter down. 'How could you be so stupid?'

A flicker of shame passed across Tom's face, quickly replaced by sullen bravado. 'I took some from Dad's room. It was just for me and Owen.'

I felt my cheeks burn, as if I'd been slapped. 'You've been in Dad's study? You've involved Owen in this?'

'No... yes. Owen went in. He said it was stupid we couldn't go into Dad's room. He found the stuff just lying about on the floor. We didn't pass any around. Anyway, it was found straight away.'

7

When was it ever possible for Tom and his friend to have been unsupervised, in this house?

'What day was this?'

'On Friday when his mum collected us from school. We came over here on the bus. Dad was out and you were at work.'

I rubbed my temples. I couldn't look at him. 'Did Owen's mother, I mean Madeleine... did she know where you were going?'

'Of course not, we went out when she had her afternoon surgery. There was something we needed from here.'

I heard a shriek... my own voice. 'Dope. You needed dope. Because you're both using it. How did you get in? How often have you done this? What on earth were you doing taking drugs to school?'

Tom raised both hands, as if to push back my anger. 'Stop asking me so many questions!'

Outside, car tyres crunched on the gravel and an engine rattled like a tractor before shutting down. It was a taxi. I waited and held my breath, listening for footsteps and Carl's key in the lock.

'Dad's home. Anyway...' Tom jumped up from the table but stayed next to me. We heard Carl moving in the hall, then the flush of the cloakroom toilet.

Honey lifted her head from her basket and gave a single bark before sighing and resting her head between her paws. Carl appeared at the kitchen door, dressed for London, his long hair brushed into a ponytail, sharpening the edges of his receding hairline. He wore a grey wool suit and a pale blue shirt, handmade for him by his London tailor. His image, secured by money, his electronic gates and me, remained secure. Only I knew about the row of identical suits and polished shoes, the safety net of someone no longer able to make choices.

Carl sat down, patting the chair next to him to encourage

Tom to join us. He grabbed at his tie. 'God, I need a drink. The flight from London was awful.'

I kept my voice low, just an innocent question, not a challenge. 'Did you fly the helicopter?'

'Of course, I've got to keep the hours up. I'll lose my licence otherwise.'

'What's the point of employing a pilot if you never let him fly? What does it matter if you lose your licence? We pay Tony to take you anywhere you need to go.'

Carl shrugged and rolled his eyes above my head at Tom, still standing at my shoulder. Nagging women, who needs them? I pressed on, unsure when I would next see Carl or even be able to speak to him.

'There's a letter here from Tom's school; we were just talking about it.'

From Carl's eyes, I saw there had been another glance between them, this time from son to father. 'She means she's been shouting at me,' Tom said.

Carl's lips curled, prepared to be amused. He jerked his head towards Tom. 'Come on, son, sit down next to me, while I hear this letter. I won't be angry.'

Tom slid into the seat next to his father.

Carl nodded, instructing me to begin. 'Go on, Alice, tell me the worst.'

I read the letter aloud, Tom closely watching his father and Carl leaning back, using his hands to sweep back his hair. I saw the tremor. We didn't have long.

When I'd finished, Carl pushed Tom hard on the shoulder. 'Don't steal my shit, you little prick, just ask first.' He cackled, like gunshot, too loud, too close. Tom glanced at Carl, then across at me, before joining in the laughter, both pairs of ice-blue eyes holding mine.

'Okay!' I banged the table, like a teacher trying to control a difficult class. 'I'll go into school with Tom, talk to the head, but don't pretend this will go away as easily as you both imagine. Having drugs on school premises is very serious. Using drugs when you're a child is very serious. Encouraging a child to take drugs is very serious.'

Carl shook his head and grinned at Tom. 'She's exaggerating, as usual. We'll offer to pay for a new computer suite. That will shut him up.'

Again, I saw the tremor from his hands as he steadied himself against the table, trying to stand up. 'I need to go up to my room for a while.'

Tom jumped from his seat to let his father pass.

'We must talk,' I said. 'Tom and Owen broke into the house, into your study.'

It was already too late. Carl's back was turned, and he weaved his way towards the kitchen door, pausing to grip the door frame as if about to pull it from the wall. He turned back to stare at me, his eyes glassy and vacant.

'Speak to Oliver,' he said. 'Tell him to upgrade the security to a level that can outwit a fifteen-year-old boy and not to employ the same fuckwit he used last time.'

Carl chuckled, lifting his thin shoulders, and winked at Tom before easing his way unsteadily from the room.

'Not if I can help it,' I said to myself, then more loudly, for Tom to hear, 'It's not funny, Tom. This isn't going to go away.'

TWO
MONDAY 8TH SEPTEMBER

I pushed Tom's door open without knocking. He had changed into a T-shirt and jeans and styled his hair to flop forward over his eyes. Music thumped from his stereo, and he didn't hear or see me come in, his head bent over his mobile. I scooped up his crumpled uniform from the floor and touched his shoulder.

Tom slid the phone under his thigh. 'Hey, Mum, it's manners to knock.'

'Sorry,' I said, without conviction. 'I'm going to the station to collect Fran. She's coming home for a few days. If you need anyone, Dad's upstairs.'

I don't know why I said it, except it was the sort of parental statement that was expected, no matter how ridiculous. Tom pulled the phone from under his jeans and began tapping the keys. He didn't bother replying.

I closed his door and stood at the bottom of the staircase leading to the attic. The sound of rock music from two generations, first Tom's, then Carl's, battled for space in my brain and I decided against climbing those stairs to let Carl know I was going out.

It was almost night-time, the sky a darkening blue. I stood on the doorstep, smelling the evening, our security system circling me in a pool of light. A fox, frozen in his traverse, stared with red eyes before fading into the dark. I retraced my route back into the city, driving the narrow lanes, the hedgerow trees pulled in close by my headlights. Between gaps in the trees, the sodium lights of the dual carriageway promised rescue and eventually, buildings on either side of the ring road rose around me like cubes of dark and light, sprinkled with windows still bright. I turned into the station with ten minutes to spare, and waited, watching the taxis inch forward to pick up a fare, their drivers sweeping back out through a regal brick arch that mirrored the one I had entered. I would not think about what I had left behind or what might be to come but switched on the radio, calmed by familiar voices, if not the words.

Fifteen minutes later, I left the car and stood in front of the arrivals board, arms folded. Fran's train was delayed by half an hour. The station coffee shop had closed. Ropes leading to a shuttered line of ticket windows held the empty space in an orderly queue. One remained open and the conversation between the ticket seller and a young couple with a baby in a pushchair, surely out too late, seemed intense. I caught snatches across the forecourt, their voices swelling and fading. It had something to do with renewing his young person's travel card and a compromise had not been reached.

Beyond the barrier, the barren, tiled corridor suddenly came alive with passengers disgorged from the London train. My throat tightened when I saw Fran, so like her father but redrawn in feminine form, except young and healthy, not wasted by drugs. She trundled her case towards me and waved, her arms and shoulders draped in layers of fabric, her hair scrunched into a ponytail. Once through the barrier, we hugged, her face and body held away from me, so that I was forced to kiss her hair.

In the car, I asked, 'So why have you got these days off work?'

'Zac needed to decorate the reception area, so he told me to go home.'

'That was generous of him.'

Fran snorted. 'I have to take it from my annual leave.'

'That doesn't seem fair.'

'Too right... hey, I saw an article today about Carl in one of those trade things that lie around in reception. His photo was on the front, that's what made me pick it up.'

'It must have been an old photo...'

'I only had a quick glance. He didn't look much like he does now.'

'What did it say?'

'I didn't read it all. It was so boring and anyway we're not supposed to read at the desk. Zac says it looks bad. A smiling face and smiling eyes, that's what our customers want to see when they come through the door.' Fran imitated her boss's accent in a sing-song voice. 'He's a twat.'

'Enough!' I reprimanded her, but Fran would mostly try to be helpful, and her sweet, pretty face and expensive telephone manner would do no harm to Zac's business.

'The headline said he's a reclusive multi-millionaire. We're not millionaires, are we?'

I paused before I replied. 'How many girls of only twenty have their own flat in London, paid for by their dad? Ella does too and she's just qualified. Neither of you pay any rent.'

'I don't want to be rich and I don't want anyone to know he's my father. My friends will take the... make fun of me. I ripped the article out and put it in the bin. Anyway, we don't act like we're millionaires.'

'You mean we don't meet film stars and throw big, expensive parties? All our money is tied up in the business. Do you understand what I'm saying? It's not really ours. I don't spend much do I?'

Fran glanced down at my faded jeans, grubby from my walk in the woods. 'You could if you wanted... perhaps you should. But why are they saying he's reclusive?' I could hear something, there was a catch in her voice, a slight clearing of the throat. She was anxious, but I couldn't pin down why. I waited; would she say more?

'Why are they saying he's reclusive?' she repeated. 'I mean, he's a weirdo right but he does go out?'

What is she really asking? I pressed on, hearing the quickening in Fran's breathing. 'Most people haven't seen Carl for ages. When he goes to London for meetings, he flies himself there and back and he only sees a very few people, but we can see him whenever we want.' We both knew this wasn't true.

'He's home right now,' I pushed on. 'He's probably fallen asleep in his office.'

We drove in silence until I spoke again. 'Dad doesn't seem to be too well. You might not see much of him.'

'Good... I've only come home because I'd nothing to do tomorrow. And don't call him Dad. To me, he's Carl.'

'Fran!'

'He's a smackhead. It's his own fault he's like this. Why do we put up with him?'

'He's not a smackhead,' I replied. 'I think we'd cope with heroin. He's addicted to crystal meth, it's totally different. We've been over this before.'

'Blah, blah... it is his fault, he decided to take it, nobody forced him.'

'He made a really bad choice, years ago. There's nothing we can do now except manage it. He can't live without the meth, but it will kill him.'

'I don't suppose you've told Tom yet.'

'No, I haven't. I don't think he'd understand.'

'You love secrets.'

My mouth fell open at this accusation, but it was true. The number of secrets I was keeping blocked any protest.

'Tom's in trouble at school. I'll let you talk to him about it, he'll probably open up to you. It seems he's been caught selling a small amount of cannabis.' Did the words 'a small amount' make it seem better?

'Not another addict in the family!' Fran protested.

'Yes, that's my worry too.'

Whenever Fran and I spoke about Carl, we would approach, circle around each other and then she would pull away, hiding behind resentment and anger. There were things that Fran needed to say to me about Carl, but she couldn't find the words and I had never been able to help her. A memory surfaced, one I preferred not to remember, when we were together in the kitchen of our old house. I can almost feel the warmth, smell the basil I'd torn with my bare hands. There was a tug on my hem, and Fran had her thumb in her mouth, grasping the scrunched-up corner of my skirt in her fist, using it to stroke her cheek.

Even now, I can feel her weight as I lifted her onto the kitchen worktop and wiped a smear of mud away from her nose with my fingers. Her hands and fingernails were caked with earth. Fran sucked on her dirty thumb while I washed her other hand with the sink cloth, then pulled the thumb from her mouth. It came away like a cork from a bottle. Her body felt hot and smelt sharp and dank from the leaf mould on her clothes.

'Daddy in garden,' she said, turning her grey eyes towards me at last. 'Daddy sleeping.' Fran struggled with this sound and at first I didn't understand.

'Daddy is sheeping in the garden?' Fran nodded and sighed.

'He's upstairs, Fran, not in the garden. Why don't you go and play with Ella?'

Fran shook her head and put her clean thumb back in her mouth, resting her head against my breast. I briskly rubbed her back; the casserole needed my attention. I put my arms under her armpits to lift her onto the floor, but she gripped my skirt, looking up at me.

'Daddy digs the flowers. In the garden.'

We found Carl where Fran had left him. People say that injured bodies can look like a pile of rags, and this is true. I thought the girls had thrown bedding out of an open window, but it was their father, face down in the freshly mulched soil. He had fallen from an upstairs window and the soft earth had saved him. Fran had dug the earth away from his mouth so that he could breathe. My little girl had watched him fall, had witnessed the madness of the fall. She was three years old.

I shook my head, trying to focus on the road now that my headlights were all that separated us from high hedgerows, guiding us back through a tunnel of foliage towards home. What was Carl taking, seventeen years ago? In the hospital, they said it was likely to be LSD, but it could have been a mixture of anything Claudio was able to supply him. For certain, it wasn't crystal meth. That came later.

Did Fran remember being praised by the paramedics, or was she still troubled by thoughts of Carl's ashen face and startled eyes? She'd been allowed to sit in the driver's seat of the ambulance as they'd worked to stabilise her father, and Ella had raged with jealousy when Fran was allowed to switch on the siren. We've never spoken about it since, never shared the memories. We have to do this before it's too late, but how to start?

At home, Fran dumped her bag in the hall and ran up to Tom's room. I sat alone in the kitchen, not bothering with the lights, my eyes adjusting to the dark shapes of kitchen appliances, the flashing digital clock on the microwave and the unwashed detritus of our last meal, still waiting on the counter. Nothing had changed except the certainty of time, for me and for Carl.

I felt my insides drop. The children might live their adult lives without me. If I didn't survive, I wouldn't be there to help them. Tom was still young, a child. Carl might become his sole parent and then Tom would lose him too. There was no one else, only Beatrice, Carl's mother, a woman who had failed Carl in every way possible a mother can betray her child. That woman wasn't getting her hands on Tom.

I began to cry, quietly and shamefully, not that there was anyone who could hear me, not even Honey, who had rested her head on my feet, snoring. I imagined bursting into Tom's room and turning off his music or shaking Carl awake from his stupor and shouting at them both. 'Look at me. Listen to me. You think I exist just to make everything all right for you, but things are going to change. We haven't got enough time left... we've left it too late to put things right.'

Instead of acting out this feverish scene, I stumbled upstairs and lay on my bed, first pausing outside Tom's room to eavesdrop. I heard nothing over his music, not even a murmured conversation between Tom and Fran. There were no sounds from Carl's attic; no music, no footsteps above me, not even his voice as he habitually mumbled to whomever he thought was listening. I was too tired, too wounded, to bother right now but I would check on him later.

THREE
MONDAY 8TH, TUESDAY 9TH SEPTEMBER

I climbed to the top of the house and tapped on Carl's study door. He didn't answer, so I pushed against it and felt the unlocked door drag against the deep carpet pile. The room was dark apart from the glow of three computers and a library lamp bent forward over the desk. Carl stood, a shadow by the window, backlit by the moon. He took one step forward and a smaller step back, forward, and back, forward and back. This was bad. I closed the door and sat in one of his armchairs.

'Carl...' I tried to make him aware of me, but he took three long steps over to the computers and began to tap rhythmically on each keyboard.

'Please sit down,' I said.

He crossed the room towards the desk and emptied a tin of pencils, lining them up by colour and length.

He didn't look up. 'Who is downstairs? Who is it that you've allowed in?'

'It's only Fran, she's home for a few days.'

He took three strides and dropped into the chair opposite mine, leaning towards me as if he had something important to say, some secret to reveal. I leaned forward too.

'I don't want her in here, in my study, not now she works for Zac.'

'For goodness' sake,' I argued. 'Apart from Tom's recent escapade, the children have never been near your study. Zac deals with the media so what secrets could he possibly want from you?' This was pointless, I knew.

Carl began to rock, gently at first and then fiercely. I put my hand on his knee and he paused, staring at my fingers as if a strange object had landed on his leg. He brushed my hand aside and began to pick at the fabric of his trousers. A collapse was imminent. I knew what I had to do but we had to speak before I lost him.

'I'll sort this thing between Tom and the school on my own,' I said. 'We can't risk losing another school place, but I need money, Carl, a lot of money. I need to know what I can offer.'

The head shake, imperceptible but there. He was listening to me. 'Talk to Oliver,' he said. 'I don't do money.'

'Oh, Carl, this isn't a business matter. You're Tom's father, take some responsibility.' The words *for once* spoken only in my head.

'You know what Oliver's like,' I continued. 'He'll put up all sorts of fake barriers if he thinks it's only a request from me. I need something to show that you approve before you...'

Carl flapped both hands towards the screens. 'Something's happening, Alice. Something big is going to happen. Look over there.'

I left my seat and went to look. Each screen was filled with data I couldn't interpret. 'What does all this mean?' I said, trying to suppress my impatience.

'It's all going down. Everything will fall.'

I returned to kneel in front of him, firmly holding both his hands to stop his frantic brushing at the arms of the chair. It was already too late for reason or argument, only reassurance would do.

'Nothing will fall. You're safe in here. I'll bring your stuff up as soon as it's delivered.'

Carl snatched his hands away from mine and groaned. He leaned forward, arms wrapped around his waist. A light flickered from the control pad on the wall, warning us that someone needed entry through the gates. Not a moment too soon.

***

I waited on the top step, my arms crossed over my chest. Every cell of Carl's body was wrecked and without meth, the alternative was palliative care and a pain-limited death. He had made himself clear; he needed to keep using, meth kept his ideas alive and he wanted as much time as could be bought, even if it was only a few more days of frenetic normality, refusing food and working through day and night, until he fractured. We'd reached this crisis point too often now, but his recovery was shorter each time, the next collapse even sooner. One day, the renaissance wouldn't come at all. His personal medical team responded on speed dial, a team who would not argue with their client, as I would not argue with his dealer. I had no choice but to act as a go between.

A black, chauffeur-driven Daimler nosed through the gates and crept towards me as I waited, shivering in the dark. An arm hung from the open rear window. I walked down our steps to greet the man we called Claudio, which he said was his name. He called me Mrs Williams with a formality that hinted at mockery.

'How are you, Mrs Williams, and the old man?'

'As if you care. Just hand over the package.'

The driver was invisible beyond the tinted windows and Claudio's face was hidden in the depths of the car, but I sensed two of them on the back seat. I heard him 'tsk' as if deeply offended.

'I care about my customers, especially those who've dealt with the firm for so many years.'

I stretched out my hand. 'Claudio, give me the package.'

The arm disappeared and returned holding a brown paper parcel, carefully tied with string as if he were a last-century fishmonger and not a dealer. I had to walk forward to take it and saw his long, manicured fingers, the phosphorescent glow of an immaculate white cuff, dark body hairs encroaching from underneath.

The window whirred upwards, and Claudio's hand flickered a farewell. I waited until the car was gone and the security system registered that the gates were locked before I left the steps. Inside, I leaned against the door and folded the package against my chest. This was Carl's only way of fighting back. I had to give it to him.

Next morning, I tapped on Fran's door and waited until I heard 'mmm?' from inside. Honey slept at the end of the bed. I sat down next to the dog and pulled on her ears. She lifted her head and gave a squeaking yawn of recognition.

'What on earth are you doing in here?' I asked, certain that she'd been in her basket when I checked last night. Honey thumped her tail.

Fran threw back the duvet and rolled her head on the pillow. She didn't open her eyes. 'What's up?'

'I've called the team for Carl, but you don't need to be involved, they know where everything is. I'll stay until they've arrived, but I have to go into the office, just for a short time. Remember, Tom's at home. Could you keep an eye on him and check the work he has to do for school?'

'I'm too thick for that.'

'Well, just make sure it's done.' Too late, I remembered I should have challenged Fran's inarguable difficulty with the GCSE syllabus. Carl had donated a new all-weather sports pitch to persuade The Mount to keep her on for sixth form.

'Keep away from Carl's study. Once the medics have seen him, he'll be fine on his own. I'll only be an hour.'

Fran opened one eye. 'What's up with him?'

'I think he's about to crash.'

'Not again!'

'Yes, again. I expect you and Tom won't even be up by the time I'm back, so don't worry.'

Fran closed both eyes. 'I'm not worried,' she murmured. 'I don't even care.'

I bent to kiss her, but she turned over, her face pushed into the pillow. I kissed her hair instead, smelling the herbal scent of her shampoo. Automatically, I picked up clothes from the floor and draped them across a chair. Honey lifted her head to try and track my progress across the room but sighed and settled back to sleep.

At the university, I went straight to the common room and piled dirty coffee cups into the sink, wiping the stained laminate surfaces with a furious energy while the kettle boiled. I crashed clean mugs onto the draining rack and threw the tea towel into the corner by the kettle. What on earth am I doing here, leaving Fran and Tom at home with Carl?

'It's okay,' I said aloud. 'It's only one hour.'

The office nameplate said 'Professor David Adams.' I was his research assistant, a grand title that amounted to very little but gave me a safe place where I could send emails from David's account, bargaining that the university's computer network was secure enough not to be compromised by Carl. David paid me what he could from his research grants, which diminished every year, but he had come to rely on me to answer his emails, and otherwise organise his life. The arrangement suited us both.

I logged on using David's password, and sipped my coffee. Of course, there was no milk and I wrinkled my nose at the bitter taste. Dan would be at his desk, waiting to hear from me. At home, Dan and Sarah opened and read each other's emails. He ought to mind this lack of privacy, but after arguing about it, we'd dropped the subject and settled on contacting each other at work. Knowing too much about your lover's life at home was one of the hazards of an affair. Dan assumed much about my domestic arrangements, based on his own, and I had chosen not to explain why secrecy and deception were already at the heart of mine, even before I'd started an affair. Our routine now seemed so ordinary, I'd almost forgotten about the risk.

In my handbag, I rummaged for the old mobile phone I used exclusively to contact Dan and sent a text to let him know I'd arrived.

On the computer, I tapped out my message.

```
To: Dr Dan Lewis
From: Professor David Adams
Subject: Abject Apologies
My love, I'm so sorry I was vile yesterday. I
should have been honest. I'm having
investigations for cervical cancer and I'm not
confident it's going to end well.
A xx
```

Dan answered immediately.

To: Professor David Adams
From: Dr Dan Lewis
Subject: My Fault Entirely
I should have encouraged you to talk. I
noticed you were distracted. Try not to worry
until you have definite news. Whatever happens
will make no difference to us.
D xxx

I tapped out my reply.

But what if I have to have surgery, then
treatment? Everything will change.

Dan's response arrived in seconds.

There will be changes but we'll find a new
way. My love for you won't change. Can you
meet for coffee?

I quickly typed my answer.

Carl is ill — I have to rush home. Tom was
found with drugs at school. If he's
permanently excluded, do you think our local
school would take him?

His response was slow, in his Dan-like way he would
consider carefully how to respond.

I'm afraid they wouldn't. No school would be

keen to offer a place to a child who's known
to be using drugs. Was Tom selling to other
students? Your nearest school has an
outstanding reputation, so it's highly
unlikely there will be space for him. Try to
persuade his own school to keep him. The main
thing is to get the story. Where's the money
coming from to fund drugs? Is someone else
asking him to sell on school premises? I can
email you the address of a drug education
service for teenagers — one of mine brought it
home from school yesterday. Kids are a worry,
and you don't seem to have much support at
home. You must be frantic. Pity about the
coffee but I understand.
Dan xxx

Of course, Dan was right, but did he need to sound so
smugly right? I'd held on to a fantasy about the meeting next
week, one where I would take charge and announce that I'd
already found Tom another school place. In truth, I was
powerless. My best option was to keep Tom at The Mount if
they'd have him. There was no choice but to contact Oliver.

Seconds after the text left my other mobile, supplied by
Carl's business and certainly monitored, Oliver phoned.

'Alice, how are you? Got your message. Sorry to hear Carl's
on his way down again. Getting more frequent, isn't it?'

Apart from Carl's medics and me, Oliver knew more than
anyone else about Carl's health, because he paid the invoices.
He listened to Carl's paranoia and almost believed some of it to
be true, even encouraging him, so that he could hold on to Carl's
trust and his own place in the business, even if this meant
undermining me. I hated him.

'I don't want to talk about Carl; his health is a family matter. We have a problem with Tom's school. It's going to be expensive because I think he's run out of chances. We may need to make a generous offer... something they'll accept. If we have to find another school, that will be expensive too.'

'Sorry, darling, you know the rules. I can only talk serious money with the big guy. He needs to countersign any shift of money out of the business, especially a sum as large as this is likely to be. As we both know, you're not a signatory. You have a generous allowance for your own use, and I don't interfere with that.'

'So, you won't help?'

'I can't. You already know this.'

'Before he collapsed, Carl said all I had to do was ask you.'

'If he said that, he's wrong. I'm the company accountant, Alice, you must show me written evidence that he agreed the transfer of funds.'

Silence followed, where we matched each other's breathing. 'You know it's too late for that, Oliver. Let's be clear, you're offering nothing to help Tom stay at his school.'

'That is correct. I'm sorry but I have no choice. Look, I'm about to start a meeting. Is there anything else?'

'Carl asked me to talk to you about security at the house. Tom and a friend managed to break in and they took drugs from Carl's study.'

'Right... that is serious. I'll send someone round.'

'Wow, you'll pay for it without Carl's consent?'

'Don't be sarcastic, Alice. I assume you'll find the time to be at home later?'

'Of course, I will,' I protested. 'I'm leaving for home right now. What are you implying?'

'You have called the medics, haven't you? I hope you haven't left Carl alone. Where are you calling from?'

I swung around, as if a hidden camera might be watching me.

I crossed my fingers and lied. 'The team were there when I left. He's warm and safe. There was something urgent I had to sort out at work, because I might have to be away for a while. Anyway, Fran is with him.'

'Well, well,' Oliver said, returning my sarcasm. 'Left with Fran. Your husband *is* in good hands. Ask the medics to send me the bill as usual. Got to go... take care.'

I placed the company phone on David's desk and sat for a few moments, breathing deeply, blowing out my fury through cupped hands.

There was time for one more email before deleting the thread.

My darling Dan, I love you but why are you always right?

Dan replied:

At least you still love me. I knew my last email was a bit sanctimonious. Let's talk soon. I love you too. Sorry, sorry, sorry. Dan the Prig xxx

FOUR
WEDNESDAY 10TH SEPTEMBER

I t was Wednesday morning, and I hadn't seen Carl since I delivered his package late on Monday night. He didn't welcome company or food when he was losing control, and could be unreasonable with anyone who intruded. The medical team had visited yesterday and were due again today, so I knew he was safe. All through the night, I heard him through the ceiling, pacing above me, accompanied by heavy bass notes thumping from his music system. Early this morning I had been woken by the dry rattle of his persistent cough, but now all was quiet.

My hospital appointment was this afternoon, and I lay still, stroking my belly, wondering how I would feel tonight. Would it be relief, tinged with embarrassment, to have wasted everyone's time, or would I have crossed over into the world of the sick?

In my pyjamas, I climbed up to the attic rooms and listened. Nothing. I used my key to open the door, and through a thick, fetid warmth, saw Carl prone on his day bed. This collapse had been so sudden, he hadn't been able to reach his bedroom. Without rousing him, I began the familiar routine I had been taught. I opened the window to let out the sweet, pungent aroma of marijuana but kept the curtains closed, since Carl was distressed if woken in daylight. An empty wine bottle lay on the floor under the bed. I tucked it under one arm before picking up the glass next to it and standing them both on the side table. One of the computers was still alive and I paused to log out, first taking care to save the incomprehensible data left on the screen. The room darkened once the computer shut down and my eyes readjusted to the shadows.

A slice of light carved through the dense air where I had not fully closed the curtains and fell across Carl's pallid face, his hair darkened with sweat. I was reminded of a pre-Raphaelite painting; the colourful tapestry of the day bed just visible in the half light, a man lying asleep or drugged, his shirt wide open, cuffs splayed, an image of Edwardian decadence. I hesitated before touching Carl, standing quite still, taking a deep breath in order to find the strength, or courage, to do what came next. I bent over Carl and checked the pulse in his neck, as I'd been shown, then lifted his eyelids to gauge the response of his pupils. More roughly than was necessary, I pulled the blanket away and undid his trouser belt, before removing his shoes and socks. There was a polythene box under the bed with all his supplies and I reached down for it, my movements automatic and unhurried.

Curling up my nose, I removed Carl's trousers and underpants together in a practised movement with one hand and perfunctorily wiped between his legs with a moistened tissue in my other hand.

'At least there's no shit,' I said aloud. 'Apart from you.'

I threw the tissue into the waste bin but missed and it lay there, curled up on the floor. Unexpected tears coursed down my cheeks, and I felt heavy with shame. I sat down in the crook of Carl's bent knees and took his hand. 'I'm sorry, I didn't mean it. It's just that...'

Carl groaned and shifted his legs away from the pressure. I took another wet tissue from the packet and wiped my face, holding it crumpled in my hand.

I gestured to the empty room. 'You threw it all away. Without the drugs, without all this, we might have worked things out, had a normal life, like everyone else.' I knew this was fantasy, but it helped to keep on pretending.

I lifted Carl's thin legs and placed a nappy under his flaccid backside, pulling it up between his legs and fastening the tapes. In case he was sick, I placed a towel under his head. In his bathroom, I dampened a clean cloth and wiped his face and hands, making sure he rested on his cheek.

From the polythene box, I pulled out a pair of rubber gloves, lifting a syringe from the table next to the day bed and another from the floor, then brushed ash and ends of spliffs into a bag with one smooth swipe of my hand. I removed the rubber gloves after sealing the bag with its adhesive tape and threw everything into the sharps bin. Locking the door behind me, I left the room, returning with an adult's feeder cup full of water and the kitchen cloth, soaked in antibacterial spray. I wiped the bedside table and placed the water close to the edge so he could reach for it when he woke. The keys for the filing cabinet dangled from the open top drawer and I gently pushed it closed and turned the lock, tucking the keys under Carl's pillow. His first action would be to search for them.

At the door again, I paused and scanned the room, completing a mental checklist. The wine bottle and glass were still on the side table, and I walked back towards Carl to pick them up. He gave a deep, snorting breath and I turned to him, as if he had spoken.

'What if I need this too, Carl?' I said. 'Will you do this for me?'

FIVE

WEDNESDAY 10TH SEPTEMBER

I t's cruel to bring women who might be about to lose their womb to the same place they had their babies. I hadn't been here for twenty-four years, the night when Ella was born. Before I left the car, I sent her a text.

Just off into women's gynae!

I added a smiley face, more for my reassurance than hers.

Can we speak tonight?

She was the most junior of doctors, always harassed, always exhausted. When she wasn't working, she was sleeping. I'd learned that contact had to come from her.

There was already a queue for the car park. I found a space after several circuits and as I stepped out of my car into the thick, hot afternoon, I reached into the back of the car for my sweater, in the unlikely event the NHS had invested in fans to keep the waiting women cool. Ahead of me a young couple struggled towards the maternity unit. The father carried a small suitcase and strode in front of the mother, her hair damp with sweat. Every so often she stopped to breathe through a contraction, one arm resting across her huge, dropped belly, and he waited, shifting the suitcase from one hand to the other, then walked on ahead. Each time she caught up, he set off again at a faster pace. I stopped and asked her if she needed help, but she shook her head and groaned. I hurried on, keen to arrive at the clinic in good time.

Tattered beige files were piled at both ends of the reception counter and as I waited to be noticed, nurses lifted them onto trolleys which looked as if they had once been used to transport vegetables to the kitchens. The receptionist looked up from the screen to pass the nurse another file and her eyes flickered across me, apparently without seeing me. Behind her head, doctors' names were written on a smeared whiteboard, and I wondered which one I would see. The phone rang and she answered it, chewing on a fingernail.

A small queue had gathered behind me and when the receptionist ended her call, I coughed, then said, 'Excuse me,' surprised at the sharp tone of my own voice. Slowly, as if focusing on a distant object, she reached for my letter and turned back to the screen. Without looking up she passed the letter back and asked me to take a seat.

I put my bag on the chair next to me. Reading the letter and leaflet again distracted me for a few minutes, then I sent Fran a text to make sure that she and Tom were okay at home. Fran replied immediately, saying that Carl's team had been and gone and they were watching an old film on TV.

Has anyone taken Honey out?

Fran answered:

Way too hot for that! You should take her out later.

I removed my glasses to look around. The patients sat passively in rows, reading, or talking quietly. Most of the women were accompanied and I felt cut by a sharp edge of self-pity.

Even if he had been in a good phase, it would have been unthinkable to ask Carl to come with me. It wasn't just that he no longer interacted with the real world, but keeping information from him was a habit that still felt necessary. The less Carl knew, the easier things were. It wasn't too late to text Dan and ask him to come, but his refusal, no matter how carefully worded, would hurt.

The clinic workers moved fast and filled the space, carrying cups of coffee and calling out to one another across the heads of the waiting group. A radio, playing a local station, was on too loud. I was an intruder in someone else's place of work, a tick on a box, a task for the day. Some people have to survive every day like this, an outcome or a product, their lives spent as service users. Because of Carl's money, I had choices but this was my medical problem and I didn't want it to become Carl's, or worse, Oliver's. I could have used the same private hospital that looked after Carl, but how safe would my medical records be at The Haven, if Oliver paid for my treatment? With naïve certainty, I believed that the NHS, like the university, would have firewalls that not even Carl's surveillance techniques could break. I would gladly put up with being one of a long list of patients, and wait my turn in a queue, if it meant my medical records stayed secret.

'Helen, is Claire in today?' a nurse shouted above the noise of the radio, and we all looked up, interested to know the answer. We belonged, just for a short time, to the world of Helen and Claire and others we hadn't met.

'No, she's still off sick,' Helen replied. The woman seated opposite shrugged and tapped her watch.

'What time's your appointment?'

'It's at three forty-five,' I replied. 'Do you think we'll be seen on time?'

'Not if Claire's off. They'll be short-staffed. Mine's at two thirty and they haven't called anyone yet.'

'You've been before?'

She leaned towards me and whispered, 'I had some laser treatment. One or two bad cells. Now, it's only check-ups. What about you?'

'Only investigations. I'm sure it's nothing serious.'

She nodded and returned to flicking through a magazine, licking her thumb as she turned each page. A large man squeezed into the empty seat next to mine. I could smell his hair gel and chewing gum and the hair on his arms brushed against mine. He apologised and lifted both arms, as I pulled at the arm of my sweater trapped under his elbow. I noticed that he held the hand of a pale, red-eyed woman and I thought of Dan. The emptiness of needing him beside me, allowed fear to creep up the back of my neck and over my scalp. I pushed away the worry; it would be nothing, it always was.

A group of women laughed as they completed a questionnaire. The waiting patients turned to stare, including me.

'How many times a week?' one shrieked. 'I'm changing it to year.'

I glanced at the man next to me, who gave me a timid, shy smile before turning away. The nurses exchanged disapproving looks and the women fell silent, with occasional whispers and giggles, like schoolgirls who had been told off for joking about sex in class. Thinking I should have been given a questionnaire, I approached the desk. A nurse now sat at the computer. She had a square face with an upturned nose that supported a pair of wire-rimmed glasses, and I was reminded of Mrs Badger from one of the children's picture books. She had the same elegant, upward sweep of dark hair with a white streak at her brow.

'Can I help you?' she asked.

I nodded towards the disgraced group. 'Should I fill out one of those questionnaires?'

She looked at me over the top of her spectacles. 'Not every patient gets one. It's randomised. That means...'

'I know what randomised means,' I snapped. 'I'm a researcher in the Sociology Department at the university.'

Mrs Badger's eyes creased at the corners. She was about to laugh. 'You will be called soon. Try not to worry. Please take a seat, Mrs—'

'Williams,' I interrupted.

She turned to speak to a nurse who was helping an elderly woman shuffle past the desk. 'There's birthday cake in the kitchen, Myra.'

'Just sit down there, love. Whose birthday is it?' Myra asked.

'It's Denise. Twenty-one again.'

'Many happy returns!' one of the men in the waiting group called out and both nurses glared at him. Back in my seat, I felt sorry for the man, who had been 'shushed' by his wife. We don't belong here; we wait our turn, polite, obedient and then we drift away. I imagined describing this to Dan later, how I would make this strange hospital world seem light and funny. It must be, it had to be, because the whole thing was a false alarm.

My name was called and a nurse waited for me, my beige file clasped to her chest. I followed her to the consulting room.

'You're lucky to be seeing Mr Wales,' she whispered, as we

travelled together down a long, utilitarian corridor, with closed doors on either side. We entered the consulting room and Mr Wales stood up to shake my hand. He introduced me to the nurse and a newly qualified doctor, who looked hot and uncomfortable in the airless room. I sat in the chair offered and tried to answer his questions:

'Yes, I'm forty-eight.'

'They're getting a bit erratic now, but I think my last period was two months ago.'

'Ella was born here but Fran and Tom were born at St Catherine's.'

'I've noticed bleeding after having sex.'

'For about a year now... I should have seen my GP sooner. I hope I haven't left it too late.'

I bit my lower lip. 'My last smear was five years ago and it was clear, but I had to cancel the most recent one.' I'd missed it because I'd been with Dan, using the GP appointment as an excuse to be out of the house.

The nurse weighed me and checked my height before I was taken into an adjoining room and asked to undress. I lay on my back in a hospital gown, with my legs suspended in stirrups, exhaling slowly, opening and closing my hands to squeeze out the tingling in my palms. Fear was easy to control. I'd had plenty of practice with fear.

She put her hand on my knee and said, 'It's cold in here, isn't it? Don't worry, he'll be with you in a minute, he's just talking to some medical students.' I could hear a low murmur from the other room and nodded, trying to smile, but found the corners of my lips were trembling. I blinked to keep tears away and the nurse patted my leg again.

'It's a bit uncomfortable but it'll soon be over and then you can go home and forget all about it. Is your husband here to drive you home?'

I shook my head.

'You can rest in the day ward afterwards for as long as you like,' she continued. 'Don't drive until you're ready.'

I wasn't reassured by this talk of resting. The booklet had said that if any suspect cells were found they would be removed immediately but there would be another quite innocent reason for my bleeding. There would be no need to rest. My body wouldn't let me down.

The door opened and Mr Wales appeared, not immediately recognisable in a gown and cap. He folded his arms and spoke, focusing on my knees.

'I'm going to put some dye into your cervix. Any cells that are a bit iffy will show up immediately. Sometimes we can remove them straight away, sometimes you have to come back for more treatment. Anything I remove today will be sent for biopsy. Do you understand?'

He lifted the cover and sat on a stool between my legs. Only the top of his head was visible. I felt the cold, metal phallus of the speculum inside me. There was silence and we waited, the two women, patient and nurse, expectant. I became aware of far-off noises, the wail of an ambulance and the intermittent whine of a train. We glanced at each other. Something was different, something was wrong, even for her. It was taking too long.

Mr Wales sat up, leaving the speculum in place and discreetly pulled the covers down. He pushed back his cap with his thumb and scratched his hairline.

'With your permission, Mrs Williams, I'd like to bring some medical students in to see you. They will simply look into the speculum and then return to my office.'

I nodded but wanted to refuse. I didn't mind the students viewing my cervix but there shouldn't be anything worth seeing. This couldn't be happening.

'That's okay,' I agreed. 'My daughter is a doctor. I know it's important.'

I caught the words, 'Won't see this often these days' from the other side of the open door before my nurse tried to cover his indiscretion with chatter. The students trooped in, shoulders slumped, so young, so awkward and I tried to smile at them, thinking of Ella. I could be your mother, I thought. They wouldn't look at me.

Once the students had seen whatever there was to see, Mr Wales placed himself again on the stool and the nurse passed him a syringe with a long needle, which he waved for emphasis as he spoke.

'I'm just going to freeze you and take a sample for biopsy. You'll feel a bit of a sharp push and then a cold sensation.'

My voice sounded hoarse, as if I needed to clear my throat. 'Will you remove any bad cells today?'

'I'm afraid you've been unlucky, Mrs Williams. You'll need further treatment.'

There was silence. I flinched from the strike of the needle. Cold spread through my belly followed by a sharp, chemical smell. The nurse pressed down on my shaking knees until Mr Wales's head appeared from between my legs. 'We should get an ultrasound done in maternity. May as well do some of the preliminaries while she's here.'

He turned to speak to me. 'I'll see you here next week, in clinic. That's my Monday clinic. Don't get dressed. We'll take you to the day ward to rest and get ultrasound to fit you in as soon as they can. We don't want you to have to wait around over there. I'm sure you remember what it was like from your pregnancies.'

We laughed together, more loudly than was necessary. The nurse was tense and I wished I knew why. Something about me, about my case, had been difficult for her. I was helped across to the day ward, incongruously wearing my hospital gown and shoes while she carried my clothes. Left alone while she went to fetch water, I sat on the hard bed, conscious of the comforting but scratchy bulk of the sanitary towel between my legs. Sunlight from a high window scattered diamonds of colour across the dull bedspread and the leaden sky from earlier had cleared and was now blue, filmed with pale cloud. There were five other empty beds. Why was no one else here? I was getting tired of this. I wanted to be normal. If I left now, just walked out of that door, I could go home.

Footsteps approached and the nurse carried a carafe of water and a glass to my bedside. 'You need to drink it all. Your ultrasound's booked for five o'clock.'

'What did he see? You know but you're not telling me.'

'I can't say for sure because you need more tests. Mr Wales will talk it over with you next week.'

'I'd prefer to get dressed.' I sounded petulant even to myself. 'I don't want to go for a scan in this gown. You're treating me as if I'm ill.'

She smiled. 'You can dress, of course. Put your clothes on when you're ready and walk over there by yourself but do come back here before you go home, so that we can make your appointment. Mr Wales can be a bit... insensitive... but he's very good. You'll like him once you start your treatment.'

The nurse left, her steps echoing back down the corridor. After I dressed, I sat on the bed to drink the water, swallowing the tight bands in my throat with each hard gulp. I'd crossed the threshold from well to sick, stepping out of my life into one that had been hiding next to mine. The anxious wait I'd had, since the appointment letter arrived, had been a rehearsal, one that now seemed ridiculously insincere. My body had let me down after all.

In the ultrasound suite, I was led to a cubicle where I changed back into a hospital gown, leaving my clothes neatly folded in a basket. Two others were waiting, and I thought I recognised the older woman. They were mother and daughter. I wondered if the girl was a pupil at Tom's school and hoped I wouldn't be recognised. Too late, the mother smiled and walked across the room to sit next to me.

'My daughter's struggling with her bladder... she's bursting. Hope we don't have too long to wait. How are you? How's Carl?' Ah yes, I could place her, a neighbour from our first home in Leicester. She'd given up inviting me for coffee because I never asked her back. Carl didn't like strangers in the house, even then.

She nodded her head towards her daughter. 'She's pregnant, only eighteen, but they've been together two years. I'll be a grandma and I'm only forty. It was a shock at first, but we've got used to it. We're quite excited really, even her dad.'

The woman was nervous, and I allowed her to talk, nodding in the right places and making sympathetic noises, but I wasn't listening. Please don't ask about me, I thought. When the moment came, I wasn't ready. She stopped talking and peered closely at me.

'You're not pregnant again, are you? I heard you had more kids after you left Courtauld Road.'

'Yes, after Ella we had Fran, she's twenty. Then Tom, he's fifteen. I'm not pregnant, I only wish I was.'

I knew I'd sounded abrupt and hid my face behind a magazine, riffling through the pages.

'Good luck,' she said, leaving my side to sit with her daughter. I raised my head at her farewell and tried to smile.

Like the girl, I was aching to pee. The cold weight of the

scanner slid through the gel on my belly, and I squeezed my fists when the technician pressed down on my bladder. The light was low, the warm room hummed. We were silent but I watched her closely, trying to measure her expression for any fleeting surprise or alarm. I could see the screen but its grey pattern of light and dark was meaningless. There was no waving child.

'Okay, two healthy ovaries,' she said. 'Whoops, that one is just sliding away from me.' I was surprised, as if a monk from a silent order had spoken.

'What else can you see?' I dared to ask.

'Things aren't very clear... something's in there. It could be fibroids.'

If it's fibroids, there's still hope. 'Fibroids are safe, aren't they?'

'Okay, that's all done. I'll do a report for Mr Wales.'

'He needs it before Monday,' I reminded her.

She chewed on her lip, biting back a grin. 'I'll do my very best.'

In the cubicle I stripped off the gown and looked down at my skin, drenched a strange colour from light filtering through the green curtains. Woven with the scars of three pregnancies, my belly was still tight and flat. I pressed my palms hard against it, then ran my hands down my legs, resting on the bench before pulling my knees up towards my chin. I crouched forward, gripped my toes hard and sobbed.

SIX
THURSDAY 11TH SEPTEMBER

P aul Harris, Tom's head teacher, opened the door of his study and gave a small bow as he gestured widely for us to pass through. 'Mr Williams not joining us today?'

'No, he's working I'm afraid. Something he couldn't cancel.' Tom threw me a look of contempt.

We sat down in two chairs angled together next to a coffee table. On the other side was a single chair intended for Mr Harris himself. I felt transparent. The absence of a fourth chair made it quite clear that Carl wasn't expected but the informal grouping gave me hope; this wasn't a disciplinary meeting. A pile of the new school prospectuses spread across the table like a hand of playing cards, each one a uniform distance from the next, the angle of separation perfect. If Paul Harris had laid these out before we arrived, then he was anxious too.

Mr Harris walked across the room to his desk to pick up what was presumably Tom's file. Like many heavy men, he was light on his feet and stepped daintily across the carpet. He sat down, more solidly than I expected and made a play of finding, cleaning, and placing his glasses on his nose. He read the file in silence as if neither Tom nor I were present.

'This isn't the first incident of its kind.' Mr Harris looked at Tom over the top of his spectacles.

'We should have been told,' I interrupted.

'Thought it best to deal with it in school, under the circumstances.' Mr Harris turned to me with an expression intended to express concern, but which actually held more in the way of prurient interest.

'What circumstances?' I challenged, looking from Tom to Mr Harris. I ran through the list in my mind. Could it be illness, drug addiction, my affair with Dan?

'Tom told us that you and Mr Williams have separated. Please don't be angry with him, boys do come out with these things here. We know how to deal with it, helped to explain the cannabis in school... three occasions I think... yes, three.' Paul Harris hesitated, flicking the pages in Tom's file.

'But we're not...'

'This time we were more concerned,' he said, cutting across my rebuttal. 'This time we're sure he was selling. The question is, Mrs Williams, where is he getting it from? We should have brought in the police...'

I knew the script. 'But you have the reputation of the school to consider?'

'But we have the reputation of the school to consider.' Paul Harris finished his sentence, staring at me with one eyebrow lifted. He leaned back in his chair, relaxing now that the difficult bit was over. One of his shirt buttons was undone and I could see his pale flesh, flecked with strands of dark hair, creeping through the gaps in the straining fabric.

'Of course, as Tom's mother you are no doubt full of worries,' he continued. 'What's he getting into? Who is he mixing with? As a parent myself I share your concern, but I have responsibility for all the pupils in this school, the whole school community.'

Paul Harris fixed me with an expression of suitable gravity and leaned forward to emphasise his point. I pulled back, wanting to escape, to be anywhere but here. If it felt like this for me, what about Tom? I tried to catch his eye.

'Of course, we have a long history with your family. Ella and Fran made such a success of their time with us.'

I nodded, as if I agreed, but how much I wanted to contradict him, to say, 'No, you told us Ella had an attitude problem and we had to beg you to keep Fran on for sixth form.' I hated this pompous little man, but I needed him.

I heard a roaring sound in my ears and wanted to shake the sanctimonious insincerity from Paul Harris's small mouth and piggy little eyes. If I could have reached my son, I'd have shaken him too, until he dropped his silly grin. If only I could make a grand gesture, announce that Tom was going to a boarding school in the Outer Hebrides, tomorrow... no, tonight. If only I could boast that I no longer required the services of this jumped-up little establishment, chosen for Carl's needs, not Tom's.

I couldn't do any of this. Rage thumped against the back of my eyeballs and my throat tightened. I searched in my pockets for a tissue. Mr Harris noticed this small movement and stood up.

'This is difficult for you. I'll see if Sheila can make us some coffee.' I blew my nose and watched him waddle out of the room, arms and hips swaying, before I turned on Tom.

Questions tumbled out, spattered with anger. 'What on earth is going on? Why did you say your father and I were separated? You've lied to get yourself out of this mess. How much did you take from Carl's study?' Tom shrugged and studied the carpet between his shoes, his head bent forward, hands dangling between his knees.

I heard him whisper, 'You lied to him too. You lie all the time.'

'What on earth do you mean? I'll take you away from here,' I hissed, 'even if they agree to have you back. Is that what you want?' Tom shrugged again, his cheeks burning. He turned his body away to face the wall.

The routine of coffee served, sugar passed, biscuits refused, allowed us both to regain our composure as Mr Harris's eyes held mine, as if he was expecting... waiting... for something from me.

'Tom has behaved very badly and his father and I deeply regret the harm caused,' I said. 'Is there any way we could put things right, so that Tom can stay here?'

Paul Harris nodded. 'The governors will consider all options, Mrs Williams. I'm afraid I can't make any promises but if you were to let me know what you might be considering...'

'I can't make any promises either,' I said, draining my coffee cup and reaching under the table for my handbag. I flicked my eyes at Tom, to let him know we were leaving. 'I will discuss the matter with my husband's business partner. Given the *circumstances*, is there any way Tom can return to school, until the governors' meeting?'

'Of course, of course, we'll do everything we can to help. Other pupils in such a situation... not many I might add... have remained in school under a sanction we call Headmaster's Detention. That means they work in isolation and don't mix with the other students. But they are in school every day.'

Tom stormed out of the office without looking back. I wanted to do the same but politeness forced me to shake Mr Harris's hand and even thank his secretary for the coffee, as I passed by her desk.

In the car, Tom's face burned with resentment. 'That detention is only for kids whose parents can't be arsed to find anyone to look after them,' he argued, breaking into the silence of our miserable drive home.

'Well, that sums us up very nicely,' I said, trying to make a joke, but my attempt sounding more like sarcasm. This was the moment to tell him everything; the truth about the life we faced, my illness, the inevitable conclusion of his father's addiction, but I wasn't brave enough.

'Tom, I can't find anyone to look after you. Fran will be gone tomorrow. I know you're fifteen, but Carl is too unwell right now to act like a parent. I can't leave you alone with him. I will be home sometimes, of course I will, but I need to work.'

'Dad says you don't really have a job. You just pretend to work so you don't have to stay in the house with him.'

'That's not fair and it's not true,' I argued.

'You don't earn any money. If he's so ill, why don't you stay at home to look after him. Then I could be there too.'

We arrived home without another word spoken. I burned with indignation at Tom's disclosure, this evidence of father and son chats happening behind my back, rehearsing the row I would have with Carl as soon as he was able to listen. He was undermining me, as he always had, but now he was belittling me to my son. How dare he poison Tom against his mother, break the pact we had made. We had agreed... I would hide his addiction from the children, pretending all was well between us, as long as he stayed out of their way whenever he was using, which in the last few years was all the time.

I already saw the smile play on Carl's crooked lips as he explained to me, with his habitual patience, that he understood my deception about my work. In truth I was unemployable, we both knew this but he couldn't bring himself to lie to Tom about my so-called 'job' at the university.

Tom thundered upstairs to his room, and I followed behind, taking the stairs to the second floor to check on Carl. The medical team had left him clean and warm in his bedroom, with fresh water. He opened his eyes but didn't see me. Soon, he would surface.

Together, Fran and I cooked supper, and I asked her if the medics had left a message. She shrugged and said, 'I just let them in and showed them out.'

I called Tom down to eat and watched the struggle between the furious teenager and hungry boy as he stared down at his plate. Hunger won, and he bent over his food, forking pasta into his mouth. I let him eat, talking with Fran about things of little importance or interest, bargaining that good food might ease his sense of injustice. As soon as he had finished Tom stood up, his chair scaping against the kitchen tiles, but I put my hand on his arm.

'Please sit down, Tom.'

Tom looked everywhere except at me, but he did sit down. 'I want to go back to my room,' he said.

'How often have you used cannabis?'

'Dunno... twenty, maybe thirty times.'

'But where do you get it from? Is it always from Dad's room?'

'Yes, of course it is. He doesn't mind. You heard him.'

'I don't want you going into Dad's study. It's not allowed. You know that.'

Tom stared at me, his eyes narrowed. 'Yeah so, I do go into his room. I go in and talk to him.'

'What else have you done in there... I mean what have you seen?'

'Just some weird stuff on the computers. Dad's shown me

47

his CDs. He says I can borrow them.' Tom leaned back in his chair, confident that this particular battle was won.

The world shifted under me and I grasped the table as if I could push back a sucking tide.

'Tell him, Mum,' Fran whispered. 'You have to tell him now.'

I had forgotten she was there, frozen in her chair. Unrehearsed and unplanned words tumbled at random from my mouth.

'Tom, listen to me. Please don't go into Dad's room. It's fine to talk to him but let him find you, because he... there have been times, lots of them, when you would have been frightened to be around him. He doesn't mean it, he's...'

Tom stared at me, struggling to hold back tears and his hands twisted around each other.

'It's your fault. You keep him away from us. He told me.'

'No, he's ill. He started using something a bit like cannabis when he wasn't much older than you. Please don't do the same.'

Now Tom was crying and his voice cracked as his pitch rose.

'It *is* your fault. It's all you... you keep me away from my dad. Cannabis is okay. You heard what he said.'

'Tom, listen to Mum,' Fran shouted. 'Carl is an addict. He's chosen to kill himself with fucking crystal meth. Why should we care about him?'

I glared at her. 'Okay, Fran, leave it alone. Tom, we might be able to find you another school but for now, you have to go back to The Mount, until the governors' meeting. You have no choice.'

Tom jumped up, knocking his chair to the floor. Startled, Honey climbed out of her basket and sat between Fran and me, panting with fear, but determined to keep her women safe.

'You're a bitch, a fucking bitch,' Tom screamed, his voice now fully that of a ten-year-old. 'No wonder he stays in his room. He has to keep away from you, both of you. And I'm not going to that shite school tomorrow. I'll stay here. You can... you can just fuck off.'

Tom lifted his chair. I thought he would throw it, but Honey barked a warning, and he placed it back upright on the tiles, shaking his head with the effort to hold back more tears. Because he stayed, I knew it wasn't over. I was trembling, shocked at the hatred he'd hurled at me, but I would take charge of my son before it was too late.

'I'm sorry but there's no alternative, you will go to school tomorrow.'

'You can't make me.'

'Tom, you have to go to school, it's the law.'

'Stop protecting him,' Fran shouted. 'Tell him everything.'

'Tell me what?' Tom's breath shuddered, his eyes searching my face.

'Dad has been very ill before, many times, but I've kept it hidden from you. His care team visit while you're at school. I've lied to you, I've said he was away on business but he was in his rooms all the time. That's why it was such a shock to find out you've been going into his study on your own. Goodness knows what you might have found... might have seen. It's awful when he's having a collapse. I don't want you around him.'

I looked at them both; Fran's eyes ringed with shadows, Tom's face mottled with red blotches. Since we were telling the truth, I ploughed on.

'I'll find out next week, on Monday in fact, whether I'm ill too. I might have cancer. I'm going to be okay... of course I'll be okay... but this house is going to seem like a hospital for a while. You really need to be at school.'

Tom slumped in his chair and swept his fringe back from his forehead. 'When did all this happen?'

I swallowed, struggling to control the tremor in my voice. 'I had some tests yesterday but nothing's certain.'

It was Fran's turn to stand up, her eyes blazing. 'You've known about this for ages, haven't you? Thanks for telling me, Mum.'

Her voice sounded different, not vulnerable but hard. 'I don't want to stay here either,' she whispered. 'I'll go back to London tonight. Don't bother with the car, I'll call a taxi.'

SEVEN
FRIDAY 12TH SEPTEMBER

Tom stabbed at the buttons that controlled the audio system, folded his arms, and turned away from me to look out of the window. We drove in silence, my questions about how he had passed his first day in isolation, ignored with a shrug. The radio presenter's accent was hard to place. She spoke like most of David's students, an emphasis on the vowels, a bit of London, a bit of Australian, yet a hint of posh too. I changed the station to Radio 4 and finding yet another analysis of the state of the world since the attack on the Twin Towers seven years ago, I switched it off.

Without a focus, my mind drifted through years of picking up Tom and the girls from school. How Carl would follow me into the hall and hold my wrist, just before I left the house. 'Don't talk to anyone,' he always said, tightening his grip. Always. Those years are gone now but like a wound that will not heal, the feelings still fester. At first I complied, afraid of the consequences, then as each child grew, I allowed myself small acts of rebellion. Once I was taking Tom to school, I persuaded myself that winning meant rolling my eyes at Carl as he snatched my arm and chatting freely with other parents at the gate. But that wasn't winning at all. I was still playing his game.

In the hall, Tom threw his bag onto the bottom step and turned to me as if speaking to hired staff.

'I'll eat in my room,' he announced.

The slam of Tom's bedroom door startled Honey, making her whine, so I stayed in the kitchen, lifting the fur on her ears and rubbing the hard mound of skull between them. The silence, save for the hum of the refrigerator, felt like a vacuum. I checked my mobile. Nothing from Dan. No missed call from Ella.

Dan's family crowded him. I understood it was hard for him to text but couldn't he sneak away from them, just for a few minutes, to be with me? I stared at the tiny screen. The signal climbed and fell, climbed and fell. Nothing.

Last night, Fran slammed out of the front door and her absence, the echo of her leaving, hurt even more than her livid presence. I'd got it wrong with Fran... again, and Tom hated me. No wonder I kept secrets. But cancer had blown away the smoke and smashed all the mirrors I used to hide from the truth. My daughters kept their distance, my son was out of control. Having a lover was not enough compensation for the emptiness I shared with Carl.

To create some sound, I switched on the small television in the kitchen, the six o'clock news dominated by the election in America and something about Fannie Mae and Freddie Mac, who sounded like disobedient twins. I screwed open the top of a bottle of red wine, enjoying the fluid sound of filling a glass, and carried it through to the library, holding on to Honey's collar to help her follow. Standing at the window with the lights off, the shapes of the garden crept back into focus. A blackbird protested over an invisible intruder, probably a fox.

I inhaled the fruity scent from my wine and swallowed a

deep gulp. When Tom was born, Carl still seemed normal to outsiders, or what passed for normal, a man fully in control of himself. What he hid, with my collusion, was that he had already withdrawn from the world, working from home in his study, a forbidden place at the top of the house. The children had accepted this without question, as they had accepted so much in our abnormal reality. It was my decision to have another child but Carl took the news well; after all, there was plenty of money. His business was making an impact in the new world of communications and the children were only part of his life when he chose.

In our earliest days together, Carl used drugs to give him enough confidence to have sex and we had shared many loving times, where I gently encouraged him to take risks with his body and mine. His later choice of substances gave him a fake energy and strength which drove our physical relationship more than love or desire. In the years before Tom was born, sex became rarely consensual and often, close to violent. It wasn't hard to conceive.

Ella and Fran weren't happy when I told them about the pregnancy. Ella was seven, forging her own life beyond the family. She was clever, bold, popular, and always out with friends. She couldn't invite them back, but it didn't seem to matter. I had prepared the ground, making it clear to other parents that Carl worked from home and couldn't be disturbed.

Whenever she was at home, Ella lay in her bedroom with Sugar, Honey's predecessor, and read boarding school stories, pushing a chair against her bedroom door so that Fran couldn't come in. Fran would lean on the other side and whine. When Ella learned I was having another baby she glared at Fran and said, 'Not another one.' I smiled, remembering her saying this, but it wasn't funny.

I gripped the stem of my wine glass, and pushed on the

window ledge for balance, my knee resting on the window seat, peering outside as the security lights suddenly lit up a circle of the garden. Something rustled outside, startled by the light. After Carl's fall, Fran lost me. She tried Ella, but Ella had other ideas. Poor Fran didn't want to share me, she was still searching for a mother. At the time, I probably laughed at her but right now, I felt only shame.

Once Tom was born, things changed. It was as if the girls knew the role they had to play; to join me in hiding the secret that ruled the heart of our household.

In my memory, I can hear Fran's small voice above me, on the landing. 'Mum. Come up here.'

She wasn't looking at me but at something else, something I couldn't see. I was next to her in three long strides. Carl was at the end of the corridor, standing where the stairs led up to his attic. He was agitated, pacing and muttering, wiping at something on his arms. I could hear the words, 'Ants, ants, bloody ants,' as he swiped at an imaginary army of insects swarming over his body. Ella had followed me and grasping the situation in a single glance, stepped in to protect Tom. She twisted her athletic, twelve-year-old body into a parody of menace, circling Tom and chasing him back downstairs. She allowed him to weave around her in the hall, even taunt her, then she reared up to capture him, Tom screaming with delight as she tried to pin him down, but always failing, always allowing him to escape, but only just.

Carl was in no danger, except within his crazy delusion but Fran was standing alone, seeing but not understanding. I helped Carl back to his study, but I should have abandoned him to his fantasies. It was Fran who needed me.

I sighed and tipped back my head to drain my glass. Did I speak to the girls about what they had seen that night, after Carl had again been taken away by paramedics and Tom was in bed?

If only I had held them close, explained to Fran that there were no insects and thanked Ella, but I'm sure that didn't happen. We pretended it was nothing and we conspired to allow Tom to believe his father was the best parent in the world. Methamphetamine gave Carl a complete sense of invulnerability and power. For Tom, he'd been more than a father; he was a superhero.

I rested my empty wine glass on the sill and sat down, turning away from my image mirrored in the dark window, tucking my bare feet under my bottom. That night was the first time Carl was admitted to a specialist drug unit. He didn't recognise me for two days but when he came home from hospital he had changed. The medics said he had become delusional, not only about insects crawling over his skin but he believed I was conspiring with others to kill him. When she told me this, the nurse had rolled her eyes and laughed. But Carl was only wrong about the conspiracy. In that moment on the landing, I despised what he had become and wanted him gone. He must have seen my disgust, felt my rejection, understood there was nothing left between us, at the very point he was losing his control over me.

Honey lifted her head and whined, sensing rather than hearing Tom's pounding descent of the stairs. I heard him open the fridge door and slam it closed, then a scraping sound as he searched the kitchen freezer. The microwave whirred, then pinged.

'What are you doing in here, boozing in secret?' Tom stood silhouetted in the open door, chewing on a drooping slice of pizza.

'I'm having one glass of wine, keeping Honey company and thinking.'

'Wouldn't do too much of that if I were you,' he said, his mouth full. 'It didn't do you any good last time.'

My stomach squeezed at the smell of hot cheese and tomato. 'Ha-ha, very clever,' I said. 'Any pizza left?'

'I'm planning to eat it all, since there's no dinner.'

'When you've finished, will you take Honey out? Just around the garden. I'm going to check on your dad.'

Tom flopped onto the carpet, next to Honey, dangling small bits of pizza in front of her eyes. She didn't react, so he held a piece under her nose. Honey sniffed the air, then snatched it out of his hand.

'Did you see that?' he said. 'She's blind as well as deaf.'

'I know,' I agreed, 'but she's still happy.'

Between his teeth, Tom dragged cheese from the last mouthful of pizza and stood up. 'I can't take her out,' he mumbled. 'You'll have to do it. She takes too long, sniffing this, peering at that. I'm not into old lady dog walks. Anyway, I have homework to do, or have you forgotten that I'm in detention on my own with a psychopath called Mister Twatface, or something. He's likely to check my work, don't you think?'

'You're on your own?'

'For God's sake keep up, Mother! How many kids at The Mount are turning up every morning, just waiting for the day they'll be expelled? Only me.'

I knelt on the floor and rested my head on Honey's back. 'I'm sorry, it hadn't occurred to me you would be on your own all day with a tutor.'

'Well, you weren't paying much attention in the meeting, or perhaps you don't know what isolation means?' Tom said. 'Do you remember Hippo Harris telling us that I'd be alone at break and lunchtime as well?'

Honey staggered out from under my weight, then lowered her head to sniff my hair, wagging her tail as if apologising for her brusque and thoughtless action. 'I do remember now. It

56

seems a harsh punishment but I don't see that we have any choice until the meeting. Don't call him Hippo Harris.'

Tom changed the subject. 'It's the weekend in case you've forgotten. I want to meet some friends in Leicester. I'll be out all day tomorrow. Can you give me a lift in and pick me up?'

A mother with greater backbone than me would have refused but there was more at stake here than making a point. I had no idea what the future held for me, Tom or Carl and it seemed petty to refuse.

'Okay,' I said, 'but in the morning, you'll stay until your dad's care team have been. I want you to meet them. No more secrets, right?'

Climbing the stairs with Honey was an effort for us both. I tapped on Carl's bedroom door and heard a murmur from inside. The room smelt of his sweat and I opened a window. Light often hurt his eyes, so I didn't put on a lamp. He turned his head, his pupils two shining points, reflecting moonlight from the gap between the curtains.

'Would you like something to eat?' I whispered.

Carl shook his head. 'What time is it?'

'It's nearly eight, on Friday.'

Carl gave a soft moan and turned his head to stare at the ceiling. In the soft light he looked spectral, his long hair spread over the pillow, his skin taut and luminous. I sat on a chair by the bed, Honey's head resting on my slippers, and reached for his hand. It lay passive in mine.

The phone rang in the hall, and Honey startled, staggering to her feet, and barking at me as if I were a stranger. Carl turned over and groaned. 'Shut that dog up!'

I helped Honey make the difficult journey back down, one

hand on her collar, the other supporting her back. When we reached the final stair, the ringing stopped. I checked the number and rang back.

'Hello, Ella.'

'Where were you?'

'Up at the top, with Carl and Honey. I had to help the poor old girl down.'

'Really, really sorry I haven't rung before now, it's just been mad. How is Dad?'

'The team from The Haven came again today. I thought he might have to be admitted tomorrow, but he reacted when Honey barked, so perhaps it won't be necessary.'

Ella spoke with the confidence of a newly qualified doctor. 'It's not looking good is it... it'll be his kidneys, liver, and heart now, as well as the brain.'

'This is the worst collapse he's had,' I agreed.

'Hey, Mum, what was that text you sent about a gynae appointment? Fran has just been on the phone. She says you might be ill too. And what's all this about Tom? Everything's falling apart and you haven't told me.'

'I don't like to text about it. Fran has probably told you everything. She encouraged me... well... pushed me really, to tell Tom that Carl is an addict.'

I heard Ella's sharp intake of breath. 'How did he take it?'

'At the moment he's too preoccupied with his own grievances. I've sent him back to school, until the governors' meeting. I think they'll ask him to leave.'

'Oh God, I hope you're wrong. You've got far too much to deal with right now, thanks to that useless...'

'Okay, Ella, I hear you. How's the job?'

'I'm either bored stiff or rushed off my feet. The junior doctors get given all the worst shifts. I haven't had a weekend off in months and when I am off, all my friends are working.'

'Come home when you can, I'd love to see you.'

'What's wrong with you... your health. Fran was a bit mysterious about it.'

I swallowed, wondering how to say the words. She heard the hesitation.

'It's nothing serious, is it?'

'It could be, I'll find out the worst very soon. It might be... they think it's cervical cancer.'

'Oh, Mum, it can't be cancer. You can't manage cancer, not with him the way he is. This is so unfair.'

'I'll just have to get through it, Ella. Everyone does, in their own way.'

'I'll come home, I'll come home tonight.'

'Sweetheart, please wait until things are clearer.'

'Where are you being treated... at The Haven too?'

'Of course not, only the NHS will do for me!'

She praised my good sense and loyalty but how could I admit that my choice had been made because Oliver would have to pay for my private healthcare, just as he paid Carl's, and I was certain he would make it his business to find out about my treatment. My secure medical notes would not stay secure. The fine detail would make no difference to Oliver but Carl and I no longer had sex. If he was shown my answers to Mr Wales' questions, it would become obvious that I was in a relationship with another man. Carl no longer had the capacity to hurt me, or Dan, but Oliver always followed instructions.

'Mum, are you still there?'

'Sorry, I *was* listening. Honey's scratching at the front door. I think she needs to go out.'

'I have to go too,' Ella said. 'The ward manager's tapping her watch. I'll ring again very soon, I promise. Let me know as soon as you hear anything.'

EIGHT
MONDAY 15TH SEPTEMBER

On Monday morning, Tom went to school without protest. It happened easily because Owen's mother took him in her battered Land Rover as she did every Monday and tonight, she would also bring him home. I had forgotten that this was Owen's first day back at school, after being caught up in Tom's scheming, but for Owen, there would be no governors' meeting. This was the end of his punishment.

I gambled that Tom would not make a scene in front of his friend and I was right. Whey-faced, Tom climbed into the back seat and Madeleine closed the rear door on the boys. She paused, hesitating, but avoided looking at me. We both waited, and a few awkward seconds passed. I hadn't telephoned, I hadn't tried to explain or ask her how Owen was coping. It was my responsibility to speak first.

'Madeleine,' I said, 'I'm sorry Tom involved Owen in all this. I should have phoned.'

She looked down at the toe of her riding boot and kicked mud from the wheel arch.

'Owen told me that *he* took the cannabis from Carl's study, so don't feel too bad. They were in it together. But I don't know how they made it to your house and back again before I picked them up from soccer club. I don't think we're getting the truth.'

'I'm just so embarrassed that we had it lying around for them to find. Carl's been so careless. I'm really sorry.'

'For goodness' sake, Alice, we all have alcohol lying around the house.' Madeleine's deep, androgynous laugh reminded me how much I liked her. 'What's the difference?'

'Don't blame Owen,' I said. 'Tom's done it before apparently, taken stuff from Carl's room. He's in really big trouble this time because he's been selling at school. He's in detention until a governors' meeting next week. What happened to Owen?'

'Not so bad, probably because it's the first time he's done anything like this, and it was Tom who had the drugs on him. He's banned from rugby for the rest of the term, which is as close to the death penalty as you can get for Owen.'

'I'm so sorry.'

'Look, Alice, it's not your fault. If anyone is responsible, it's Carl, he should lock it away. The boys have both been bloody stupid, but we can't watch them all the time. I hope Tom's given a second chance. What about you? You're looking peaky.' Madeleine peered at me with interest, although since she was a vet I wasn't convinced by her observation.

'What about coffee sometime?' she continued. 'I'd love to hear how those beautiful girls of yours are doing and whatever Carl is up to these days.'

She grinned and climbed into the driver's seat. I watched the Land Rover roar through the gate, scattering the gravel, my hand raised. Tom didn't look back.

Owen was Madeleine's only child and so far, he had been a work of perfection. Her understanding was remarkable. When all of this was over, we'd be friends again.

In the kitchen, I made coffee and waited for the intrusion of Carl's team. The strong, frothy coffee filled the kitchen with its tantalising smell, and I carried a mug out to the gardener. We stood side by side, taking small sips, chatting about his tasks for the day and grumbling about the lack of rain.

Back inside, I sat at the table, glad of the cool, shady kitchen. At last, there was a text from Dan after his weekend embargo, wishing me luck with my hospital appointment. I couldn't stay angry with him. To keep our relationship secret, we had agreed to keep texts to a minimum. It wasn't his fault that sometimes I changed my mind.

In the quiet house, I heard some movement from above and decided to visit Carl in his attic. The study was dark, but he was awake and working, tapping at the keyboard of one his computers, his thinning hair tousled. He was wearing his sickness uniform, a grey T-shirt, and jogging bottoms that made him look like a prisoner.

Whispering seemed to be the correct approach, so I spoke softly. 'Carl, I've brought you some coffee.'

Without turning around, he said, 'Put it there,' gesturing with his elbow at the desk to his left.

I sat down in one of his winged armchairs. 'Carl, I've got something to tell you... well, two things actually.'

He carried on tapping out his message, fingers flying across the keys. 'Go on, I'm listening.'

'I've had some tests. I'll have more this afternoon. It looks like... they think I might have cancer.'

Carl paused. I heard him breathe and waited, the shadows around us gaining substance as my eyes adjusted to the half light.

'And the other thing?' he said.

'Do you remember that Tom was caught selling cannabis at school? I met the head teacher last Thursday. There's a governors' meeting next week and I think they'll expel him. We might be able to change their minds with a generous donation. Can you please talk to Oliver? We need Tom to be at school.'

Carl reached for his mug and took a deep swallow. 'Do you remember a concert in the student's union, our first summer at university? It was a band called Planet Gong.'

'Does that really matter right now?'

Carl swung around in his office chair, to face me. 'We should focus on what's important.'

I folded my arms, sighed. 'Was that concert really important, Carl?'

'Yes,' he said, his tone one I was familiar with. It was how he dealt with a stupid woman who needed everything explained. 'That was the night I fell in love with you. You hated the music, but you stayed. It has meant so much that you've always been here, even though there are times when you've hated me. I can't allow you to leave.'

Was this a stream of jumbled thoughts from his drug-addled dreams or had he already guessed at the thoughts I had shared with no one. The skin on the back of my neck prickled. Carl was always one step ahead, knowing my plans before I was sure of them myself. This time, whatever happened, I would leave. There was no doubt.

I stood up and reached for his empty cup. 'Not even you can stop me leaving if I'm dead. Your control doesn't reach that far.'

Carl's eyelids flickered and he clutched the arm of his chair. I helped him to his feet and slowly, with shuffling steps, walked him back to bed. His eyes closed as soon as I pulled the covers under his chin, and he appeared to be deeply asleep. As I opened the door to leave, he whispered, 'Tell my mother.'

I wasn't expected at the hospital until eleven, so stayed at home until Carl's carers arrived. His team had grown over the years to include a neurologist and heart specialist, but it was only the care assistants who visited patients at home. On crash days, my routine was to alert the hospital and if I felt confident that Carl could be left for an hour, I would go to the university. They have their own keys and the tasks they follow are theirs not mine.

Three of them filled the hall with coats and bags, bringing with them a smell of mown grass from the gardener's work outdoors. I recognised one of them, she had been here on Saturday, but I couldn't remember her name. Immediately, the young man asked if he could use the toilet.

The older of the two women smoothed her hair in the hall mirror. 'Getting warm out there already unless it's my hot flushes. Too hot for September, don't you think? Didn't expect to see you here, Mrs Williams. It was lovely to meet your boy on Saturday. He's a fine lad. How is the Mr today?'

In the crowded kitchen I filled the kettle, but the women made our tea, clearly familiar with my kitchen and where everything was kept. Honey, sensing company and possibly biscuits, eased herself from her basket and sniffed their shoe covers.

'He's been unconscious for longer than usual,' I said. 'He did come round a bit this morning and we spoke, but he didn't make much sense.'

'What sort of night did he have?' The younger woman joined me at the table and pulled a notebook from her tunic pocket. 'Two sugars for me, Barbara,' she called over her shoulder. 'What did you say, love?'

Ah yes, her name is Barbara. 'He was pretty restless. I turned him every three hours, but I could hear him moaning through the night.' It felt important that my care was noticed and recorded. They should hear that I nursed Carl too, just as I had been shown, so I repeated myself.

The woman making notes turned and spoke to Barbara. 'When was I last here? Was I with you or was it Karen?'

Barbara squeezed the dripping teabags into the bin. 'It was about two months back.' I noticed streaks of brown tea trail across the cream lid.

'It wasn't me,' she continued. 'I was in Lanzarote in July. Must have been Karen.'

'Were you here yesterday, Mark?' Mark lifted his head from stroking Honey's ears and nodded.

I interrupted, impatient with this meandering conversation. 'I think his crashes are getting more frequent. Are you monitoring how often he has them?'

She removed her glasses and smiled at me. 'Of course, the doctor would never forgive us if we didn't.'

Barbara handed her a mug of tea. 'Here you are, Lynne.'

And she's Lynne. 'Lynne,' I continued, 'it's getting harder to manage Carl with Tom around. After you've checked him today, could you ask the doctor whether he needs to be admitted?'

'Is he aggressive before he crashes?' She looked up from her notes then turned to Mark. 'Pop upstairs, love, and check on Mr Williams. We'll be a few more minutes here.' She frowned at Honey. 'Wash your hands first.'

'He gets very irritable... sort of agitated, but he hasn't been openly aggressive towards me or Tom.'

'Is he still working?'

'Only when he's fuelled up with meth and then he works for days at a time and through the night as well. If he has a business meeting, he plans his use to make sure he times it properly. It wouldn't do his reputation any good if he started being obsessive... I mean lining up pencils or rocking on the spot. And he still pilots his own helicopter.'

She tutted and shook her head. 'What about his appetite? Do you prepare food for him?'

What was that question supposed to mean? 'Yes of course I do,' I said. 'But he eats very little. He's lost a lot of weight.'

'We thought so too, last time we were here, didn't we, Barbara? No, sorry, it wasn't you, it was Karen. Come on then, onwards, and upwards.' She nodded to Barbara who poured the last of her tea into the sink.

'We'll speak to the dietician. Nice to see you again, Mrs Williams. I'll let you know what we think about Carl before we leave. Is it okay to phone you at work? I'm guessing you're off out now.'

NINE
MONDAY 15TH SEPTEMBER

'Is there no one with you, Mrs Williams?' The nurse at the reception desk looked over my shoulder as if a friend or partner might still appear by magic. I shook my head. This was the same clinic as before but it was hushed, like a church, with only three couples scattered amongst the rows of seats.

The Bad News Clinic, I thought, looking at the bent heads of the women. If anyone spoke at all it was in a whisper. One couple held hands. I held my own hand, very tight, and pressed down on my stomach to push the fear away. It returned in my legs, like a viral shiver, and I stretched down to rub my ankles.

Fear made me think of Carl's mother, Beatrice. There had been no contact with her for so long she held no terror for me now, but my first meeting with her had been petrifying. We were still sharing a flat, Carl, our friend Euan, and me, and it was almost finals. Beatrice was giving a talk to the biochemistry postgraduate students, which finished at midday, and I'd been instructed to make lunch for us all. It was the first time we'd met and I knew almost nothing about her. I was already pregnant with her first granddaughter Ella. Carl and I had planned a tiny wedding at the Leicester Registry Office and this was his chance to tell his mother.

I'd made a fish casserole with expensive haddock from the fish market but the fish had disappeared into a pulp. My nerves meant that I didn't pay enough attention to the rice and it ended up as overcooked sludge. Everyone forked politely at their pile of white mush and almost everything was left. Euan poured wine as if he had been born to a life of drinking expensive French wine at lunchtime, and tried to shower his natural charm upon Beatrice's immovable carapace. He was so used to winning even the most recalcitrant over to his charms, it took him sometime to notice that no one was even looking at him.

'Sorry, Ma,' Carl said, his unsmiling eyes fixed upon my face. 'She's got a lot to learn in the housekeeping department. Perhaps she'll get better after we're married. Since she'll have nothing better to do, practice might make perfect.'

'Nonsense,' Euan bellowed, 'it was delicious!' His irony always struck me as more hurtful than Carl's criticism and in my embarrassment, I felt my lips twist with the ominous threat of tears.

'Don't be ridiculous,' Beatrice snapped. 'You can't marry *her*. I mean, who is she?'

Carl feigned boredom, slouching further into his chair, and took a deep swig of wine. 'It's all settled. We're getting married on the fifteenth of August. You're welcome to attend, if you're not too... busy.'

Beatrice stood up, glaring at me. 'I need my coat,' she snapped.

'It's in the hall,' I said, heading towards the tiny, damp space that separated our front door from the rest of the flat.

She squeezed beside me in the small entrance and snatched at my wrist, pressing hard on the bones.

'I can see what's going on here,' Beatrice hissed, peering at me so closely I could count the black hairs sprouting from her chin. 'If you have any sense, young lady, you'll make a run for it. He's no good... you won't be able to save him.' She poked at my belly. 'Take this child with you, if you know what's best.'

A nurse called me into a cubicle. I was reminded of the order of the day, in case I had forgotten my letter, or had not understood my letter or had torn up my letter in anger and dismay at the sheer, utter, unfairness and cruelty of it all. I was told there would be more tests so I would need to get undressed. 'Once you're ready, just wait out here and you'll be called,' she said, passing me a basket and robe. 'Can I call you Alice?'

Back in the waiting area, I felt fear creep back into my fingers and shook them as if they were wet. A woman across from me looked up and smiled, then quickly turned away. A nurse brought round menus for us to choose our lunch. Of course, I thought, today we are patients. This is our first day. I ticked lamb stew with dumplings, which I knew I wouldn't eat, followed by rice pudding. The other women were also now in robes, their baskets neatly stored under their chairs. Their men looked out of place, overdressed and hot.

My nurse... how soon I felt possessive of her... came and sat with me, her feet tucked around the chair legs and her hands folded in her lap, holding my plan. 'We'll take some blood and then you'll have a CT scan because Mr Wales needs to see right inside you. After that, you can dress and have your lunch.'

'Will I talk to him in the afternoon?'

'Yes, but I'm not sure when. There's not many of you in today, so not too late I think.'

'I need to get away to check on my husband, he's unwell.'

She frowned in sympathy. 'He's got to look at all your test

results together, which might take a little while, but you can count on being away by half past three because he has to collect his little boy from nursery at four.' We smiled, sharing an unspoken thought about important men caught up in family trivia.

I picked up a magazine and flicked through the pages, feeling shivers squeeze my stomach and bowel. I tried to focus on recipes and holidays. One by one the other three women were taken for their investigations. The men vanished, a little too hastily I thought, but who could blame them? I was given a cup of viscous liquid to drink and told that my turn would come soon. I watched the nurse draw deep red blood from my vein, laying the phials in a neat row across a white cloth. My blood pressure was high. 'Only to be expected, nothing to worry about.' My weight was less and my height remained the same. We laughed... I hadn't shrunk!

I was left alone. I took out my phone to text Dan but changed my mind. There was nothing new to say. I turned to a clean page in my notebook and wrote down the heading Cervical Cancer which I underlined twice, then a subheading Treatment Plan, which I did not underline but followed by a colon. I left two blank pages and created a new heading: Options for Tom's Future. I wrote a list of numbers down the side of the page. I would write down each idea in turn as it occurred to me. When I felt a tap on my shoulder, number one was still blank. Half an hour had passed.

I had to lie very still while the machine hummed and whirred across my pelvis. The nurse had squeezed a liquid into my bottom before she and the radiographer rushed behind a screen. I felt desperate to empty my bowels. It was like being a child again, an infant child new to school, having to wait outside closed toilet doors, desperate not to have an accident.

I was rushed to a cubicle with a toilet alongside. The water exploded from me and I curled over as I heaved and retched in painful spasms. I dressed slowly, my trembling arms and legs forcing me to sit down and breathe deeply after each minor triumph of tights and sleeves.

A nurse came to collect me and I joined the other women in the clinic. The men were still absent. Our lunches arrived on a trolley and gave us a reason to talk. We wouldn't mention our cancer but we could safely talk about hospital food. I ate my rice pudding, the comforting sweetness settling my stomach, but I could not eat one mouthful of the lamb stew, which smelled of farmyards and school dining halls. We left almost everything.

The men returned from their own solitary lunches in the hospital cafeteria and I was called first to see Mr Wales. I hoped this wasn't chance and felt proud of my nurse.

He was waiting for me and looked up, gesturing that I sit down on the chair next to him. He angled his own chair to face me but kept his body turned towards the desk so that he could read the papers in front of him. He removed his glasses and rubbed his eyes and I thought how old and tired he looked, grey hair, grey skin, grey suit. I wondered about his nursery-aged child. Was it a second marriage or a late baby?

'Mrs Williams, I'm not sure if it's wise that you have no one here with you. It often helps, not least because the patient so often forgets what is said. Do you want me to ask one of the nurses to sit in?'

I shook my head. 'I think I know what I'm going to hear. I've known all along. I've brought a notebook so that I can write down what you say. Do you mind?' He shook his head and I searched my bag for my notebook and pen, turning over keys and mobile phone, purse, and tissues, feeling my hands shake and my head tighten. A band gripped my throat.

'Take your time, there's no rush.' Mr Wales spoke softly. I looked up at his weary eyes and thought that next to Dan, he was now the most important man in my life. I opened my notebook at the page and held my pen, as if ready to take dictation.

'You have cervical cancer, as you suspected, but the good news first. It is a Stage 2 tumour which means that the cancer has spread but not too far. The bad news is that you have Grade 3 cells. These will move fast if we don't get rid of them soon.'

Mr Wales was at work. It was an obvious thought but it struck me as very profound, like the moment when I first truly understood that I would die, that death didn't happen to everyone else except me. He is at work. This is my life but he is just working. I ticked the heading Cervical Cancer and wrote underneath, watching my hand shake as I tried to control the pen, 'Stage 2'. Below that I wrote 'Grade 3'. We sat in silence for a few moments then he continued. 'Is there anything you want to ask at this point?'

'What do you mean when you say the cancer has spread? Where to?'

'The CT scan shows that it has not gone far, just into the upper part of the vagina. Before your surgery, we will look more thoroughly when you are under anaesthetic, but I'm as confident as I can be that this is still a locally advanced cancer.'

'If I hadn't missed my last smear, it might have been caught?'

Mr Wales scratched his eyebrow with a thumbnail. 'In my experience women always try to blame themselves for this particular cancer and it's part of my job to stop you doing that. It doesn't help. For what it's worth, the smear before the one you missed was completely clear. I've checked it again. You have a fast-growing cancer. It could easily have been overlooked, even if you hadn't forgotten the appointment.'

Silence again. Just the ticking of a clock and footsteps from the corridor outside. The air felt thick and sounds were muffled.

'Take a few minutes to think about what I have said. Take as much time as you need.'

I watched Mr Wales read through my notes. He had tufts of wiry hair growing from his earlobes and his hair lay grizzled and untidy over the collar of his shirt. I had already decided that he was divorced and wondered about his first wife and whether she was coping. Had he met his new partner at the hospital? Had she been married before? Once I knew him better I would ask.

'No more questions?'

I shook my head.

'Okay let's talk about the treatment plan. I want you to try to hear this bit very clearly. I'm telling you that recovery is our goal and is a very realistic outcome. You will be free of this cancer in six months, but we have a hard journey ahead of us.' He looked at me without blinking and I saw that his eyes were grey too. I nodded. I heard the rest, but it was just words. What I understood was that I trusted him.

'I'll operate in a couple of weeks, on the third of October. I would have liked to do it sooner, but I have to go to a conference in Copenhagen on Friday. Write down the date and time in your notebook so that you can tell your family tonight, but we'll send you a letter anyway. Now, if you will just bear with me a minute, I'll dictate a letter to your GP. I want you to hear what I'm saying to her so that you're confident I've held nothing back.'

The fear and waiting were over. We had a plan and I was no longer alone. I felt safe.

Again, Mr Wales turned to face me. 'One last thing. I don't want you to be alone for your surgery. Who will you bring?'

I knew the answer to this. 'I'll try to bring my eldest daughter, Ella. She's a doctor, just qualified.' Mr Wales nodded and stood to shake my hand. When I rested my hand in his, he placed his palm over mine and pressed down firmly. This man will do, I thought.

The other women, still waiting, raised anxious, careworn eyes as I passed through the clinic. I smiled at them, feeling an inexplicable sense of relief and joy. I would fight for my life. I would deal with Tom and Carl... I would manage Oliver. I would live.

TEN
TUESDAY 16TH SEPTEMBER

My euphoric mood didn't last. The prolonged heat wave gave us another shimmering morning, but everything seemed too bright. My eyes hurt, the colours weren't right. The sky was too pale, washed with a brush of thinning cloud and any leaves still hanging on to tree branches were crisped and jagged in the unseasonal warmth. When I reached the city, it was a relief to find the landscape brown, littered and clotted with pollution. If I had to die, maybe leaving all of this behind would be okay.

After I'd dropped Tom at school, I went to work. The arrival of Carl's team would feel like an intrusion and I had nowhere else to go. Arriving late at the university meant that I couldn't find a parking space. When an attendant turned me away from the third car park I tried, I started to cry. A kindly man, he was distressed by my tears, but could not create a space for me. There are some things that can't be changed, like cancer.

I emailed Dan from David's desk. *I need to see you.* Five minutes later my secret mobile rang.

'I've been worried,' he said. 'You didn't text me after the hospital. Are you okay?'

My throat hurt, and my chest ached. 'Can we meet?' No more words would come.

He said my name, soft on an exhaled breath. 'Alice...'

'I thought I could manage this. Today I can't. I'm sorry.'

'I'll be with you in an hour... are you in David's office?'

'Yes, but what about your work? You can't drop everything. Don't come.'

'I've got a tutorial, but I'll cancel. Unexpected sickness; that's the truth.'

'Dan?'

'Alice, I'm coming... wait for me.'

I stayed in David's room, the door ajar so I could hear Dan's tread. The habits of an affair are hard to break, even when one of you is dying. It still mattered to me that we shouldn't cause any gossip. A department secretary passed the door, then leaned backwards to speak.

'Didn't think you'd be in today, Alice, with the Prof away.'

'I thought I'd take the chance to organise things a bit, you know what he's like.'

'Are you okay? You look terrible.'

I shook my head. Tension throbbed at the back of my eyes and twisted in my throat so that I had to cough. I couldn't look at her and clutched the desk in case I floated away. She hurried towards the desk and lifted me up by the elbow, gently steering me along the corridor. I could smell her body, her early morning shower gel or shampoo. There was a roar in my ears, like the rushing sound from inside a seashell or an ebb tide sucking away from the shore.

'Think you had a little turn back there,' she said, easing me into one of the chairs in the staff room. 'I'll make tea with sugar. That's good for you if you've fainted.' I shook my head. No sugar. But I drank the hot, sweet tea anyway, letting it scald my tight throat.

'Should you be at work? Can I call someone for you?'

'I'm not well,' I whispered. 'It's cervical cancer.'

'My sister-in-law had that, three years ago. She's fine now.'

'Is she?' I reached for this, grasping at good news. 'How far gone was she... when they found it?'

'Quite bad, I think. Stage something or other. I can't remember now. She has to have checks and things, but she looks better than me these days.'

'Did she... what treatment did she have?'

'Surgery, chemo, radiotherapy, you name it. Who're you seeing? Who's your consultant?'

'Mr Wales.'

'Same as Paula, that's my sister-in-law. He's lovely. You'll be okay with him.'

Traffic sounds drifted in through the open window. An ice-cream van played a tune I knew but couldn't name. I swallowed the tea in deep gulps.

'I do feel better. Thank you, you've been very kind. You must have loads to do.'

'Do you want me to take you home?'

I shook my head. 'I'm waiting for a friend.'

Dan and I walked through the park behind the university. There was a small café near the war memorial favoured by street drinkers. The fossil lodged in my throat would not allow me to speak and Dan kept silent, reaching for my hand as we left the open grass of the playing fields for the shady, mottled light of a small copse of trees. Dan was easily diverted, particularly if he saw the chance of sharing some knowledge. He stopped to look at a signboard badged with the city council logo which reminded us the trees had been planted in honour of the Queen's silver jubilee. Dan touched the bark, remarking how tall they had grown in only thirty years. His wife and daughters must have grown bored of this habit, years ago, but one of the things he loved about me was that I was still interested. I loved this man, his unshakable interest in detail.

The path led to a bench outside the café, and we sat down, still in the shade from the trees, listening to squirrels click and whir as they darted and tumbled along the narrow branches. A group of men sat in a circle on the grass, surrounded by cans and bottles without labels. They listened intently to the one talking, who jabbed the air, his fingers stabbing his points home. I still couldn't speak because if I let go of the stone, I was afraid of what might follow. I rested my head on Dan's shoulder and could sense the scuff of his hair on mine.

'Why did I tell all that to someone I hardly know? She's one of the department secretaries but I can't remember her name. She knew mine... it's embarrassing.'

Dan shrugged and I felt his shoulder lift. 'Embarrassing because you don't know her name or because you told her your medical history?' He didn't wait for me to reply. 'Because it's easier to talk to strangers, I suppose. Maybe we have to practise the words first, like a dress rehearsal. Try to get them right before we tell the people that really matter. I don't know, I'm just guessing.'

'Dan, I have cervical cancer, I'm sorry.'

'Christ, Alice, don't apologise. I should have noticed that something was wrong. What made you think there was a problem?'

'I'm bleeding after sex. I left it far too long to see the GP.'

'After we've had sex?'

I pulled away so that I could see straight into his eyes. 'I don't have sex with anyone else.'

He dropped his gaze. We never discussed the fact that he still had sex with his wife.

Sometimes I felt as if I had sex with her too, that our bodies were linked by his hands. I knew what she liked because of the way he touched me.

The street drinker's discussion was becoming an argument, but we stayed and listened. It was about something that had been said and who had said it. A small man with a huge hat jumped up and swung a wild punch. He staggered and fell, and the group laughed. It felt tense, possibly dangerous.

Dan spoke again, lifting his head to find my eyes. 'What is it you're most afraid of?'

'Right now, it's whether those men will turn violent.'

'We're quite safe. They're not aware of us.'

I paused, reluctant to shape my thoughts into words. 'I'm afraid of dying, not of death itself but of leaving Tom alone with Carl. When I've thought about the end of my marriage, I've imagined every other horrible scenario but not this one. I expected Carl to die first. In fact, I thought he would die quite soon.'

Dan stared at me, frowning. 'Slow down, Alice, you haven't even had your treatment yet. Try not to imagine the worst. Take it one step at a time. And why on earth would Carl die?'

I reached across for his hand. 'It's time I told you everything but not today. I must go home.'

ELEVEN
TUESDAY 16TH SEPTEMBER

I still have my first year Sociology notes in a ring binder, hidden amongst the books in the library. The cardboard cover is frayed, softening at the edges, releasing minute paper fragments like asbestos. The edges of the lined paper are yellowed, and rust has spread around paperclips which grip the blue smudged handouts. They still smell of ink. My name is written across the front in faded blue biro, *Alice Catherine Bowles*. Around my name, in hearts of various colours, I have scattered declarations of love for Carl. The library captures the best light in the house. It's a room where I always feel warm and safe, the pleasure of warm sun on new carpet never fading. I carried the folder over to the window seat, crossing my legs and tucking my feet under my bottom, remembering the pen I'd used to write those words of love. There were at least twenty different colours, every one released from a carousel with a single click. After I used up the ones I liked, the pen seemed worthless. My sister Hazel bought it for me to take to university in 1978, just before she left for Australia and I had packed it amongst my jeans and T-shirts, my Rod Stewart albums, and my Rupert Bear with only one eye. My precious things.

I flick through the pages of notes and handouts, but the underlined titles and lines of neat handwritten notes mean nothing to me now, even though I work as David's research assistant. Carl and I had both studied Sociology and he used to enjoy quoting theory, names and dates, especially if it meant undermining me. I wondered if talking about the past might help bring him back to his present. With the folder tucked under my arm, I climbed the two flights of stairs to his rooms. He was asleep on his day bed, his head thrown back on the cushion, his mouth open. I crouched beside his bed and watched his chest rise and fall. Occasionally he frowned and muttered. Who was he talking to?

I pushed myself up from the carpet and brushed threads from my jeans, pacing the room, then settled into the chair by the attic window. Below me, russet tree crowns bunched together in dense folds of sepia and taupe and my thoughts drifted to the autumn, almost thirty years ago, when I first met Carl.

The first year Sociology students had organised a wake for the death of Keith Moon, the drummer of The Who. Carl stares straight ahead, his old school scarf tight around his neck, like an old-fashioned binman and his hair, dyed black, stands erect in sticky peaks like a Goth version of the royal icing on my mother's Christmas cake. He wears a collarless shirt, probably from a charity shop and an antique waistcoat I later learned had been handmade in France for his great grandfather. His trousers were intended for someone pounds heavier and years older and were tied around his waist by a dog lead. His boots, highly polished, would have done credit to an officer of the Coldstream Guards. He stands at the edge of the room, one hand deep in a pocket of his trousers, the other lifting cup after plastic cup of beer to his mouth before he drops them into an over-spilling bin. No one speaks to him.

His isolation makes him appear special and exotic and I am fascinated. We weren't at an exciting university. It hadn't been hard to get in although most of us had struggled to achieve the already low grades we were asked for. Carl's absence from fresher's week only made him seem even more mysterious. In the second week of term, he turned up at lectures, sitting apart from us, always at the front, the first to arrive and the first to leave.

I am dazzled by a strobe light as I push my way through the dancing students, their body shapes frozen in slow motion, and crunch towards Carl through the litter at his feet. I try to speak to him, but 'Substitute's' pounding rhythm sweeps my voice aside. At first, Carl pretends that he hasn't heard then he leans towards me, one arm folded across his chest, the other cupping his chin. He peers at me over glasses he might have borrowed from John Lennon and raises his eyebrows. It's a gesture I have come to know well.

We've left the party and are sitting on a bench in Victoria Park. It's early October and I shiver after the heat of the student's union. Carl unwraps his scarf, links it around my neck and turns it twice. It's too tight and I protest. He slowly unwraps it, a curious smile flickering across his features. 'I'm sorry,' he says, but I know he didn't mean it.

Carl tried to give the impression he missed fresher's week because he disliked organised fun, but the truth is simpler. He arrived at our glass and concrete university through clearing. Beatrice put him on a train... this was to be her last parental act, although neither of us knew it at the time... paid his fare and waved him goodbye. Carl knew the name of our city, but he didn't know where he was in relation to any other place. He was a stranger to the world. Later, I learned that Carl's life had been bounded by his mother's home in Oxford and his school, a school with a name. Everything else about the world he learned from textbooks or the television. Of course, he went outside but only the outside that was permitted to a boy who was at prep school from the age of six and whose mother left him in the charge of a housekeeper.

That night, I opened the door for Carl to take over my world. He loved me as if he had never loved before, which was probably true, but even at the start, he didn't seem to like me. There was too much about me to dislike. I embodied everything his mother had taught him to despise. Carl said he hated ordinary things, like shops, the houses lived in by most people, families like mine, yet those were the things that had made me. He hated Sociology, but it was the only course that clearing could find for him. He mocked my notes, the underlining, the lists I made, but relied on copying them out for his tutorials.

I only found out his mother's name was Beatrice when my father died. At the funeral, my sister and I linked arms and walked amongst the bouquets spread out on the grass and my mother asked who had sent the expensive white lilies. I crouched down and turned over the card. It said *Deepest regrets, Beatrice Williams.* I stood up and brushed my hands, although they were not dirty.

'Carl's mother,' I said.

'That was nice of her,' my mother whispered, already moving on to the next bouquet but even then, I had winced at how much Beatrice would detest the word 'nice'.

The knee curled under my weight became stiff and numb and I shifted my position. I looked at my watch; two hours before I needed to collect Tom from school. I remembered that Dan was picking up his younger daughter today too, as she had a music exam. Sarah worked, of course, as a primary school teacher. If she wasn't his wife, I expect I might have liked her.

I walked alongside Carl's bookcase and pushed my folder amongst his books, at the same time pulling out a photograph album. It was one I'd bought in Woolworths just after we graduated. Its plastic cover stuck to my fingers as I knelt down and turned the pages, my back resting against the bookcase. Carl snorted and I startled, as if I had been caught prying. I hadn't seen these since Euan died, was not aware that Carl had even kept the album.

At first, there are only photos of Carl. I owned the camera and he never offered, or I didn't ask him, to take any of me. I notice now, primly, that he always had a beer or a cigarette or both in his hands. He was always posed and never smiled.

A few more pages of photographs, hard to distinguish underneath the bubbled cellophane but I angle the album to avoid glare from the window and see Euan, and Carl, playful in Monty Python poses. There's one of Euan at a protest march outside the library, demanding something, his fist tight by his cheek. Carl is tagging along as usual, but his hands are folded across his chest, as ever. I'm there to take the photographs, already cast as an observer of their remarkable lives. They wanted everything to be recorded, as if they knew.

Carl didn't make friends, he only wanted to be with me and if I made a friend, he would belittle them, so they soon gave up. His chance meeting with Euan at the medical centre in the student's union was a miracle. Carl always made a fuss about being ill and if he was neglectful of his lectures and tutorials, he was diligent about making and keeping appointments with the doctor. I remember my surprise, seeing Carl and Euan walking towards me, their heads already close together in the deep companionship that would become their signature.

We're sitting at our kitchen table, candles burning low amidst the debris of my chicken casserole. The plates are cold, with skin and bones congealing in fat amongst the overcooked carrots. Our breath, as we talk and smoke, is caught in the guttering of the candles. Euan's eyes shine, his pupils reflecting the flickering flames, and Carl is mesmerised by his talk of their potential future. I am equally bewitched, but by the beauty of my flatmates, the angles of their thin, earnest faces chiselled by the soft light. I watch them and listen to their talk through a haze of love and wine, oblivious to my exclusion, or pretending not to mind.

I rise to clear away, dipping my hands in warm, soapy water, absorbing the mothering scent of washing-up liquid. My reflection in the kitchen window is ripped apart as a train rattles past the end of the garden. I think about the passengers and whether they see me, a young woman at a window in love with two boys, Carl so vulnerable and Euan so fascinating and unreachable.

That was the first time that Carl didn't come to bed. Through the night I heard the thump of music, and I woke ragged with exhaustion and loneliness. The sitting room floor was scattered with papers and empty wine bottles and the flat was cold and smelt stale. The bathroom door stood open, but Euan was in bed, his neck stretched and mouth wide open, just as Carl's is now. His clothes were tangled on the floor. I found Carl lying on the sofa, fully dressed. I shook them both awake, fiercely slapping their tousled heads. They had lectures at nine and I couldn't allow them to be late.

This became our pattern. Carl and Euan lived for each other's minds and my role was to be an admiring audience and mother, someone they needed but didn't respect. My failure to grasp their lifestyle and the choices they made was simply another reflection of my pedestrian, middle-class thinking. Carl reminded me of this whenever I tried to contribute and Euan would look at me, apologetic, wistful even, when he heard Carl's harsh judgements, but he didn't disagree, he only shrugged in sympathy. They missed lectures, more and more often, yet passed exams by begging notes from other students and working through the night. To compensate for the alcohol, they started using something to keep them awake. I hated feeling left out, but something important was happening. It should be enough, I was reminded, to watch and admire from the margins.

Euan thought he knew about everything and one night at the beginning of our final year, when Carl was asleep, we sat up late and talked about my assignment, due the next day. He snatched the course text from my hand and scanned the photocopied articles at my feet, his finger stroking his upper lip as he read, dropping each one back onto the stained, matted carpet. Then we talked or at least he talked, and I listened and gradually I was aware only of his lips. The top one was so much narrower than the lower and I noticed how his dark brown hair fell across one eyebrow and that he had down on his earlobes. Euan paused, his eyelids lowered, leaned towards me and we kissed. That was the first time we had sex, but there were many more, as Carl gradually turned his days into night. I can't remember there ever being another girl for Euan, at least not one I met. I still miss him. We both do.

Euan graduated with a first in Maths. I scraped a lower second, any hope of doing better destroyed by constant morning sickness. Carl passed with a third but said he didn't care. The business he and Euan had started would give us everything we wanted, especially me, who would struggle to find a career anyway. My mother came to my graduation, but no one was there for Carl or Euan. I turn another page in the album and here are the photographs. My mother took one of me in my gown and mortar board but I'm frowning and looking away from the camera, as if I'm thinking, *Where are they?*

On that day, I actually made a cake, and we ate tea together in the flat. My mother was puzzled by my living arrangements but still too bereaved to ask questions. Her face was alert and smiling whenever she spoke but fell away once she was silent. She knew I was marrying Carl, but I hadn't told her I was pregnant.

Honey scratched at the door and whined. I wanted to stay here, in Carl's study, with my past but she must have been desperate to climb three flights of stairs to find me. I glanced at my watch; there was just enough time to walk her before collecting Tom from school. Sliding down the bookcase, I rolled into a patch of sunshine, stretching my arms out above my head and pointing my toes, before calling out to the anxious dog, 'I'm coming, Honey, I'm coming.'

Before I left, I gave Carl some water. He opened his eyes but without recognition. The care team were happy with his progress, had reassured me he was slowly surfacing and all he needed was time. There was nothing to stop me taking Tom out of school tomorrow. We would go in search of Beatrice. If we didn't see her, we would only waste a few hours in the car, and what else did either of us have to do?

TWELVE
WEDNESDAY 17TH SEPTEMBER

'How come I can suddenly miss school?' Tom spoke at last, after we had been driving for an hour.

I hesitated, caught out again by guilt and uncertainty.

'Some things are more important than a day in detention. I thought you should meet your grandmother. The hospital team will visit Dad while we're gone, around lunchtime. He'll be okay.'

'This is the first time I've heard about a grandmother.'

'You've always had a grandmother. She just divorced us, I suppose. She didn't want your father and I suppose she didn't want me either.'

'Lucky her. Why are we going to see her? Remind me.'

I was unsure of my motives and felt needled by his questions. All that was actually required was to inform Beatrice that Carl was ill. I could have written a letter to her old address or telephoned the university to pass on a message.

I glanced at Tom, but he stared straight ahead. 'Carl wants his mother to know how ill he is. She needs to be given a chance to see him again. Don't you think that's important?

'I'm not sure if she still lives in Oxford,' I continued. 'I don't have her telephone number anymore. She isn't listed in any directory and she's not the kind of person to own a mobile. I admit this visit could be a wild goose chase.'

Tom sneered. 'We own a surveillance company. You could have asked Oliver to track her down.'

'I don't want to involve Oliver or encourage him to snoop on private individuals. When your dad and his friend Euan set up CU.com they hoped it would help the world be a safer place. I don't trust Oliver and I want us to manage family things ourselves.'

Tom frowned. 'You're wrong about him, Mum. I really like Oliver, he's cool.'

I plunged on, determined to put into words the thoughts that had kept me awake through the night.

'Tom, I'm worried about you being at home this summer with Dad and me, both of us so ill. Even if The Mount take you back, it will be hard for you to see friends. Ella will be home for a few days when I have my surgery but that's all. I was thinking you could go to Australia and stay with your aunt, my sister Hazel. I can email her, if you like. It would be such an adventure.'

'It's okay, I'll stay at home,' Tom said with forced politeness.

'At least think about it. They live in Queensland and there's beaches and surfing and they have two grandsons about your age.'

'I said, I'll be okay at home.'

'Madeleine texted last night. If The Mount ask you to leave, you can help out in the surgery in the afternoons and meet Owen on the nights he doesn't have rugby. It's really generous of her, especially as Owen isn't supposed to see you. I want to say yes.'

Tom turned to look at me. Even as I drove I felt his blue eyes staring, hard and icy in the way that only he and Carl could manage. 'I want you to stop talking about me to other people. I don't want help from anyone.'

Those were the only words we spoke and now Tom bounced on the balls of his feet, hands in pockets as I rang the doorbell. This was the same front door, with its cracked panes and peeling paint but I was twenty-four years older, heavier, my face more lined. Standing by my side, curious and impatient, was a boy that had not yet been created or even considered the last time I was here. The house continued unchanged but there was no longer any trace of me, that heavily pregnant young woman. A neighbour confirmed that Professor Williams still lived in the house, so I knew we would see her. We might have to entertain ourselves in Oxford for a few hours, but I would wait.

Ten minutes later, I heard a muffled thud and shuffle from inside and a shadow moved towards the leaded lights. I took Tom's arm, but he snatched it away. Locks and chains scraped and rattled and Beatrice slowly opened the door, her eyes darting between Tom and me.

'Oh, it's you.' Like her house, Beatrice was unchanged. Her face was narrow and pointed and framed by a halo of frizzy grey hair which supported a pencil and two pairs of glasses. She wore a black T-shirt, faded from washing and her unfettered breasts had settled at her waist. Her thin legs were covered by black leggings, also faded to a mottled grey and her feet were bare. 'What do you want?'

'I need to speak to you. Can we come in?'

'You can say everything you need to right there.'

I saw Tom smirk.

'I'd like to come inside, talk to you properly. I've got some news of Carl.'

Beatrice rolled her eyes, but she opened the door wider and we entered the hall. While she fussed with the chains, I felt again the silent, ticking, claustrophobia that had overwhelmed me on my first visit. We followed Beatrice into her study, where she cleared piles of newspapers from the chairs. There was a strong smell of cat.

She frowned and pulled a pair of spectacles from the bird's nest of her hair.

'And who is this?'

'This is Tom, your grandson. You know about Ella but you didn't hear about your other granddaughter, Fran. She's twenty.'

'Never heard of contraception?' Beatrice snorted. 'Can't understand people who don't learn from their mistakes. I make just one and what do we get? A bloody dynasty. No wonder the planet is over-populated.'

Beatrice examined Tom over the top of her glasses, like a biological specimen and I studied her. Carl looked so like her, now that he was older and thinner. I wondered why she was unchanged then remembered that she was only nineteen years older than her son, which would make her sixty-seven. She was still in that phase of middle-age we think will last forever until old age unexpectedly trips us up. Her toenails were thick and yellow and the smell of cats was now masked by a sour smell from her unwashed body. I couldn't imagine that she was still working but the room was unchanged; drawn mud-coloured curtains, and toppling piles of academic journals on the floor, the carpet almost hidden. On the walls hung the same sepia prints I had once pretended were absorbing, allowing me to hide from the acerbic verbal games that Beatrice and Carl seemed to enjoy.

'And do you go to school?' Beatrice asked Tom.

Tom was comfortable, even cheerful. 'I'm about to be expelled,' he answered, adding 'selling drugs' for impact.

Beatrice turned to me. 'So, what do you want? Is this why

you're here? Want to send him to a boarding school. Needing money?'

Tom yelped with laughter and I could see this had annoyed Beatrice. She wasn't used to being humiliated, although it was one of her favourite activities with other people.

I shook my head. 'Of course we don't need money. Do you know nothing about Carl?'

'Not interested. Once he'd made the mistake of marrying you he was off my hands.'

'Well he doesn't need financial assistance.' I sounded abrupt. As much as I had sought this visit, I was now keen for it to end. 'He's an addict and the drugs he uses are killing him. It might be a few months, it could be longer. I thought you should know, and I wanted to tell you myself.'

Beatrice flinched, but her mask was so quickly back in place that I could not be certain. 'You want me to go and visit him? Beg his forgiveness? Have a touching mother and son reconciliation at his bedside?'

'Something like that, yes.'

Silence. Beatrice was thinking. She pulled her other glasses down and stood up to rummage on her desk. She found a piece of paper in a drawer, yellowing at the edges, and passed it to me. 'Write it down. I'm not promising anything.'

I found a pen in my bag and wrote our details and the address and telephone number of the hospital. Beatrice looked at the paper and gave a small nod as if she had decided.

'You'll want to let his father know.'

'His father?' I gasped. 'Carl has a father?'

'Your knowledge of biology is somewhat rudimentary, my dear, everyone has a father.'

Tom sniggered, enjoying my humiliation but I ploughed on. 'He has a living father?'

'Yes, he's alive. Still lives in Oxford. He was my tutor. No one very exciting after all. He never acknowledged the child. Would've been sacked. An affair with a student was a serious offence in those days. Expect they're all at it now.' Beatrice made a honking sound that I remembered was her laughter.

I had nothing to lose, I wasn't afraid of her now. 'Why did you have the baby? An abortion would have been easy in the circumstances, even in the late fifties.'

'I wanted him to see the child every day, so that he would never forget. Nothing gave me greater pleasure than wheeling that pram past him in the street, especially if he was with his wife. They didn't have any children.' Beatrice's shoulders shook with the memory of her cleverness.

I pulled out my notebook and turned to a clean page. 'Write his name and address here and your own telephone number.' While Beatrice wrote, I felt leaden with pity that Carl had been born out of spite and revenge. I looked at Tom and saw his excitement; he was gripped by a saga that would become his family myth. He would tell this story to others around dinner party tables and they would laugh together about the evil grandmother and his poor, naïve mother. But Carl was still living this narrative and he would have no other.

We stood up to leave. I hated asking, as if it were just the nonsense that fills these parting moments, but I needed to know. Uncertainty was no longer tolerable at the end of Carl's life. I wanted his story to be complete, even if he didn't care.

'One more thing, why didn't you come to our wedding? Were you really at a conference?'

Beatrice kept her back to me and fiddled with the locks and chains on the door.

'Boredom. It would have bored me. A whole day with your tedious mother and that odious oaf you and Carl lived with.' She shrugged. 'There we are. Water under the bridge. I couldn't face it.'

'When you say, "odious oaf," you mean Euan?'

'That's the one. Surely you don't expect me to remember his name.'

'He died, Beatrice.'

She turned to face me, her lips twisted in a sarcastic grin. 'You have much to learn, my dear. An odious person remains odious, even after death.'

Tom was transformed on the journey home. 'Okay,' he said, grinning, 'a grandmother, a grandfather and an aunt in Australia. Any more relatives you want to surprise me with?'

I shook my head and taking my eyes from the wheel, glanced at him. 'Beatrice terrified me when I was young. I hate the way she spoke to us about your dad. What did you think?'

'I didn't like her, I enjoyed her,' he said. 'I thought a lot of it was an act. She knows how to wind you up.'

Clearly, Tom was delighted to have witnessed Beatrice's fun with me, to have discovered a grandmother of such rancour.

'And you enjoyed that?' I asked.

'Yup, it was funny. When I get home, I'll look up my grandfather on the internet and see if I can track down Beatrice's parents too. I mean... weird or what? Thanks for taking me, it was great.'

Tom pushed the earphones of his portable CD player into his ears and fiddled with the switch. The conversation was over. My pleasure in the ordinary was not his and even his father's particular form of weirdness was of limited interest. Tom was bored with us, that much was clear, but perhaps a family of nasty academics had potential.

I drove on, thinking about Beatrice and her relationship with Carl. Even when he was a small child, she had rooms in college, where she spent most of her time, claiming she needed to be 'on hand' for her students. By her own admission, she had satisfied her spite by giving birth, but after that, she didn't want him near her, even in school holidays. Boarding school had given him a paper-thin veneer of charm and confidence but underneath, he had been left deeply vulnerable. Carl had been a victim of his mother's cruelty. In turn, I was his.

We arrived home and Tom thundered upstairs to his room. The television was on in the den, but I was quite sure it had been off when we left. I tiptoed to the door, peering into a darkness lit only by the dancing flicker from the screen. Carl was there, his eyes dark and the shadows beneath his cheekbones sharpened by ripples of blue light. My stomach turned. I should have been here.

I sat down next to him, forcing a bright, artificial tone into my voice. 'Goodness, you're awake. Should you have come all the way down here without help? There's a TV in your study.'

'I was looking for you but you weren't here. You must see this. It happened a couple of days ago, but I'm just catching up. They're going to let them fail. It's unprecedented.'

I peered at the screen. 'Who's failing?'

'Lehman Brothers. The US Treasury aren't going to bail them out.'

'Does that matter?'

'Of course. Financially, everything and everyone is connected all around the world; if one falls, we all fall. Investments will be worthless.'

I turned to face him. 'Our investments?'

It was as if I hadn't spoken. Side by side we watched the changing pattern of diagrams and charts on the screen. To me, it was incomprehensible. I decided not to tell Carl about visiting Beatrice, for reasons that were unclear even to me. If anyone had asked, I'd have justified myself with the argument that he was already stressed enough by this financial news but maybe it had more to do with me and secrets. Perhaps I did like keeping secrets, at least until I was ready to share them, until I could measure the consequences.

Carl rose with difficulty. Once standing, he pushed his sleeves above his bony elbows and scratched at the scabs on his arms. 'Oliver's coming here at eight. Could you tell him to come up to my study? If you're planning on cooking something, bring up a tray for him.'

He hesitated. 'Nothing for me, thanks.'

I stretched an arm along the settee and spoke over my shoulder. 'I don't think you're fit enough to see Oliver but I'm not going to argue about it. At least let me help you climb those stairs.'

'Okay, on both counts,' Carl said, one hand resting on the back of the settee, securing his balance before starting his unsteady progress towards the door. I followed closely behind as he clutched the banister and placed both feet on each step, climbing the stairs with slow precision. He hesitated on the landing outside Tom's room, taking shallow, rasping breaths. We couldn't miss the sweet smell seeping out from under the door.

'Shall I look in on him?' Carl asked, panting.

I shook my head. 'He's probably using something in there. Let's get you upstairs and then I'll check. If you're well enough tomorrow, he needs to talk to you about the governors' meeting. I've tried but he's not willing to speak to me about it. If you're seeing Oliver, could you have the conversation about Tom's school? I need to know what our options are.'

Once Carl was settled into an armchair in his study, I crept down the attic stairs and hesitated outside Tom's room but I couldn't face him. In the morning, I would turn out his schoolbag and once he left for The Mount, I would search his room, but right now, I needed peace and quiet to prepare for Oliver. Downstairs, I switched off the television and remembering poor Honey, unfed and without a walk, went into the kitchen. I crouched down and let her lick my face.

'I'll cook some steaks for us all, even for you,' I said aloud. Honey thumped her tail as if she had heard. 'Why not? Who cares about stupid money.'

I met Oliver in the hall, talking to Tom. I'd heard the whine of the electronic gates and had his food ready on a tray.

'You can take this up,' I said. 'Carl is waiting for you. Don't stress him out.'

Oliver's eyes scanned the steak and chips. 'Oh dear, in a mood, are we? This smells delicious.'

'Tom, please carry this up to the attic and see if your father wants a drink. I need to speak to Oliver... in private.'

Once Tom reached the landing, I hissed, 'Drop the flattery. I need to know what to say to the governors at the disciplinary hearing. Are we looking for another school or should I offer some sort of financial compensation, with the promise of no further incidents. Carl won't discuss it and you control his money.'

Oliver's eyes narrowed. 'Carl and I have bigger problems to deal with. You allowed this to happen, Alice.'

I tried to defend myself, 'Oliver that's...' but he held up his hand, thrusting his palm into my face.

'I'm only telling you what the governors will be thinking. Carl isn't involved with your children, that's delegated to you, and you've made a mess of it. Sort it out yourself. If the worst happens, you'll have to pay for a home tutor.'

He began to climb the stairs but paused when he reached the landing, looking down at me, his lips stretched into a fake, mocking smile.

'If you can't be good, be careful,' he said. The smile fell away, his eyes hardened, and he repeated, 'Be careful, Alice, be very careful.'

THIRTEEN
THURSDAY 18TH SEPTEMBER

I rose at five, woken after only a few hours of sleep by the throb of music from Carl's attic rooms and sounds as if furniture were being dragged across the floor above me. After Oliver's visit, I had tied myself in knots of worry about what his parting words meant. He had always been critical of me, following Carl's lead, but last night I had felt threatened.

Further sleep was impossible, so I rolled onto my back and behind my head, twined my fingers on the pillow. Carl must be feeling considerably stronger if he were able to shift furniture. Perhaps he would recover after all. Next time, perhaps not, but for now I might be able to hold the status quo. If Carl's death had once seemed like a passport to freedom, my vulnerable health had changed everything. I had to be unwell and allow myself enough time to recover before making any life-changing decisions. Oliver must be kept at bay, even if his words had only been a cruel, teasing taunt. To manage him, perhaps I needed Carl, the only person Oliver respected.

I carried a coffee into the garden, the sky pink with the promise of another hot day, and followed Honey's meandering path as she tracked the night's scents across the wet grass. I felt a burst of the type of energy that comes with organisation. There were plans to be made for my hospital stay and the weeks afterwards when I wouldn't be strong. If Tom was at home, permanently excluded from school, a home tutor must be found. There was much I still had to say to Ella and Fran and it was important I didn't handle this the wrong way. I pulled my thin dressing gown around me and shivered, sitting on a garden chair that had been left out overnight. Dew soaked through my nightclothes to my thighs.

'Come on, old girl,' I spoke to Honey, who had finally settled her chin on my knee, sighing with relief that our wandering had stopped. 'There's no point hanging around, I'm going to get dressed.'

Carl was alert and working. At his insistence, I cancelled his medical team but Tom could not go to school. From under his covers, he groaned that his throat hurt and when I checked his forehead, he did have a temperature. I left him in bed with a drink, a note Sellotaped to his bedroom door to say where I was going, and drove out of our locked compound into the city centre. It was still early for most shoppers and I had my pick of places on the ground floor of the car park. In Caffè Nero, I bought coffee and an almond croissant and sat by the window on a high stool, watching elderly couples, poor sleepers too, help each other through Fenwick's heavy doors. The women walked badly on swollen ankles, rolling from side to side like string puppets. The husbands, uniformly turned out in beige anoraks with tartan collars, gallantly assisted their wives. I poured a sachet of sugar into a perfect circle at the centre of my cappuccino and watched it sink, drowning the raft of chocolate. I bit into my warm croissant. To hell with calories, I thought, and felt almost happy. There was still today, there was still now, this moment. I decided to text Dan and tell him how much I loved him.

Dan and I often played at imagining our early-morning routine, as if such conversations mattered, as if we might actually wake up together one day. I told him I wore pyjamas, preferred to drink coffee and rose early. He said he slept naked and I wondered if he might feel sticky to touch in the middle of the night. It wasn't fair on Sarah but Dan told me she wore old-fashioned nightdresses, which he hated. She liked brown toast with tea and worried about fat on her bottom and the veins on her legs. Because we discussed these things I thought we would be together, but I had mistaken fantasy for plans. Now, it's no longer important, because there might be no future and sometimes, but only sometimes, that can be a relief.

I finished my coffee and walked through the parts of Leicester that pretend to be a market town. A middle-aged woman sat alone on a bench, wrapped in a sleeping bag. Her cheeks sagged into deep lines down the side of her mouth, and tendrils of greasy hair framed her face. An empty coffee cup sat beside her and I dropped a five-pound note on top of the few coins.

'Would you like me to get you something to eat?' I asked. Her eyes opened and she stared at me but said nothing. I strode away, desperate to hang on to the fragile hope of the morning.

In Marks and Spencer, I bought three sets of pyjamas and a warm dressing gown.

'Going on holiday?' the assistant asked, pushing the receipt into the bag.

I hesitated, on the cusp of telling everything to a comfortable woman with time on her hands. My mobile rang, and I scrambled to find it at the bottom of my bag. At first, I could barely hear the voice. It was Tom, hoarse and speaking in no more than a whisper.

'Mum, come home now... please. It's Claudio, he wants some money.'

'What on earth is he doing there?' A pointless question that didn't need a reply. 'How much does he want?'

'Five hundred quid.'

'I'll get it. Don't let him into the house. I'll be home in half an hour.'

The gates opened to allow me onto the drive. I saw the waiting group, Claudio leaning against the car, his back to me. It was the first time I had seen anything of him other than his arm and the flash of his dark glasses. Tom and Honey sat side by side on the top step. At the sight of me, Tom stood and folded his arms and Honey staggered to her feet. My car circled the fountain and I stepped out into the late morning heat, burning from the gravel. I shaded my eyes to better see them, absorbing the dry, yellowing grass on the lawn and exhausted foliage in our stone troughs. Apart from the sound of Honey's nervous panting, no birds sang and the cows in the adjacent fields were silent.

Claudio pulled his body away from his car bonnet and threw down a cigarette. Honey drew back her lips in a warning snarl. Tom came down the steps, gripping her collar and stood between Claudio and me, unexpectedly taller than us both. Honey finally grasped I was home and grinned in relief.

I stared at Claudio's dyed black hair, vivid red lips, and unnaturally pale skin. 'I understand we owe you money,' I said. 'What could have happened to your payment?'

The small man screwed his already narrow eyes so they appeared shut. 'Wasn't in the account, Mrs Williams. Thought I'd come around and collect, in person. Didn't mean to worry your lad.'

Tom straightened up and pushed back his shoulders, hooking his thumbs in the pockets of his jeans.

'You didn't have to do that,' I said. 'You know we always pay. Something very simple must have gone wrong.'

'Thing is, Mrs Williams, you're the fifth default this week. I have to pay my suppliers. It's business. Supply and demand.'

'I've got your money here.' I pulled the wad of notes from my handbag. 'I'll check the problem with our accountant. Now, I'd be grateful if you would leave.'

He took the money from my hand and flicked through the notes with his thumb. I was sure he wanted to count it but noticed his hesitatation, guessing he was caught between old-fashioned politeness and his more natural conviction that he was being cheated. The hand dangling from the driver's open window tapped the car door and Claudio startled, giving me an incongruous bow before disappearing into the rear passenger seat.

I wrapped my arm around Tom's waist and he gripped my shoulder. We watched the car disappear through the gates, then together tumbled onto the hot, stone steps, giggling in relief. Honey barked, sensing all was well at last.

'You were brave.' I propped myself onto my elbows, feeling the sharp edge of the step against my spine. 'When did you get to be so tall?'

Tom screwed up his nose so that his freckles formed a dark shadow across the bridge. 'I'm not scared of Claudio. Dad told me all about him.'

I knew nothing of Claudio, except for his shadowy presence in the night-time car. 'What did Carl say?'

'His name isn't Claudio, it's Colin and he lives in Shepshed. He used to be a milkman, that's when he started dealing.'

I laughed. 'Colin might not be scary, but who's that with him, in the driver's seat?'

'Dad says it's his mum.'

I leant my head back against the step, feeling a deep, throaty laugh rise from my belly. Remembering that Tom was meant to be ill, I reached out to touch his brow. 'Are you feeling better? Let me check if you're still hot.'

Tom clutched at his neck and made a choking sound. 'My throat kills but I'm okay. I probably caught it off that stupid learning mentor.' Tom made speech marks in the air, either side of the words learning mentor and added, 'He was sneezing all over me yesterday.'

Honey licked my face and I sat up to push her aside, a worm of fear crawling across my skull.

'Tom, why didn't you ask Dad to speak to Claudio? He was awake and working when I left this morning.'

'I tried his door. It wouldn't open. He didn't answer my knock.'

I remembered the heavy sounds from earlier, furniture being moved. Had it been a rehearsal? 'We'd better check on him... now.'

With our combined strength, the well-upholstered armchair propped behind the door moved just enough to allow Tom to squeeze through.

'Move the chair,' I called through the gap.

'Mum, he's dead. I think he's dead.'

'Let me in.' I shouldered the heavy chair out of the way.

Tom stood next to the door leading to Carl's bedroom. 'He's on the floor. In there.'

I knelt beside Carl and felt for his pulse. 'He's not dead, but he needs help. I don't know what he's taken, or how much.'

It was only ten minutes before The Haven's private ambulance arrived but in that time, Tom's skin took on the pallor of his father's.

'Come with me to the hospital,' I begged, but Tom refused, making an angry, fierce gesture of contempt with his hand.

I tried to put an arm around him but he shrugged me aside.

'Let me ring Madeleine, so you're not alone,' I said. 'I can take you there on my way.'

'We have to leave now,' a paramedic interrupted, glancing between us. 'Who's coming and who's staying?'

I gave in; arguing with Tom would only waste more time. There was no choice but to leave him behind with only Honey for company.

I followed the ambulance to the hospital, fearing for Tom, not his father. Until very recently, he had been a child sheltered from all harm. Today, without warning, he had joined the rest of us, the secret society who protected and cared for Carl. This wasn't going to go well.

FOURTEEN
THURSDAY 18TH SEPTEMBER

I t felt as if I had been away for days instead of hours. Tom's trainers lay on the hall floor but apart from the low hum of the electronic monitors, the house was still and silent. That wasn't unusual; Carl's architect had designed the house to be soundproofed, so he would not be disturbed by screaming children or barking dogs. I went into the kitchen, not putting on any lights, and breathed in the smell of dog and rubbish which had been left a day too long without being emptied. I heard a creak from Honey's basket and her characteristic squeak at the end of a yawn. I splashed my face with ice-cold water and looked out of the window towards the kitchen garden, grey now in the last of the daylight. A young deer, no more visible than a darting shadow, crossed the grass in front of me and stopped to scent the lopsided seat of the children's swing, hung by Carl from an apple tree the year after Tom was born.

I put lights on in the hall and climbed the stairs to face him. My legs felt stiff, as if I had been to the gym, and I stopped when I reached the landing to inhale deeply. I felt weak and remembered I had not eaten since breakfast. There was no sound from Tom's room. I tapped on the door. No response. I pushed my way in, my access partially blocked by his jeans and bent to pick them up so that the door would open fully. The light from the landing picked out his sleeping body, fully dressed, in a parallelogram of colour set against the grey shadows of the rest of the bedroom. He lay on his side in his running kit as if in full stride, his legs suspended in the act of pounding the pavements. Disturbed by the light, he turned over, muttering a few words I couldn't catch. The movement released a smell of sweat and sheets that needed to be changed, and from the floor, vinegar rose from a half-eaten plate of chips, the remains of three spliffs pushed into the ketchup. I sat at Tom's feet and as my eyes adjusted to the dim light, a room caught between childhood and adolescence gradually became solid. There were posters on the wall but an aeroplane mobile still hung from the window frame, turning in the draught. I leaned over to pick up the plate and saw his teddy under the bed, next to a pile of magazines. Kneeling beside the bed, I brushed Tom's hair from his brow. He opened his eyes.

'Mum...?'

'It's okay, I'm back. Do you want anything?'

Tom yawned and stretched, shaking his head, and I smelt again the damp, earthy smell from his body.

'I'm going out for a walk. You go and shower and get to bed properly.'

'But I wanted to talk to you.' Tom sounded petulant. 'How's Dad?'

'He's fine, we'll see him tomorrow. You need to sleep.'

Tom grunted and eased his legs off the bed. He staggered towards the door, picking up a towel from the bedroom floor.

'Tom...?'

'What?'

'Use a clean towel.'

'For fuck's sake...'

I needlessly called out a farewell against the pattering cascade of the shower, before opening the front door and striding out across the gravel drive, tugging at my reluctant dog. It was warm and just dark, a streak of light still visible behind the beech trees that crowded the squat bulk of the church. On evenings such as these, no one thought to close their curtains and I had a chance to stare into the lives of my neighbours. Mrs Tindall sat alone, her hands folded in her lap, alert, straight-backed but leaning forward to catch the late evening news. The young couple in the neighbouring house were trying to calm a crying baby, passing the hot bundle between them, hoping that one of them might have the magic touch.

It was like the peep show machines from the seafront at Skegness. My father would give me a penny and I would light up the rooms one by one, creating from darkness the warmth and light of a family home with just the press of a button. I believed the funny little wooden family, with their crowded rooms and posed positions, had a secret life when I wasn't there to watch them. I pestered my parents to visit the doll's house every day and they humoured me, but I was never quick enough to catch the stiff figures rushing back to their places. My parents bought me a doll's house for my birthday but were disappointed by how little I played with it. My mother made tiny curtains and cushion covers and my father papered the walls so that it would look like our house but they didn't understand; the peep show family really had been alive.

A middle-aged couple in the next cottage curled up together on a sofa watching television. Their plump bodies seemed to mould, as if they had sat like this for years and their bodies were now shaped to fit together. I remembered cuddling up between Euan and Carl in the flat, but without Euan there to give legitimacy to acts of affection, Carl made it clear such intimacy made him uncomfortable and it vanished from our marriage.

This ordinary love was what I wanted now, but with Dan, not Carl. I pulled my phone from my pocket, hoping he'd replied to the text I'd sent him from the hospital, but there was nothing.

I pushed on upwards, climbing the slow incline towards the green, waiting for Honey as she explored the night scents of the street. My father had never expected to be more than a prison officer, we had lived in prison housing and at the weekend we went to the officer's social club. My mother stopped work as soon as Hazel was born, her role defined by the demands of her house, her children, and my father. After my father died, I realised how narrow her life had been. She had no ambition, no friends, opinions, or interests. My father owned all of those. All she ever wanted was for everything to be nice: a nice cup of tea, a nice bit of beef, two nice little girls, a nice house, a nice garden.

'Oh, that's nice,' was my mother's comment on everything. I don't think I ever heard her say that something was 'not nice'. Not nice didn't exist. My father wasn't nice but it took me years to see this. Hazel fought back against his control, but I learned to be his compliant, good girl and never felt the back of his hand or the lash of his tongue. We were his prisoners, kept meek and compliant by the very real threat of violence but in those days, we didn't understand what was happening.

My first and only act of rebellion was to escape, through having more brains than I deserved and ending up at university far from home, only to fall victim to Carl. I listen to Women's Hour, I read books, I watch daytime television and I know how domestic violence works, but I didn't then. None of us did. Carl swamped me with a claustrophobic love that excluded everyone else. For the first time in my life, I felt important. The care he gave me, the advice, the restrictions, seemed only natural from someone who loved me so much, who only had my best interests at heart. I couldn't see his love masked a creeping, insidious control, and a growing rejection of everything I valued. It didn't seem personal, at first. We all rejected 'nice' and it had seemed especially cool to join in with Carl and Euan's jokes at the expense of ordinary people like me, families like mine.

My brain burned with looking inside and I dropped down onto a bench on the village green. Despite Carl, all I have done is try to be ordinary, to hide the total disorder of my life and pretend to the outside world that we are a normal family. But Dan and I can be ordinary, we can meld like that couple, watch the evening news together, shake our heads at the politicians, make a nice cup of tea before bed, have slow, sleepy, middle-aged sex. I know what I want and I can have it.

'I want him,' I said aloud. Honey yawned and lifted her head from my shoes. 'I will get well and then I'll take him away from the wife and family who love him. I will destroy another family, I'll destroy their ordinary, taken for granted lives. I'll do it for me and it won't be nice.'

I ate a banana, barely chewing the slimy mouthfuls as they slipped over my tongue, and dropped a piece for Honey, who tracked its path to the ground with pricked ears, followed by a fruitless search of the earth under the bench for something better.

We headed home, passing the tree Tom's playgroup had planted in honour of Nelson Mandela becoming president of South Africa. I knelt at the base of the sturdy, adolescent tree and read the plaque, tracing the faded, mossy words with a finger. Tom had walked hand in hand from the nursery in the village hall with George, a plump little red-haired boy who often invited Tom to play but was never asked back. Where are George's parents now, do they still live in the village? I ought to know these things, any ordinary person would.

At home, I called Oliver from my bedroom.

'What a shocking thing,' he said. 'He seemed fine last night.

Something must have set him off. Does the hospital think it was deliberate... an overdose?'

I thought of the chair pushed against the door. The hospital hadn't mentioned suicide but it was possible. I shook my head, as if Oliver was in the room. 'The news from America, I think... all this financial business has troubled him. Because of his paranoia, he might believe CU.com is next. There's nothing else, apart from Tom's school situation, which he doesn't seem too bothered about.'

It was unlikely that worries about my health had precipitated Carl's sudden collapse and I saw no reason to share something so personal with Oliver. 'You know that Carl's condition can only get worse,' I added. 'You're the accountant, you pay his hospital bills.'

'The thing is, Alice,' Oliver continued after a brief pause, his tone confidential. 'I've spoken to the hospital this afternoon and the doctors don't feel Carl is fit enough to make any business decisions. You may not know this, but a few months back, Carl gave me power of attorney to act on his behalf, if the worst happened. I must now action this agreement. If you need money, you must come to me.'

'We've always taken whatever we need from the business,' I argued. 'Carl doesn't even have a salary. As his wife, I should have equal access to our money.'

'Can't be done. You're not a business partner, you're not even a co-owner of the flats and houses. That's how Carl and Euan set it up, right from the start. I'm sorry if this is news to you but perhaps you should have checked. Anyway, financially things aren't looking good, every company is feeling the pinch. You're right that Carl never paid himself a salary but I treated the money he took from the business as a dividend and paid the tax. Right now, we can't afford any more expense.'

'The governors' meeting is on Tuesday. I might have to find

fees for a new school, possibly send Tom away as a boarder. At the very least, I'll have to pay for home tutoring. You're saying I'm on my own with this?'

'I'm afraid that's the case,' Oliver replied. 'What's to stop you staying at home yourself, give the lad some time and attention, teach him yourself. It's what he needs.'

'You know nothing about what Tom needs,' I protested. 'What's going on, Oliver? Carl's dealer turned up this morning, claiming he hadn't been paid.'

'Ah yes, that was unfortunate. Look, Alice, we're going to have auditors crawling all over the accounts. I've had to stop the payments to the dealer. I'll sort out some more money for you, set you up with a carer's allowance or something, but it won't be much. It's too late to start paying Carl a salary. We couldn't afford him!'

Oliver laughed at his own joke and ended the call, claiming an obligation to his dinner guests.

I ran a deep bath, pouring rich oil under the pounding taps. Blood rushed to the surface of my skin as I slid into water that was too hot. I lay still until it cooled, using only the tips of my fingers to create small currents and whirlpools in the clouding water. Afterwards, I dried myself with a rough towel and smoothed my wrinkly feet and hands with lotion. I should have heeded Beatrice's warning. In his belittling of me, Carl had found a willing partner in Euan and now I knew that both of them had conspired to shut me out of the business, from the very start, as if I wasn't to be trusted. Would Carl have excluded me from power of attorney without a recommendation from Oliver, feeling justified by Carl's paranoia? I would find out what power of attorney meant and once I was well, I would fight it.

It was midnight and I was hungry. In the kitchen, I pulled down a packet of breakfast cereal and scooped the bits out with my hands, tipping oats and grains into my upturned mouth. In the fridge I found ham, which I ripped apart and ate with my fingers while I defrosted bread in the microwave. I padded down to the cellar in bare feet, treading lightly on each concrete step so that the cold wouldn't seep into my toes. From the chilled wine cabinet, I chose two bottles at random so that I could escape quickly from beneath the sterile strip lights. My bare breasts chilled under my thin bathrobe as I tucked one bottle under each arm and climbed back up the steep stairs, dragging fabric behind me like a bridal train.

My fingers, greasy from the thick butter I'd spread onto hot bread, slid upon the wings of the corkscrew, as I tried to open the wine. I poured a glass, condensation frosting the sides and swallowed it in three deep gulps before tipping another into the glass. Licking my fingers, I placed the bread and wine on a tray and rummaged in the fridge for some cheese. In the family office, I sat in the glowing light from our shared computer, stuffing bread and cheese into my mouth while I tried to draft an email to my sister. Glass after glass of wine disappeared until the bottle lay upended on the tray, glistening with butter. My rambling email to Hazel about Tom and his future in Australia made little sense, but I pressed send anyway.

Checking my phone again, there was still nothing from Dan and I started on a second bottle of wine. My disappointment leached into hard, bitter self-pity. How could he choose not to text me, why couldn't he hide away from his family just for a few minutes? Everyone except me had someone they could turn to, even Carl still had a mother. I held my breath. I had forgotten to tell Beatrice.

After two bottles of wine, it was hard enough to find the letters on my phone, never mind spell easy words, and I had to delete three attempts at a text. I felt her presence over my shoulder, standing behind me and scowling at my pathetic attempts to write coherently.

> I have bad news. Carl is in hospital. You should come. Alice

Would she open it right away or put her phone down to read the message later? If she put it down, there was a chance it would never be seen.

FIFTEEN
FRIDAY 19TH SEPTEMBER

We drove to Carl's hospital with a CD playing at full volume. I was too tired to speak, even to ask Tom to turn down the volume, but when we reached a Little Chef just before the hospital entrance, I parked and mouthed one word. 'Lunch?'

The café was deserted but we were still asked to wait for a table. The décor was a washed-out throwback to the 1980s and the air hung with a smog of burnt fat. I wasn't hungry so ordered coffee, but Tom wanted an all-day breakfast. The food took a long time to come and for a while it seemed as if the staff had abandoned the restaurant along with the customers. Tom fiddled with packets of sauce and I stared out of the window, watching lorry after lorry turn at the roundabout outside, like a children's fairground ride. The smell of frying, stale fat and remnants of other people's meals, made me want to gag. I swallowed mouthfuls of my coffee, wiped my mouth, and broke the silence.

'I spoke to the hospital earlier and Dad is better today but he's still very ill. You'll find he looks thin and pale and he's attached to a lot of wires and tubes. He gets tired very quickly.'

'What's the matter with him, I mean apart from being an addict?'

'The methamphetamine... some people call it ice or crystal... has destroyed him. He's taken it for about twenty years. Before that it was other stuff.'

'Fuck...'

'His whole body is affected, including his mind. He thinks things that aren't true. He sees things that aren't there, like insects crawling on his skin. It's killing him.'

Tom's food arrived. He fussed with sachets of ketchup then picked up a chip with his fingers, stabbing at the egg and mixing yolk, sauce and beans until his plate became an inedible jumble. He looked at me, tears running down his face, and wiped his nose, streaking his cheek with sauce.

'What about you, are you dying too, I mean apart from your alcohol problem?'

'Okay, okay,' I blustered. 'I know I overdid it last night.' I tried to lift my voice to sound confident. 'Of course I'm not going to die. I'm going to be fine. I need some treatment, that's all.'

'I want to stay at home. I can look after Dad, and you as well. I'll catch up on schoolwork later or you can find me a tutor. I don't need a job because I'll take over from Dad. I can run the business, after he's...'

The solitary waitress stopped wiping tables and stood by my elbow.

'Is everything all right, do you need anything else?' She looked at Tom's food and then at his face. 'Is the lad okay?'

'Just some water, thanks. Yes, please take that away,' I replied, gesturing towards Tom's plate.

Tom went to the cloakroom to wash and I waited outside. When he swung out between the glass doors, I steered him to a low wall, where we sat with our feet surrounded by cigarette butts. He rested his head on my shoulder and I felt his shuddering breaths gradually slow.

'Do I have to go?' Tom asked, without looking at me. 'I can't stop thinking about how he looked when we found him. What do I say to him?'

'We'll check with the nurse. If he's too poorly, you won't be allowed in anyway. But if he's well enough to see you, I think you should try. I'll ring the hospital now and tell them we'll be there soon.'

Carl's hospital was at the end of a long drive, which wound through manicured parkland. Sometimes the hospital was visible from the road, its mock Georgian windows glinting in the afternoon sunshine, at other times it was hidden from view. I parked under a tree in a small copse, at some distance from the house.

'Can we walk the rest of the way?' I asked Tom, although it wasn't a question. 'I need to clear my head.'

He shook his head but didn't protest and I guessed he was glad of the extra time to prepare. A breeze lifted at the hem of my cotton skirt, now horribly crushed, and I pulled a jacket from the back seat before locking the car. The drive crossed a stream before it swept up to the house and from the bridge we stopped to watch weeds sway in the water. I felt reassured by Tom's presence, happy I wasn't alone. I swung the strap of my bag over my shoulder and we left the road, striding across the grass. This year's lambs, overgrown and adolescent, skittered away from us, bleating for mothers who lifted their heads, indifferent, then returned to grazing. I felt the prickle of sun on my bare legs and memories of what my surgeon had said returned in fragments. I wouldn't be the same, not like this, for a long time.

We stepped from the bright heat of the day into the deep shade of the hospital reception and a smell of freshly made coffee. I approached the desk and told the receptionist we had come to see Carl Williams. Tom took a seat but I walked around the foyer where there was a display of photographs. The original owners, I read, built the estate in 1880 but it was already a nursing home for wounded officers by the end of the First World War. It became the flagship of *The Haven* private healthcare in 1978 and had been opened by Rt. Hon. Margaret Thatcher MP. The date seemed significant. Carl and I met in 1978, the same year the hospital was born. For Carl, this is where it might end.

Tom made room for me on a leather sofa and I sat next to him in front of a fake gas fire, flickering in the grate of an elaborate marble fireplace. On a coffee table, a bowl of lilies fell across a crisply folded *Times*, placed next to a new copy of *Country Life*. Carl's designated nurse, Jack, appeared from the end of a corridor, dressed in white trousers and a white tunic, giving him a spectral appearance until he became solid and reassuring. Once a frequent visitor to our home as part of Carl's care team but never in Tom's presence, I introduced them and watched my son's shoulders relax as Jack chatted about cricket and music. The leather of the sofa felt cool and solid against my bare arms and a welcome draught stroked my temples, easing the headache that drilled into my brain. I smelt the raw scent of the lilies and ran my fingers through its yellow pollen, sprinkled over the table.

'How is Carl?' I asked.

'He's much better, in fact he's sitting up beside his bed.'

'Is he well enough to see Tom?'

Jack turned towards Tom to include him. 'Of course, I'm sure he'll be very pleased to see you both.'

Tom acted as though there had never been any question of whether he should visit his father and pushed ahead as we walked the length of the corridor to Carl's room.

Carl patted the edge of his hospital bed. 'My boy, sit here.'

Jack carried a chair for me from the other side of the room and left, promising to return with tea. Carl's chin suddenly fell to his chest and I thought he had fallen asleep. I was about to call for help when he lifted his head and focused his gaze on Tom.

'So why aren't you at school?' Carl's voice was soft but grating, as if he hadn't spoken for a long time. 'What are you doing here, visiting your old dad?'

I was about to jump in and protect Tom but he answered for himself.

'I'm suspended from lessons, because of the drugs thing, so Mum let me come. You remember that letter I showed you last week, before all this happened.' Tom's eyes tracked the machinery in the room but didn't settle on his father's face. 'I have to see the governors on Tuesday. I'll be expelled but it's okay, I want to be.'

Carl's shoulders began to shake and he made small, choking sounds that I realised were laughter. 'You're impossible, Tom. Just like me, when I was–'

'No he isn't,' I interrupted. 'You were really quiet at school. Oliver says that no one even knew who you were until...'

'Ah, Oliver.' Carl sat up, his fingers plucking at his blanket. 'Where is that lazy shit? I need to talk to him. Tell him to come and see me today... no, tomorrow. Where's my mobile?'

Carl scanned the room. 'They won't allow me anything in this place. They try to keep me from my work. It's control. No one wants me to work. They're scared of my ideas. Don't let anyone control you, Tom, stay in charge. Ask me anything... I'll tell you how things really are.'

I pressed the buzzer. Carl's eyes had become bright and his hands were scratching at his shoulders. Past experience told me that Tom should leave right now. A nurse entered immediately.

'Call for Jack,' I barked. 'Mr Williams is distressed.'

Jack arrived, out of breath. 'Please take Tom for something to eat. We'll help my husband into bed.'

Alone with the nurse, we lifted Carl from his chair, and I smelled an odour from his body, like a decaying log. I recognised this, from when my mother was dying. He didn't have long.

Once the nurse left, I tried again to speak to Carl. 'We need to talk about Tom. We have to decide what to do. He wants to stay at home, but he can't be around all this sickness. He needs normality as well as an education. I'm thinking of sending him away. I thought your mother might be persuaded to take him or he could go to my sister in Australia. Are you listening?'

Carl's eyes were closed but he turned his head towards me and answered, 'He's not going to my mother, that old bitch. He's not going to Australia. It's a big house, designed for privacy. He'll only see what we show him. Get him tutors. Ask Oliver to set it up. Tell him it's an instruction.'

'It's not just the illness. I want him away from...'

'Me?'

'I want him away from drugs, right away. I think... I believe... it's his only hope. He's an addict, Carl, he just doesn't know it yet. I can see the signs.'

Carl coughed and paused before speaking, his voice hoarse. 'Send him away? With both of us ill? You're worse than Beatrice.'

'It will be so difficult for him at home. Ella and Fran will do what they can, but they have their own lives.'

Carl's breathing fell into the rhythm of sleep. I listened to the noises of the room, one that had the pretence of an upmarket chain hotel, with its dressing table that elided into shelves, a wardrobe, and abstract prints in pastel shades on the walls. After several minutes he whispered, 'You must plan for Tom... do what you like... sort it out with Oliver. I want to think about ideas. That's all I've got time for.'

'I can't sort it out. Oliver says there's no money.'

'Sell a flat or something.'

'I can't, Carl. Everything belongs to the business and the business is in trouble. The flats, everything we own, probably belongs to some creditor. You gave power of attorney to Oliver, but not to me. Remember?'

Another silence. Instead of music from an in-built stereo, there was water bubbling through pipes, the slow whirr of a fan and the steady beep from a monitor attached to Carl's arm.

'I've been thinking,' Carl said at last, 'about creating a mobile phone that converts thoughts to words and sends them as a text. The technology is almost there. You'd only need a headset. Imagine the potential in a place like this, with head injury patients. Tell Oliver I need to speak to him.'

I touched his brow, dry against my fingertips and sighed. This was pointless. 'I think you'll find Oliver is a little tied up. Fran and Ella are on their way. They'll visit you this evening.'

'Tell them not to waste their time or mine. I've got work to do.'

I collected Tom from Reception and we strode across the pasture, neither of us speaking. In the car, he stared straight ahead but his knee jiggled frantically, despite resting his hand there to keep it still.

'Are you okay?' I asked. 'Did you manage to find something to eat in the coffee shop?'

'Yup,' Tom said, without a glance in my direction.

'I'm sorry you had to leave,' I said, guessing at the source of his hurt feelings. 'I thought Dad was about to get angry. He was fine in the end, quite calm actually. He talked about his plans to create a device for converting brain signals to written text.'

Tom turned towards me, his words weighted with scorn. 'I know what you're trying to do. You think by telling me about his weird plans, you can make up for sending me out of the room, like I was a kid. You just don't get it... I want to be included. I could have helped you. Okay?'

It crossed my mind to be grateful that my thoughts weren't showing up in text. Thank goodness he didn't know about my plan to send him away, the email to my sister sent only last night.

'I understand, Tom,' I said. 'I'm sorry, I am listening to you but I don't always hear what you say.'

After their hospital visit, Ella first dropped Fran at the station but then came home. Tom disappeared to his room after I had cooked for us all, but I stayed up late with my eldest child, sharing a bottle of wine.

Ella recounted her reaction to Carl's latest idea. 'Of course, I told him it was rubbish.'

'Oh, that was a bit harsh.'

'I know, he wouldn't speak to me for ages.' Ella tossed back her hair in a gesture that reminded me of Euan. I saw him mirrored in the way her eyes turned up at the corners whenever she laughed. 'Fran disappeared for ages, so we had to sit there in silence.'

'Fran disappeared? Where on earth did she go?'

'She went off to smoke with Jack and she was more than a little flushed when she got back.'

'No, not Fran and Jack...'

Ella arched her eyebrows and smirked. 'I think there's a definite attraction, unless I'm imagining things. You'll be seeing more of Fran. Expect a sudden enthusiasm for hospital visiting.'

Our lightness of mood could only carry us so far and we both fell silent.

Ella raised her cheek from her fist and said, 'It won't be long, will it, Mum?'

I shook my head. 'I don't think so, but no one can be sure. When do you have to leave?'

Ella glanced at her watch. 'I'd better get off to bed. I've a shift tomorrow afternoon that lasts through to Monday morning. I'll try to ring after Tom's meeting and I'm definitely staying for your surgery and all of that weekend... more if I can get the time off.'

I wandered through the house, my beautiful child, my Ella, asleep in her childhood bedroom. I opened and closed cupboard doors and picked things up, only to put them down again, Honey trailing behind me, keen that I should sit down. I tried to read but couldn't concentrate, tossing the newspaper aside.

The night she was born, there was a full moon and the earth glittered from a dusting of snow. Carl helped me down the steep staircase from our flat and sat next to me on each tread where I had to rest and breathe, his hand squeezing my knee. In the light from the streetlamp, flickering through the coloured glass in the front door, his face glowed white with fear.

The taxi dropped us outside the maternity unit, and we waited outside, hand in hand, before stepping through some gap in space or time to enter a humming place of glaring strip lights, bustling uniforms and women crying from behind closed doors like cows bellowing to be milked. It was another world and one we would not be allowed to leave without a child in our arms. When they slapped Ella down onto my belly, she studied me with a look I had seen many times across our kitchen table. I don't think Carl saw but if he did, he pretended not to notice. This was Euan's child.

SIXTEEN
MONDAY 22ND SEPTEMBER

Over the weekend, thunder clouds built and the temperature climbed further, the sky eventually collapsing into a deluge of hailstones and rain. Today, Dan was first in the car park, leaning against his car smoking one of the five cigarettes he allowed himself each day. My stomach tightened at the sight of him, still surprised that this man was waiting for me. He didn't see me drive in, so I paused to watch him draw on his cigarette and blow the smoke to one side. I studied his face in profile, his hair still dark with only a feathering of grey, as if he had brushed against a newly painted door. He took a last draw on his cigarette and crushed it under his shoe, bending down to pick up the stub and put it in his pocket.

Dan saw me and waved, his smile lifting the lines that drew down the corners of his mouth and made him look sad, which he rarely was. He waited for me to lock my car and we pushed through the door of the pub together. I found a table while Dan went to the bar, feeling the chill of a century's hoard of wind and rain trapped in the stone walls, like storage heaters in reverse. While I had longed for the end of the heat wave, an

English tavern on a wet Monday can be a miserable place. The pub's small windows, so inviting seen from outside on a winter's night, struggled to snatch at remnants of grey sky and the rooms had a damp, musty smell that mingled with a sour odour of spilled beer and wet dogs. Through the window by our table I could only see wet slate roofs from the brick cottages opposite, and I turned away to stare into an empty grate filled with artificial flowers, their colours muted with dust.

I shivered and watched Dan's slow progress at the bar. He felt my gaze and turned and winked.

With a glass in each hand, Dan sat down with deliberate care but still managed to slop some of his beer onto the table.

'Miserable out there, isn't it?' he said, nodding towards the door.

'Was it difficult for you to get away?' I asked.

Dan swiped at the spilt beer with the sleeve of his jacket. 'Surprisingly easy. The students are only just back, so the department's pretty empty. How about you?'

'It was fine. Tom's back at school but in detention. His governors' meeting is tomorrow.'

'I can't imagine how you're coping. What's happening with Carl?'

'Ella took Tom to school on her way back to London, so I managed to see him for a short while this morning. He's better than yesterday. I left him watching CNN. Something seems to be happening over there in the financial markets. Have you heard of Lehman Brothers?'

Dan shook his head and reached for my hand below the table. 'Alice, you were going to tell me about your life, not world finance. I won't go back to work, so we've got a few hours. We could slip upstairs once we've eaten, if you're okay with that.'

We've met at this pub for years. It's plain but has a few bedrooms which are rarely taken because this area isn't a honey trap for tourists and the staff indulge us by letting us pay with cash. Hiding my identity, my payments, is routine for me but not Dan. Today, I had promised to explain everything.

'Of course that's okay. I don't have to collect Tom. He asked if he could go into Leicester after school with his friend Owen and with the governors' decision tomorrow, which will likely go against him, I saw a chance for him to see a friend and us to have more time. It might be our last pub visit, for a while. What do you think, is it certain that he'll be excluded?'

'Come on.' Dan nudged me. 'That's enough about Tom. Tell me about you.'

Dan listened, resting his cheek on his palm and tracing patterns with his fingers in the streaks of beer on the tabletop.

'I met Carl in my first week at university,' I began. 'He loved me so much, I might even use the word "besotted". Yes, he was besotted with me. But he slowly started to control me, keeping friends and everyone else away, even my mother, and picking apart the things I said or did. Then Euan moved in with us.'

I paused. Would Dan understand what came next?

'I didn't mean it to happen but I started sleeping with Euan, as well as Carl. They often stayed up all night, fuelled by coffee and stimulants but because I was asleep, it took me a while to realise that Euan was also sleeping with Carl.'

I tried to judge Dan's reaction. He squeezed my hand and nodded, encouraging me to carry on. 'Euan wasn't obviously unkind, as Carl could be, but he didn't stick up for me. He and Carl were inseparable, especially as their business grew. They convinced me it was important and I thought I was part of it. I believed I was included, until I wasn't. I've only just learned the degree of my exclusion from the business and that was as much

Euan as Carl. I was stupid, naïve. I trusted them when I should have been questioning everything.'

Bar staff brought our food and the fragrant smell of hot, oily pasta and herbs brought a rush of hunger. We ate quickly, our mouths so full of hot food we could only give a frantic nod when one of the staff returned to check that everything was fine. Dan apologised for ordering chips but I shook my head, my mouth crammed with potato and sharp mayonnaise, grateful I didn't have to speak.

Once I was able to talk, I said, 'At least you didn't order garlic bread.'

Dan lifted one eyebrow and wiped his mouth with his napkin. 'There's still time,' he replied.

I shook my head and Dan sat back in his chair, his eyes waiting and expectant.

'I fell pregnant just before our final exams,' I continued. 'I should have left them, in fact Carl's mother tried to make me leave, but I didn't know who I was anymore. I didn't know if I could survive without them, or what else I could do. I wanted to stay with them both, to have their child.'

'Did Carl know the child might not be his?' Dan asked.

'We never spoke about it. Carl and I decided to marry but we both thought it would be the three of us, forever, with our baby.'

'And it wasn't?'

'Euan died a year after the wedding.'

Dan slowly exhaled, as if he had been holding his breath. 'You both loved him,' he said.

I nodded. 'Carl's drug use escalated. It was his way of coping.'

'What was your way of coping?' Dan asked.

'I pretended it made no difference. I believed I had to stay, even without Euan, for Carl and Ella.'

Dan frowned. 'There was no one left, was there, Alice? No friends, no family. That's how controlling narcissists work.'

'I'm not blind to my own situation,' I argued, aware that I might have spoken sharply. 'We all know much more than we used to about how such relationships work. As Carl's addiction took hold, the control increased because of his growing paranoia, except his methods were not so obvious. I have no evidence, of course I don't... he's too clever for that... but he started to use his surveillance methods on me. In the last few years, as Carl has become increasingly diminished by the meth, I dared to believe I could have a normal life. He wasn't capable of thinking about anything else other than managing his use. But as I have faded from importance in Carl's mind his business partner, Oliver, has become more controlling. I don't know if Carl has asked him to monitor me, or even if it's all in my imagination but I've had to become an expert with deceit.'

My voice faltered and I paused before expressing a thought that had become horribly clear only in that moment. 'Dan, I'm afraid I've taken a great risk seeing you. More than you know.'

'We've met every week for five years,' he said, shaping each word. 'We worked together before that. Why didn't I realise how bad things were for you? I'm ashamed I couldn't see it.'

'I hid it from everyone, even the children. Tom didn't know until recently that Carl is an addict. It's all about shame and fear and trying to hold on to something that isn't there. Secrecy becomes a habit and having money makes it possible to hide things. Carl has always been an outsider, the one who doesn't belong, but he turned his invisibility into a business asset. He's never known anything else.'

Dan left in search of the toilets and said he would order coffee. My eyes tracked him, the pub carpet swirling with green and brown fronds and the walls, shiny with cream gloss paint, reflecting shafts of sunlight cutting through the rain clouds.

'I feel as if I've been blind,' Dan said, pushing a cup towards me. 'I've got so many questions. I don't understand, how have you put me at risk?'

'Carl can find out almost everything about anyone and I think he's passed his methods on to Oliver. I'm not certain Oliver knows about us but he's hinting at something. It might be a bluff.'

Dan frowned and stared at the table before raising his head to look straight at me. 'I know I shouldn't ask this, but why didn't you leave Carl? Why go on and have another child?'

My attention was caught by a group of elderly women lunching together, their silver heads nodding as they chatted. It was difficult to say the words; the truth hurt. All I wanted was to run away. As if he guessed, Dan rested a steadying hand on my arm.

'I felt worthless... I am worthless. If I tried to leave, he would have hidden his addiction, hired the best lawyers and fought me for custody of the girls. The only thing I've achieved is to be a mother but like most women, I'm not perfect. There was every chance he would win and I would have lost contact with the children.'

I swallowed hard, afraid of losing control. This was a conversation I needed to have and I resented that tears might rob me of this chance.

Dan cupped the back of my head with his hand. 'Alice, you were never worthless, only brave. I can't imagine being forced to leave a child in charge of a delusional addict. There was no choice... of course you had to stay, to protect them.

'I have another question I'm afraid,' he continued. 'Couldn't you leave once Carl's addiction became obvious, once he could no longer hide it? No court would have given custody of children to a barely functioning addict.'

Around me, laughter roared and chinking glasses sounded

as if someone was smashing plates. The smell of frying food now made me want to retch. I had to confess the worst thing.

'I was waiting for him to die. I wanted him dead. I'm so ashamed but I colluded... yes, that's the right word... I colluded with his addiction. Death was the easy way out.'

Dan dropped his arm and rested his hand on my knee. 'That's not so unusual. Sarah and I had a few sessions of counselling, when we were going through a sticky patch. The counsellor told us many people in long-term relationships have fantasies about their partner's death, because it makes separation blame-free. They don't mean it of course. If their partner actually died, they would be devastated.'

'But in my case, it wasn't a fantasy. I only had to wait and everything would be resolved. No lawyers, no blame, just a grieving widow. I'm finding this tough, Dan. Is there anything else you need to know?'

Dan grimaced and stroked his chin, waiting to speak. I pulled my chair forward to allow someone to squeeze past our table. 'This one's about me,' he said. 'Why didn't you tell me before? Couldn't you trust me?'

'I've often thought of telling you, but I wanted you to love me just as I was, the Alice who works in the Sociology Department, the harassed mother of three teenagers, someone who exists on her own merit. Someone who exists.'

My throat tightened, and I forced my eyes wide to stop the prickle of tears. Dan rested his hand on the back of mine, squeezing my fingers in his palm. 'Let's see if they've got a room.'

We made love. I wasn't sure we should, because of what was inside me but I needed to be held very tight, to feel his skin against mine, to disappear into my body and only be aware of physical sensation. Dan was a competent lover, not imaginative but polite and generous, as he was in every other respect. He touched me as if any worries about my health, my marriage, our safety, were needless. Afterwards, we lay on top of the bed, my back tucked into his soft belly and a draft from the open window cooled our damp skin. The rain had stopped and I smelt the moist earth, Dan's fresh sweat and heard his breathing drift back and forth in the pattern of sleep.

I had known almost immediately that Dan and I would be lovers. The touch that might have been imagined, the way he looked at me as if I were truly there, the way his eyes travelled down my breasts and hips when he thought I wasn't looking. It felt different from the way every other man behaved towards me. He was just on the wrong side of handsome, he wasn't tall, and his shirts were rarely ironed but he carried his desirability with utter conviction. Out of all the women he met, he had chosen me, and our transition from work colleagues to lovers felt easy and natural, never clumsy, awkward, or embarrassing. Looking back, I can't believe how little I cared about the risk we were taking. Having Dan seemed inevitable and necessary.

I stirred and Dan traced the slope of my arm with his fingers, dipping into the curve of my waist and up onto my hip bone. He dropped his hand down between my thighs, then up across my stomach and cupped one of my breasts. Rolling forward, he kissed me just below the earlobe.

'I love you, Alice,' he whispered.

'I love you, Dan,' I said, catching the words, 'please leave Sarah for me' before they spilled out to cause untold harm. If I spoke them aloud, he might come to me because he felt obliged. The fine balance of our old lives had gone forever and I needed him to make the offer to leave Sarah without prompting. I turned over and ran a finger down his nose.

'It's time to go home,' I said.

Dan dried himself after his shower, different parts of his body moving in opposition to his vigorous towelling.

'How would things have been if Euan hadn't died?' he asked.

'We both lost the one passion of our lives,' I said, watching him pull on his underpants and socks. 'In the end, I've been lucky... I found love with you. Carl found crystal meth.'

I watched a thought track across Dan's face and his expression darkened.

'Are you jealous of Euan?' I asked.

'Of course I am.'

'How can you be jealous of someone who's dead?'

He turned from me and buttoned his shirt, whistling tunelessly and checking his reflection in the mirror. 'You're still in love with him, I can hear it in your voice.'

It was my turn to shower. I angled the spray so that my hair wouldn't get wet and squeezed a handful of shower gel from the dispenser. Downstairs in the pub, those grey-headed women, they must all have lost someone they still love. Surely, love never stops?

Euan's parents would now be the same age as those aged diners. He'd mimicked them with unkind sarcasm and I'd imagined a powerful couple, fiercely intelligent, but instead they were confused, tiny and very Scottish. At the funeral, his mother held out her handbag before her with both hands, in supplication. In her eyes I'd seen the love she still held for Euan, even though they had not spoken for years. I remember showing them the baby but was too riven with grief to speak to them properly, or anyone else. I have no memory of where Carl was, out of his head in the crematorium toilets no doubt.

Warm water splashed between my breasts. Hiding these grandparents from Ella had been wrong. It was never enough to send them a Christmas card every year, one that included a photograph of the children, hoping they might guess. This was a betrayal of Ella and Euan and I had to put things right, however difficult it might be.

The pub garden already had early evening customers and through the window I could hear chatter and glass touching glass. Dan waited on the bed, watching me apply make-up, and as I pretended to peer at my skin in the dim light, I checked his reflection. Without awareness of my scrutiny, Dan's shoulders slumped and the grooves on either side of his mouth deepened.

'Would you mind if I said something?' he asked. 'Something you might disagree with.'

I didn't turn around. 'Go ahead.'

'The reasons you gave for having more children, for trying to build a life with Carl, despite everything he did to you, are logical and make sense but they don't go deep enough. You and Carl clung to each other to hold on to Euan, the only person you both loved. In that way, you kept him alive, but you have both suffered. I think you've punished each other, for not being him.'

Dan's words felt like a blow under my ribs and I struggled to breathe. I wanted to argue, but there was no time for further discussion. All I could do was nod and hold him through a long, tight embrace, measuring what felt like understanding and forgiveness. He would go home and when his family allowed, he would think about my story, but ordinary life would reassert itself and soothe him. This special man, who until a few hours before had known little about my life, was trying to understand me, and that was all that mattered.

SEVENTEEN

TUESDAY 23RD SEPTEMBER

On a perfect, autumn morning like this, it was hard to believe that so much had gone wrong. I had been up since six, roaming through the garden in my bare feet with Honey following at a distance, checking every scent left by those night-time visitors who slid around the edges of her territory. The air smelt fresh after yesterday's rain, with the return of another bright, hot day still wrapped in the chill of dawn. Each blade of glass shimmered with diamonds of light. A green woodpecker tapped at the stones around the foot of the sundial and as I crept towards her she hopped away, chattering in complaint, then rose towards the woodland beyond the gate. I followed the path our footsteps had left in the dew and made coffee in the kitchen, warming each foot in turn on the radiators, now heating the house for the coldest hour. I sipped from my mug, wondering what Dan was doing at this moment.

I know his routine in the mornings. He gets up first and makes tea and toast, then climbs back into bed until Sarah wakes. He says she's often irritable because teaching wears her out, so he pours her a mug of tea, by now very strong and she sips with her eyes closed while he reads bits out from the newspaper. We should have tried harder to spend a night away. A tiny and improbable idea grew and became solid. Why shouldn't we wake up together, just once, and drink coffee. Why not? We had a few days before my surgery... Carl wasn't here. I would work out the details and ask him. He could only refuse and might well do so, but I'd rather endure the hurt, than lose this one chance.

Dan sent a text hoping that the meeting would go well for Tom. I replied, asking him if he could possibly free himself from his family for one night at the weekend. I then sent a text to Fran, bargaining she might want to be in Leicester, and asked if she could possibly stay overnight with Tom on Saturday, if I went away. She replied within ten minutes, agreeing.

I showered and dressed quickly, uncertain what to wear for a meeting where the outcome had almost certainly been decided and how I looked would mean nothing. I settled on linen trousers and a white blouse, my hair pulled back in a low ponytail, and a cashmere cardigan settled casually across my shoulders.

The sun stroked the back of my neck as I laid out breakfast in the conservatory: fruit, pancakes and coffee, food that might help us to talk. Tom ate hungrily and without a word, leaning across his plate. His hair stood up unevenly and he wore his school uniform casually and confidently, his shirt out and his tie knotted low, as if this were just another school day. I hesitated, unsure how to say the words.

'Perhaps the last day in uniform, Tom, at least for The Mount School.'

'Thanks. You're so positive.'

'We need to talk about your options, that's all.'

'Dad will sort it, he always does.'

'Not this time, you've seen how ill he is. He can't make decisions right now. We're on our own with this. We can think about what might be possible but in the end, I will decide. We'll tell Carl what's happened when we see him later and over the next few days I'll come up with a plan.'

'You're sure The Mount won't have me back?'

'I'm afraid so, because it's drugs and you were selling. And I think it's not the first time.'

Tom flushed and stared out of the window. 'It's a crap school anyway.' He drummed his fingers on the table. 'I'll just go to another one. A better one.'

'I don't think another school will take you, that's the problem.'

'So, get someone to teach me here at home, like I said.' Tom's eyes shone as he leaned across the table, his chin resting on his hands, satisfied with the simplicity of his argument.

'When they operate, I'll find out whether this cancer has spread. If it has, you must be out of the house for at least part of the day. I won't be in a fit state to have tutors here and Dad will resist having strangers around.'

Tom shook his head. 'I know I've been pissing about with all this school crap when you've got Dad and everything and all your problems, but I want to stay at home.'

'Carl and I have been, to borrow your word, crap parents but you're a child in this family and we still make the decisions. We can talk properly later but right now,' I glanced at my watch, 'we have to go and meet the governors.'

Tom and I were kept waiting for half an hour outside an oak door marked Boardroom. We could hear a murmur of voices and the scrape of chairs and plates. Occasionally there was a cough, some laughter, a chair pushed back against floorboards. Neither of us had ever been in this part of the school. We smiled at each other and touched a little, as much as boys of fifteen can allow their mothers to touch them. I reminded Tom that we had nothing to be afraid of because we knew it was over anyway.

Privately, I wished that Tom didn't have to listen to what would be said about him, not today.

Mr Harris opened the door and we were shown into a dark room, where sunlight from high windows was reflected on the surface of a heavy, polished table. There was a smell of coffee, the cups stacked on a trolley at the side, and a whiff of stale tobacco embedded in the clothing of some of those only just discernible around the perimeter of the table. Mr Harris pulled out two chairs for us, with an extravagant gesture of hospitality. As my eyes adjusted, I could see at least two reverends and one woman I thought I recognised from the school gates. The governors were introduced, and the Chair outlined the case against Tom. As she spoke, I tried to catch the eyes of those sitting in judgement, but they avoided me by writing notes or studying the titles of books that were ranked in strict colour formation across shelves that rose from floor to ceiling. Despite what I had said to Tom, I found that I held on to some hope but listening to her words I knew it was over, the meeting was a formality. I felt the disappointment like a weight in my stomach and glanced over at Tom, who looked as if he were trying not to cry. I watched the last moments of our shining little boy, who had rushed at life with joy and saw his eyes dull as he settled for the role of sullen teenager with a drug habit and a home background described in this room as 'privileged but without adequate boundaries and role models.'

Tom was asked if he had anything to say and he shook his head. It was my turn. I hesitated. I could still plead, I could play the sick and death cards; both of them. They might change their minds. I hesitated, I paused too long.

'Mrs Williams?'

I had to try. 'We have a lot of illness in the family. I have cancer. His father is very ill. Tom needs stability. He should be in school. Things have been very hard for him at home.'

The chairperson looked around the table. 'I am sorry to hear this. Do we need five minutes to discuss this new information?' There were several nods of agreement and we were sent outside once again to the plastic chairs set against the wall on the other side of the door.

Tom's eyes were bloodshot, and his skin pale. 'You shouldn't have said all that. You were begging. I don't want you to beg them to have me back.'

'I had to. It's our best chance,' I hissed. 'God knows how I will find you another school after what I've just heard.'

We were shown back to our places. Tom leaned forward and rested his forehead on the table.

'Sit up, Williams!' Mr Harris barked. I sat up sharply, as did several others around the table, but Tom lifted his head slowly and slid back in his chair, legs wide apart, studying the end of his tie. He then lifted one buttock and farted. If there had been any chance of a reprieve, it was now lost.

'Tom Williams.' The chair of governors spoke as if delivering a death sentence. 'You are expelled from this school. You are barred from the grounds and from the streets surrounding The Mount at the beginning and end of the day. If you are seen in the environs of the school we will report you to the police, on suspicion that you are selling drugs. You will have no contact with anyone, either staff or pupils. This is not a maintained school, you have no right of appeal. Our decision is final. As you leave the premises, you will hand back your locker key and library card. If you have any property at home belonging to the school, a parent or guardian must return it within three days. Thank you, Mrs Williams, for supporting Tom today. We wish you both well for the future.'

I couldn't help but look back. At the school gates, Tom threw his blazer and tie onto the ground and disappeared. It made no sense, but I bent down to retrieve them and as I stood up, I turned around to face the school. It already seemed unfamiliar and distant, as if we had never belonged. The children's voices, the bells, the shouts from lunchtime rugby practice, excluded us like the strangers we had already become.

Once at home, Tom stormed up to his bedroom and slammed the door. I wandered into the conservatory and through the open door, glimpsed the unexpected sight of Ella playing with Honey. I held my breath, seeing her height and powerful grace. Her dark hair swung around her tanned, bare shoulders and her breasts filled the top of her cotton sundress as she bent to stroke the dog. I put my palm flat against a pane of glass and pulled it back to see my hand imprinted there in sweat.

'Mum,' Ella called out, catching sight of me. 'My consultant said I should take today off, when I told her what was happening. I've made some sandwiches. Let's eat outside and you can tell me what the governors said.'

I carried a tray from the kitchen and we sat in the shade of the rose pergola, the branches now heavy with reddening hips.

Even before I sat down, I answered Ella's questioning expression. 'It's what we thought, he's been expelled. He didn't behave well in the meeting.'

'Only to be expected.'

'Don't be too hard on him. This is a particularly difficult time for you all, but he's stuck here at home with us. It's not just about our health. Things aren't going well financially, for Carl and the rest of the world. I don't know how permanent any of this is.' I gestured at the house and garden. 'If we do find another school for Tom, it's going to be expensive.'

'So I might lose my flat?'

'That's a real possibility.'

Ella finished her sandwich, her mouth too full to speak. I found I couldn't swallow and passed mine in small chunks to Honey.

'I caught something on the lunchtime news,' she said. 'All these young bankers were carrying boxes out of an office. They arrived at work this morning and were told to quit. Losing my flat is nothing, I'm well paid and can live on my salary but Fran is a different matter.'

'I'll warn her tomorrow when I ring her. She's coming home at the weekend to be with Tom. I'm hoping to spend Saturday night in London with a friend.'

'I'm sorry but I thought you didn't have any friends,' Ella teased. 'Who is she?'

Struggling with my resolve to keep no more secrets, I lowered my eyes and fussed with Honey's collar.

'It's a "he",' I said.

Seconds passed. 'You've no idea,' Ella said at last, 'how much I've worried about how isolated you'd become, stuck here with Carl. I could never understand why you stayed with him. I might have known you could look after yourself. Well done, Mum! Why haven't you ridden off together into the sunset?'

'He's married too. He's perfect for me but he won't ever leave his wife, or so he says. It seemed best that we both stayed married. If I'd been single, I'd have pressurised him to leave and I might have lost him. It's worked for us up to now, but everything's become so uncertain.'

I didn't confess that I had always been afraid of leaving Carl, believing I would never be safe from his revenge. I didn't say that I had persuaded myself to wait until his addiction made the decision for me. Ella might think these were excuses, which they were.

'I thought you'd be shocked,' I said.

'Frankly it's a relief. You need someone to love you, I mean apart from us. I won't tell Fran... you can do that yourself. She might not be so understanding.'

'I won't tell Fran or Tom until I have to.'

The sun, now lower in the sky, cut through a gap in the tangle of branches on the pergola and Ella shielded her eyes, frowning at me from beneath her hand.

'Have you any idea what you'll do about Tom? Doesn't the local authority have to find him a school place?'

'After you've gone back to London I'll ring them, but Dan, my lover, says that any school can claim to be full for his year group. They're allowed to say no.'

Ella stood up and reached for my plate. 'I'm really sorry but I have to leave first thing tomorrow morning. My shifts are awful this week, but I will be here for your surgery, that's a promise. I'll drop in on Carl on my way back to London. Mum, you look as though you need a rest. While Tom's sulking, you should try and grab a few hours' sleep. I'll do the big sister thing, take him a sandwich, and see if he'll talk to me. I might even ask him to show me whatever game he's playing.'

'Thank you,' I said. 'I am exhausted. I will go and lie down. Good luck with Grand Theft Auto.'

EIGHTEEN
WEDNESDAY 24TH SEPTEMBER

With Ella gone and Tom asleep, I sat in the conservatory to start a list of the things I still needed to buy for a hospital stay: a wash bag, some slippers, what else? I spoke to someone in Admissions from the local authority about a school place for Tom and she said they would send me a form. Dan sent a text checking whether he could call me and within minutes of my reply, my phone rang.

'I can get away on Saturday. Just so happens there's a suitable conference in London.' I thought he sounded flat, unexcited.

'Do you want to go? You don't sound as if you do.'

'I felt awful about lying,' he said. 'It seemed like a new level of betrayal.'

Normally I would have agreed, told him it didn't matter, said we should forget all about it. How often had I done that? My birthday, Valentine's Day, all the important days for couples. Whatever Sarah wanted had to take priority.

'It's only a matter of degree, Dan. You won't be where they think you are for one night, instead of a few hours. Let's spend a night away like an ordinary couple. We don't know how things are going to be... afterwards.'

I waited, counting. Dan was silent for several seconds. Had I pushed him too far?

'You're right,' he said. 'I needed to hear that you were confident, that's all. We'll do this. Now, tell me what the decision was about Tom?'

Tom refused to come out of his room, so I left him sandwiches in the kitchen, with Honey's lead next to them, hoping he'd take the hint about her walk. On my way to visit Carl, I stopped at an out-of-town shopping centre to buy hospital supplies and some GCSE course books for Tom. Feeling embarrassed and a little ridiculous, I slid into a shop selling women's underwear and found a set with a matching camisole, one that covered more than it revealed. As I fingered the pretty, rather than sexy, lace on the French knickers, my phone rang. I glanced at the contact name and pushed the phone deep into my bag, allowing it to ring on, unanswered. Of course, it was Oliver, his intrusion perfectly timed, as always. I passed the items across the counter to the ridiculously young man at the till, scrunching the garments into my fist as if I could hide them from everyone who might be watching.

At The Haven, there was a problem, but the receptionist was able to tell me little except that nurses were with Carl and I should wait in the foyer. Instead, I walked in the grounds and found a bench in a courtyard garden where the afternoon's watering pattered onto herbaceous borders filled with sedums and acers, already turning the brick-red of autumn. I had hoped to reassure Carl that his mother knew how ill he was, that she might still visit, but perhaps it was too late.

My phone rang again and I glanced at the screen. This time, I had to answer.

'What is it, Oliver? I'm at the hospital, waiting to see Carl. He's taken a turn for the worse.'

'Yeah okay, I tried to speak to him earlier but they wouldn't let him take my call. I contacted the school, heard the news, so that's one less business expense.'

'You rang the school...?'

'Perfectly entitled, considering I pay the fees.'

'The business pays the fees, you're just the broker. What do you want? I might be called away at any minute.'

'Of course, wouldn't dream of keeping you from your husband's side, not a loyal wife like you. Just do one thing for me, Alice, make sure I have access to Carl. You know what's best... for both of us.'

Oliver rang off and I slipped my mobile into my pocket. In the quiet, empty courtyard, I remembered the first time I met Oliver, in the university library. Carl was with me, as he was for most of our first year before we met Euan. His nose was running, and his cheeks were pinched with cold, so he waited for me beside the ancient radiators in the reading room, while I searched for journals in the stacks.

Carl was talking to someone, a tall, heavily built boy with tousled, curly hair. I watched them closely as I checked out my books. I'd never seen Carl speak to anyone independently, other than those paid to teach or care for him.

The stranger pressed a large hand onto Carl's shoulder, but as I approached, the heavy fingers left Carl's shoulder to shake mine. Carl's body shifted as if a weight had been lifted from him.

'Hi, name's Oliver but most people call me Olly. Can't believe that old Williams is here too.'

Olly punched Carl on the upper arm and Carl steadied

himself against the radiator, pushing his glasses back up his nose.

'Alice, Olly was at school with me,' Carl stammered.

This was all that mattered. It wasn't important that Oliver had ignored Carl at school and that they had nothing in common; they were bonded through finding themselves in the wasteland of the Midlands and pretending to each other this was where they had intended to be all along, instead of at Oxford and Cambridge, like the rest of their year group. I expected Oliver to quickly forget about us but once we were settled in the flat with Euan, he couldn't stay away. Whether it was because he smelt food or money, he always tried to be with us. Euan and Carl ignored him, as they ignored me and too often, I was left alone to talk to Oliver. He was studying Economics, read the *Financial Times*, and played rugby for the university. What was there for us to talk about? He seemed too big for our flat, sprawled in an armchair with his legs apart, still smelling of the pitch and the changing rooms. Sometimes he helped me clear up, but I didn't like to be so close to him in our tiny kitchen. Once, he wrapped a tea towel around my neck, pulled me towards him and kissed me, with Carl and Euan in the next room. I put both palms on his chest and pushed him away, leaving him to dry the plates. When I thought it was safe, I left the room I shared with Carl to lock the front door and put out the lights, but he was still there, asleep in an armchair. I think he was waiting for them to notice him, as they sometimes did, but only when he was of use. Looking back, I can see Oliver must have been lonely, and I almost feel sorry for him but I have never trusted him. For one thing, he has never forgotten about that kiss.

Our wedding day was the only time I have ever felt pleased to see Oliver. Beatrice offered to pay for everything, since my father was dead and my mother still grieving. Her decision not to attend was unforgivable but suited us all. Whatever her protestations about the boredom of the event, I suspect she found it intolerable that Carl had repeated her single mistake by having a child, and not by choice.

Nineteen eighty-one was a disastrous year for the country with riots in several cities but everyone who mattered suddenly saw the importance of information. We all had to be watched and Carl and Euan were learning how to provide us with the means. Carl was happy to leave everything about the marriage to me but apart from booking the registry office, I was clueless.

Oliver's strength was that he knew about weddings, and he had the arrogant confidence that was a by-product of his education, although this particular gift had bypassed Carl. As soon as we became aware of Beatrice's absence he took charge, although I don't remember anyone asking him.

The marriage part was easy. We queued up behind other families for our turn, said our vows and left. Our wedding party was tiny: my mother; my cousin; two members of staff from Sociology; and Carl's family, represented by his mother's housekeeper; and Euan. Carl stood next to me in front of the registrar, with Euan at his side and both men looked into my eyes when Carl repeated his vows. It was our wedding and our child. Whichever hand gripped mine made no difference.

Our tiny group crowded onto the street outside the registry office and Oliver had to wait for gaps in the traffic to take photographs. Perhaps that's why there were so few. I had chosen a dress of oyster silk that twisted and draped across my hips but in the weeks it took to arrange the ceremony, a swelling of my belly, obvious only to me, left me self-conscious and I bought a frock from Laura Ashley which made me look like a vicar's wife. I hated that dress.

Beatrice's money paid for a meal at an expensive bistro, and we walked through Leicester's back lanes, tripping on cobbles in our unfamiliar shoes and up some steep stairs to a restaurant housed in a renovated factory. Oliver organised champagne and insisted on toasts and speeches. Euan, finding himself in the role of best man, made little sense and I wondered what he might have swallowed between the registry office and the restaurant. Only at the meal, was I able to whisper to Carl whether he knew what had happened to his mother. He flushed with irritation, hating anything about his mother's behaviour to be questioned, especially with my own mother leaning across the table to hear better. Beatrice had telephoned that morning to wish him well from a conference in San Diego, where she was the keynote speaker. Carl's expression warned me not to question him further and my mother caught my eye, her lips twisted in sympathy. The rest of the day is gone from my memory, but I know I loved Carl and Euan. I was carrying their child, and I hoped the unit we had created by chance at university would last forever. What Euan thought about our arrangement was lost, like everything else about him.

I startled as footsteps sounded on the gravel behind me. Jack joined me on the bench seat.

'How is Carl?' I asked.

'He was better earlier, when your daughter was here, so much better we were going to move him to an ordinary room but around one we let him take a call from his business partner. He was agitated afterwards but then, I'm afraid I let him watch the news, which made things worse. I don't really get what's happening, but it was something about Lloyds TSB taking over HBOS. He was quite aggressive with one of the nurses, accused her of spying on him, which I suppose she was. His heart rate was all over the place and he had difficulty breathing. In the end we discovered he'd picked up a virus, so it was nothing about the call or the news. His immune system is affected, like everything else, so these setbacks are going to happen.'

'And one of them will kill him?'

'That's right. There won't be a dramatic exit. He'll go quietly with flu or chickenpox, something very ordinary.' I smiled at this, but the irony was lost on Jack.

'I can't pretend I know what's happening in the financial world either, but I suspect Carl has been aware for some time. Unless there's an emergency, I won't be able to visit again until later tomorrow, so I want to make absolutely sure that Oliver Thompson doesn't telephone or visit without my consent, even if Carl asks. Ring me if he turns up. You have my mobile number.'

'Carl's medical notes do specify family visitors only. It's our usual practice with patients who are very ill.'

'Put it in capital letters and underline it. Oliver might try and insist but I don't think it would do Carl any good to see him. He doesn't need to be worried about the business.'

We walked back to the house, side by side, the bricks in the walled garden warm from the day's heat.

'Jack, I hope you don't think I'm prying but are you seeing Fran?'

He stopped walking and faced me, hands in pockets, his skin tone pink from either the setting sun or his embarrassment.

'I've met her a few times in London. Do you mind?'

'No, I'm pleased. It could be the very best thing for her right now. I'm worried whether it's ethical, that's all. You've been Carl's nurse for so long, I'd hate to lose you.'

'I've checked. It's borderline but Fran isn't my patient, so we're okay.'

I held Jack's gaze. 'I'm going to be away on Saturday night

and Fran will be at home to keep an eye on Tom. I don't want her distracted. Can I trust you?'

'Of course,' Jack said. 'She needs to be responsible for her brother.'

He left me at Carl's room and I pushed my way through the heavy door. It was dark and my eyes took time to adjust. The only sound was the whisper of the machine that breathed for him. I sat by his bed and held his hand, but he was sedated and didn't respond.

'Carl,' I said. 'Tom has been expelled from school. Oliver didn't come up with any money, so I was powerless.'

Silence.

'I think Oliver is threatening me, but I can't be sure. Have you put him up to it?'

Silence.

'Beatrice says your father is still alive. Would you like to meet him?'

Silence.

'Jack is dating Fran, did you know?'

Silence.

'I should go home. Tom is on his own. I'll try to visit tomorrow.'

At this, I felt the briefest squeeze of my fingers. Carl was listening. I kissed his forehead and left.

NINETEEN
THURSDAY 25TH SEPTEMBER

Nothing moved in the leaf littered at my feet and in the tree canopy, no birds called from the curled, browning leaves above. I sat on a granite outcrop in the woods beyond the house and rested my elbows on my knees, my chin in my cupped hands with Honey panting at my feet. I had let Tom sleep in, probably out of cowardice, since we had to talk about his future. My sister had emailed, delighted to have Tom to stay and I had almost made my decision. He should go to Australia until the start of the new school term, if he had a school to return to at all. But what if I was making a mistake?

Worries that Oliver might try to access Carl had kept me awake and my head throbbed, my eyes tight with lack of sleep. Dan and I had been careless and even a private detective working without the resources of CU.com, would probably have taken less than a day to track down our affair. Carl and Oliver worked with governments all over the world to follow the electronic trails that every one of us leaves behind. They worked with other organisations too, but the shadier side of the business was never discussed with me. I couldn't be certain what Oliver knew, there was a chance he was bluffing, but he was certainly scared. Even I had grasped that the world was floating on a sea of unsecured debt and our company was no different. The business would collapse; Carl would die. Whichever came first, Oliver stood to lose everything that mattered to him and he believed I was his safety net.

I slipped a note under Tom's door to tell him I'd gone into work. I was actually meeting Dan, but I also needed to see David Adams to talk about my absence over the following months and organise any work I had in hand. My note was not entirely a lie.

The inside of the car felt hot and thick with the smell of molten plastic and the air conditioning roared in my face. Above that, the radio shouted about the extraordinary heatwave and global warming. I could barely touch the steering wheel. Should I tell Dan about Oliver's threats? Not yet, I decided. Oliver was powerless if I could keep him away from Carl.

Dan and I met in a corner of the university hidden from students and rarely used by staff. An old library had been converted into a coffee shop and bistro. It was private, dark, and expensive. Stained-glass windows and books held secure behind mesh grilles, created a hushed and respectful ambience that alienated most university customers. The students preferred more noise, and the lecturers couldn't afford the prices, so it was always empty. Dan sat on a deep sofa in one of the alcoves. I thought he looked wounded; his shoulders slumped and there were dark shadows under his eyes. But he lifted the corners of his mouth into a smile when he saw me and disregarding caution, leaned forward to kiss me. We sat close together and held hands, not speaking until a waitress left our drinks on the wide table at our knees.

Dan spoke first. 'How are you feeling about the surgery next week?'

I shrugged. 'Terrified but confident, if that makes any sense. Ella will be with me for the operation, and she can stay for a week afterwards. Fran's coming home on Saturday afternoon to be with Tom, while we're in London.'

Dan lowered his drink. 'I'm afraid I've lost my confidence. I feel so useless about your health, about Carl and ridiculously nervous about lying to Sarah.'

I put my cup down on the table and rearranged a paper napkin before I looked up. It shocked me to see him close to tears, this man I relied upon for good sense and strength. Uncertainty crept up the back of my neck when I thought about the risk we were taking at the weekend, but there was no future for us if we both gave way to fear. I had given in to fear for too long.

'Spending a whole night with you this weekend, away from everything, is more than enough. Right now, I can't think of anything that would make me happier. You don't need to do any more, Dan. It will be okay.'

He looked up at me and gave a small nod but whether either of us felt reassured by my show of conviction was doubtful.

He walked with me across the campus to David's office and we brushed cheeks in a farewell gesture outside the open door. I leaned against the frame, watching my friend, colleague, professor, standing behind his desk sorting papers, fingering his top lip. I thought of the first time we met, when David was a thin young man with wiry hair balanced above a forehead that was high and shiny, wearing glasses that were too thick and clothes that would have looked better on his father. Here he was now, an older man noticing me across the room, grey hair cropped close to his scalp and a pair of metal-framed bifocals on the end of his nose. His jeans, a little too tight, forced a generous stomach over the top of his belt.

David tried to be jovial, helping me pack my things but it felt awkward. I understood. It was better for us both that cancer was not mentioned, better not to try, to risk saying the wrong thing. Instead, once we had finished with the boxes, David made tea in the staff common room and we talked about Tom.

'I can understand your dilemma, Alice,' David said, after giving me his full attention. 'Don't you think that Tom needs to be with you? A separation now could make everything worse.'

'I've thought of that,' I argued. 'But I have this image of him on a beach, tanned and healthy, away from sickness and death and drugs. I can't watch over him, I'll be too ill.'

'Have you thought of asking your sister to come over here for a few months? Could she leave her family?'

This simple solution, obvious to anyone who didn't have an addict in the family, had not occurred to me. If she agreed to look after me, Hazel would have to be told everything and I wasn't ready. I stood up and lifted my bag onto my shoulder. If I stayed longer, there was a risk I would tell David about Carl.

I looked around the room and picked up a plant I had overlooked. David would never remember to water it.

'That's good advice, thank you. I'll think about it,' I said.

He reached into a cupboard and pulled out a bunch of flowers wrapped in cellophane, slopping water from its vase.

'These are from all of us. Good luck, Alice, we'll miss you. Ask Ella to let us know how you are.'

He walked with me to my car, carrying my few belongings. A student smiled at us, thinking she saw the remnants of a birthday or leaving party. I lifted the box from David, and we kissed awkwardly over the top of the carton. I watched him walk away, the afternoon sun searing my neck.

Once the seat of the car and steering wheel had cooled in a

draft from the open doors, I drove home thinking of the email from Hazel. Queensland was glorious she had said, even in the Australian winter, and she painted a picture of surfing and beach parties once Tom had made friends. Surely Tom would recognise that this was the perfect solution? But if I handled the conversation badly, I would lose him. Was it possible that first Carl and now David were right. Should I really send Tom away, to live with someone he had never met? But sending Tom to Hazel was my best and only chance to protect him and I had to take it.

Hazel was six years older than me. During the small part of the childhood we shared, I had fallen into the category of nuisance. There were only two rules I was expected to follow, leave her alone and don't touch anything. Once she became a teenager I was allowed to watch in awe and envy as she fiercely backcombed her hair, turned the waistband of her skirt over several times and disappeared after school into the coffee shops of Northampton, coming home after eleven when she was expected in at ten. From upstairs I would listen to my father shouting and my mother crying. It had felt almost comforting to hear an excess of emotion in our little household, without being responsible for any of it.

When Hazel went out in the evening, as she did most nights, risking my father's fists, I would creep into her room. Music from Z Cars or Coronation Street drifted upstairs, meaning I was safe from a homework check for at least half an hour. I opened the bottles on her dressing table and sniffed the eye-watering contents but was careful to use nothing. I stroked her vinyl records, removing them first from their cardboard sleeves, knowing that this was forbidden. I searched through her drawers, trying on her sanitary belt with a bulky pad between my legs and waddled around the room, holding up my skirt in the mirror to admire my future as a menstruating young woman. Worst of all I read her diary. She and Eric were 'doing it' but I didn't know what that meant. We soon found out. Hazel had to flee from my father's rage, without saying goodbye. We never spoke of her again but I think my mother risked meeting Hazel once or twice before they left for Australia. I couldn't wait for my turn, even if that meant being eighteen and pregnant.

Hazel had been the bad girl of the grammar school while I was the star of the new comprehensive. My teachers' hopes were riding on me to pass exams and go to university, although neither of my parents had been students and weren't sure quite what a university was for. The new, psychedelic freedoms of the late 1960s, which I was still too young to enjoy, wiped out the world of romantic ballads and coffee bars that Hazel had made her own. Claiming to be disgusted by hippies and drugs, my father insisted that if I was permitted to go to university at all, I must live at home. At the time, it seemed as if my freedom to enjoy a glamorous, exciting youth was over, even before I had started. It's hard to believe now the risk my mother took. Behind his back she helped me apply to a university far from home and when the day came, she put me on a coach to Leicester and squeezed a ten-pound note into my hand. I hate to think what she must have faced that night. I never asked and I never thanked her.

Hazel was at our parents' funerals, when she stayed with Eric's family, but I was already part of Carl and Euan's world, where relatives were either ignored or despised. In the photographs she sent every year with her Christmas card, she had grown sturdy and grey, very much like our mother. I received the same circular letter as everyone else, a little too hearty and full of her family's graduations, weddings, and births, much in the tone of a parish magazine. There had never been so much as a few personal, scribbled words to me but her recent email had been friendly, even welcoming. If she and my son became friends, perhaps there was hope for us.

Parked outside the house, I wound down both front windows and let the hint of a draft touch my cheeks and lips. I sent a text to Dan, to finalise our plans for the weekend but within seconds, my legitimate phone, resting in my lap, buzzed. I jumped. Right on cue, it was a text from Oliver.

> Carl wants 2 cu. Dr P will meet u at 2. Where r u?

I looked at my watch. It was already half past three and the hospital was thirty miles away.

> On my way now.

I texted back, after checking that I hadn't made a monstrous error and sent Dan's text to Oliver.

> Dr P will have to re-arrange.

And go and fuck yourself, I thought.

I searched for Tom, and finding no trace of him, faced a few seconds of panic that he might be searching his father's study, but he was in the garden, playing with Honey.

'I'm going to see Dad,' I called from the open conservatory door. 'Do you want to come?'

Tom shouted back, shaking his head. 'No, I don't. I mean... why are you never here?'

CRASH

I sighed and walked across the grass to where he lay with the dog, scratching her belly. 'This is exactly what I meant when I said I need you at school. Your dad is sick, I have to arrange things before my operation. I can't stay at home. I'm expected at the hospital, as soon as I can get there. There's some sort of emergency, at least Oliver thinks so. You can come with me.'

'But what am I supposed to do all day, on my own,' he whined.

I didn't have time to argue. 'Why not look at those workbooks I bought? There's food in the freezer and don't forget to take Honey out. I'll be home as soon as I can. We can talk later.'

'Forget it,' Tom said. 'I'll play on my PlayStation.' He turned his back and threw a ball for Honey, too hard. She watched it bounce off the lawn and crash into a tangled border of faded plants but didn't move.

I heard Tom mutter. 'For heaven's sake, Honey, take an interest.'

The receptionist leaned across the counter, *The Haven* logo stretched across her chest. I could visit Carl, but I must wait to speak to a nurse first. I sat in one of the leather armchairs and brought out my notebook. I turned to a clean page and wrote 'Carl', then looked back at the notes I had written about my diagnosis. There were only four words. *Grade Two. Stage Three.*

Jack walked towards me, his footsteps muffled by the carpet.

'Come in here,' he opened a door to his left. 'Dr Pritchard will join us shortly.'

Four low chairs were arranged around a beech coffee table. The door closed with a heavy sigh and it felt as if the air had been sucked from the room. No sounds reached us from outside.

159

'Would you like some water, Mrs Williams? Is it okay if I call you Alice?'

I agreed to both. 'I thought I had missed Dr Pritchard.'

'No, he's here all day. He said he would see you anytime this afternoon. Oliver Thompson telephoned earlier and spoke to the hospital's management. He insisted you should be called in. Carl's been asking for you too. We rang your home and Tom said you had an appointment at the university.'

I spoke abruptly. 'Just tell me what's happening.'

The door opened and a short man I guessed was Carl's consultant, sat down next to me, slamming a heavy bundle of files onto the table. He pulled roughly at his tie and scanned the room.

'It's too hot in here. Why do none of these windows open? Jack, can you see if there's a fan anywhere.'

Jack left us, and the doctor turned to me, holding out his hand. 'Hi, I'm Mike Pritchard, consultant neurologist. Pleased to meet you at last. We tend to talk to that Thompson chap, only because he pays the bills.'

'He has power of attorney whenever Carl has a crash, which these days means always.'

'Since when?'

'I'm not sure... I wasn't told. Oliver is Carl's right-hand man and he acts for Carl in all respects, including paying Carl's hospital fees from the company accounts. Carl was never very good at separating our finances from the business. It was his, you see, right from the start. But that doesn't mean you should talk to Oliver about Carl's health.'

'Of course. What about you? Stop me if I'm asking too many questions but why weren't you given power of attorney?'

I've never been involved in the business. Carl has never trusted me.

'It makes sense that someone who's more experienced

handles the finances,' I replied. 'It's years since I was actively involved in the business but there's something else you should know. More recently, Carl has been prone to paranoid thoughts, which focus on me.'

'I wondered if that were the case. I'm guessing he's employed someone almost as paranoid?'

I smiled. 'You don't miss much.'

'Comes with the territory. The overlap between my field and my mental health colleagues is a narrow one. I work a lot with madness and that's just the staff. Ah, at last...'

Mike jumped to help Jack through the door and as they searched for a socket, I dipped into my handbag to check my mobile phone. There was a text from Dan, telling me that he had mortgaged his house (lol) for opera tickets. He loved me, he added, and couldn't wait for the weekend.

Mike looked calmer and the perspiration had dried on his brow but I felt chilled from the fan, which was too powerful and close. I smiled at Dan's words and a flush of warmth spread across my skin. Mike noticed and as if to avoid intruding, turned away, one arm spread along the back of his chair, his free hand covering his mouth. He remained like this for several seconds, focusing on a distant point through the window. I looked at Jack, but he shrugged and folded his arms. The only sound was the occasional burp from the water cooler.

Mike turned back, his sudden movement making me startle.

'It's bad news, Mrs Williams. Thompson says your business can no longer pay for Carl to be a patient here. To be frank, we've not been paid for the last time the team visited your home. Of course, we should have told you sooner, but he reassured us, said he could sort something out. This is very difficult because Carl is seriously ill. I think he will recover from this episode, he might even find the energy to work again, but at most he has a few months to live.'

I heard a sharp intake of breath. It was mine. A memory of Carl: thin and fit, running and running, then jumping into the sky to catch a Frisbee. His jeans pull away from his stretched torso showing me a ripple of muscles across his belly and a thread of dark hair snaking below his belt. In my mind, he falls to the ground, tumbling, laughing and I pile on top of him. We kiss and roll together across the grass and then his eyes are red, streaming tears, his face covered in itching sores from an allergy to newly mown grass. We had to go home, and I'd bathed his skin with calamine lotion in a darkened room.

A weight settled across my brow and I raised my hand to my eyes.

'What if he tried, once again, to come off the meth?' I said. 'This might shock him into sticking with rehab.'

Mike shook his head. 'It's too late. Carl is the drug, the drug is Carl. His brain is damaged. He needs the meth just to be normal, but it will kill him.' He looked down and stacked the files, squaring up the edges with his palms. 'It will be quick at the end. That's the only hope I can give you.'

The fan rattled through the long pause where I was expected to speak. 'What do we do now?' I whispered.

'We can't move him today. He's my patient and I'll do what's best for him. The costs are already so high that another day or two will make no difference. The best thing for him now is care at home, rather than another hospital. Why don't you go up and see him? He's awake. I'll join you in about fifteen minutes because I want to tell him what I've just told you... I mean about the end of life not the finance. We don't like to do these things without a family member present. We can start planning Carl's care after we've spoken to him.'

Unplanned words blurted from my mouth like vomit. Talking about myself made me cry. 'I'm having surgery next week, I have cervical cancer.' I tossed my head to shake away the

162

tears and turned the pages of my notebook, as if something vital was written there.

'Look, it says so here... I wrote it down.'

Jack walked around to sit next to me and took the notebook from my hand. He tried to put his arm across my shoulders, but I pulled away. I didn't want comfort from my daughter's boyfriend.

I wiped my running nose with the back of my hand and controlled my voice, speaking each word in turn as if I were dictating. 'You don't understand, I'm going to be fine. I'm going to recover. But you must see, I can't care for Carl at home.'

TWENTY

THURSDAY 25TH SEPTEMBER

Carl had been moved to a room that had no pretensions to be anything other than a place where the very sick were cared for. Machines puffed and hummed, attached to him by wires, tubes, and clips. He appeared to be asleep, but the nurse spoke to me in a whisper and said that he would respond. I touched his shoulder and he turned to me and exhaled my name on a long, drawn-out sigh. I held his hand, sat down on the chair next to the bed and cradled his head on my arm. He closed his eyes, as I stroked his temple. I smelt his breath, which was stale but not foul, like the gravel at the bottom of a fish tank.

I didn't whisper to Carl about what we should do about Tom or money. Carl was about to learn that he was dying. He had destroyed the miracle of his life and that was enough. When I first met Carl, he must already have been certain he was unlovable and he would have been shamed every day of his life by Beatrice's rejection. In turn, he made me feel unlovable and had rejected me but even after this, I felt glad that I had loved him.

I wasn't sure what Carl understood of the stark facts Mike Pritchard gave him. He nodded when questioned but for much of the time he seemed to be asleep. After Mike left, I stayed and stroked his forehead and gave him sips of water from a cup, like the ones the children used when they were prone to spills.

The nurse asked me to leave when Carl needed support to breathe but first I helped her moisturise the sores on his skin and then washed his face and hands with a warm, scented cloth. I brushed the thinning strands of hair from his face and bent to kiss him. He opened his eyes and found mine, his pupils struggling to focus.

'I'm sorry.' It was just audible, but I knew for certain Carl had heard everything Mike had said.

———

Jack walked with me to the end of the formal gardens. He kept his hands in his pockets as we crunched across gravel paths between crumpled herbaceous borders, tangled with decaying leaves and brown flower heads. At the steps down to the path that led to my car, Jack sat on the wall and pulled a pack of cigarettes from his trouser pocket. He flicked one out for me, but I shook my head. Jack lit his, cupping his hand around the flame and inhaled deeply. The smell of new smoke, mingled with the earthy scent of early evening, made me ache for Dan.

'Are you okay to walk the rest of the way yourself?' Jack screwed up his eyes against the smoke drifting from his lips.

'Yes, of course. It's still daylight and I need to think. The walk will do me good.'

Jack nodded. 'And you're sure about what we agreed?'

'You'll keep Carl here until I'm ready to have him home.'

Jack stood up and held out his hand to me. 'Good luck, Alice.'

As I walked across the grass, I thought about Carl alone in that room and wondered if I should have stayed, but Tom was at home, waiting for me. The light was just softening within the lengthening shadows of the distant trees. The shape of my car grew solid, but its colour was indistinct. A figure was moving. There was another car, parked behind mine. I shaded my eyes, but I was still too far away to make sense of what I was seeing. Alert to danger, my senses sharpened. Yes, there it was, a man was moving around my car. I hesitated. Should I run back to the hospital?

A voice called, echoing across the parkland and the shadowy figure raised a hand. It was Oliver. My fear turned to anger. *I don't want him here.* His bulk became solid as he strolled towards me. I hurried to close the gap between us, to get this unwelcome meeting over with. I didn't greet him as we met, but walked past with my head down, planning what I needed to say. We reached the cars and Oliver opened the door of his new Mercedes.

'Shall we talk in here? It's getting cold.'

I shook my head. 'I'm hot from walking. Here is fine.' I leaned against a tree and folded my arms, brushing at grass and stones with the toe of my shoe.

'They told you about the money?'

My mouth felt dry and my tongue stuck to the roof of my mouth. I swallowed but there was no saliva. I nodded.

'Have you said anything to Carl?'

'Not yet, he's too ill. He'll stay here a couple of days, until I can have him at home.'

Oliver jangled keys in his trouser pockets. 'It's not my fault. You've seen the news.'

'You should have said something, taken some action sooner. Carl trusted you.'

Oliver looked away and even in the half light I could see a deep, red flush spread from below his shirt collar and up his neck like a port wine stain.

'The thing is, Alice, I need to hide some money, a lot of money.' I watched him struggle under my glare. His blond curls, shining in the setting sun, gave him a cherubic aura, incongruous now in one so middle-aged. 'I need to use your bank account. The auditors are crawling all over me. It might help you too, we could fund some of Carl's care.'

I felt nothing but disgust. For the first time I was glad that Carl had so firmly shut me out of the business. 'There is a National Health Service, he'll be looked after. You and Carl made choices that didn't include me. It's too late and almost certainly illegal, to involve me now.'

'You've never liked me,' Oliver whined, but still he didn't look up.

'That's irrelevant. My opinion of you makes no difference.'

'I know about you and your lover.' Oliver smirked, lifting his eyes to judge the impact of his words. 'I track every email, I know about every shag. I've protected you, Alice, but Carl ought to be informed, especially about your tryst in London... at the weekend, isn't it? The police would also be interested to hear about the drugs you keep in your home. That you leave your fifteen-year-old son alone to pay off dealers.'

The sun burned low through the trees and I heard rooks settle high above us, rattling in the branches. The threat was real. Mike Pritchard had said Carl might well recover from this episode, to some degree. If Oliver encouraged him, he would seek revenge. The best outcome would be legal or financial retribution, the worst case was that Dan might not be safe.

I spat out the words, 'You are a shit, Oliver.'

'Be reasonable, Alice. I have to walk away with something and you can too. You'll only have to hide the money for a few days, until I find somewhere more secure. If you agree, your secrets are safe with me.'

My voice cracked, betraying my fear. I struggled to control

the corners of my mouth. 'You've exploited Carl. You've preyed on his weakness and addiction. You're not protecting me, you're saving up information to use against me... to destroy me. Why are you doing this, Oliver?'

'I've always acted in Carl's best interests, unlike you.'

I shook my head. 'You bastard...'

Oliver interrupted. 'For your children's sake, I need to save what I can from our creditors. Carl is killing himself with drugs, but you haven't exactly cared or tried to stop him. I'm asking you to help me now. Come on, Alice, it's only one more lie. We're not so different you and me.'

Anger burned inside me and I felt bile rise in my throat. 'How dare you suggest that I wouldn't put my children first. And you know nothing about living with an addict. What do you know about family life? Your children have been in boarding school since they were seven. Your wife screws anything that moves. You're just trying to protect all this.' I swept my hand over his car, his suit, his puffy, prosperous face.

'You haven't exactly been mother of the year,' Oliver spat back at me. 'Your son's been expelled from school, another addict in the making and once again, you expected the business to compensate for your inadequacy as a parent. Without Carl's money, you're on your own. If Carl chooses to divorce you, he'll make sure you won't see Tom again and you'll be left without a penny. Dan Lewis won't be much help. I've heard university lecturers earn peanuts and his alimony payments will be high, very high, especially after I've tipped off his wife Sarah. A bit too late to find a decent job, isn't it, Alice?'

The evening breeze cooled, and I felt the hair on my arms prickle. Leaves whispered above me and a fox screamed. The blue sky had spread into a soft orange smeared with dark clouds, like inkblots. I watched a flock of starlings settle into the trees around the hospital, chattering as they fought amongst each other for a perch. Lights from the building glowed warm and safe and I thought of Carl inside. At last, my world made sense. Perhaps Dan was right. Oliver couldn't touch me because Carl needed me in a way that Oliver would never understand. He always had. Everything was uncertain except this one thing. I smiled and Oliver frowned, puzzled.

'Do what you like,' I said. 'I won't hide any money for you. It's over, can't you see? You can't control me, or Carl or Dan. Save yourself... if you can.'

I drove home following the red taillights of the cars ahead, as if we were all on the same journey, holding lanterns aloft for each other so that we could find our way home. I listened to the news, still dominated by the run on HBOS shares. Cows swayed over a motorway bridge after milking, silhouetted against the end of the day. I had been taken into the core of Oliver's dark heart and he knew mine, but right now, I would fight for my family and I believed I could protect Dan. My life with Carl was finished, the business was finished, Oliver was finished. These things would happen and very soon. But I wasn't finished. Mr Wales had said I would live.

TWENTY-ONE
FRIDAY 26TH SEPTEMBER

Tom burst into my bedroom at the very moment I was laying out my new lingerie and silk pyjamas on top of my duvet. I scooped the guilty underwear into my hands and sat down, crushing them underneath my thighs.

'If you're going to see Dad today, can you drop me at Madeleine's?' he asked.

'I thought you didn't want to...'

'She's got a Great Dane coming in for a caesarean and she needs my help. The dog's too big for her to handle,' Tom explained, as if this was obvious to everyone except me.

Madeleine had been handling animals larger than a Great Dane for years on her own, but I felt grateful she had allowed Tom to believe he was indispensable. 'Of course, I said, let me know when you want to leave.'

In the surgery car park, I sent Dan a text.

> Oliver knows about us but we're safe as long as he can't get to Carl. I'll do everything I can to stop that happening. This number is still okay.

At the hospital, I checked in at reception. 'Your husband has a visitor, Mrs Williams.'

Oliver. I didn't pause to allow her to check the name in the register. I slammed on the keypad for the lift with my open palm and unable to wait, climbed the immaculately carpeted stairs two at a time, hauling myself up by the brass-plated banister.

I caught my breath on the second landing. Someone called out. 'Alice, down here. We've moved his room. Lower dependency. I tried to call you. Dr Pritchard says he can go home.'

'But you said you would wait until I was ready for him,' I protested.

'That bloke Thompson insisted Carl be moved out. Told the financial director of the hospital that you're bankrupt. We had no choice once our finance people knew they wouldn't be paid. He is much better today... against all odds. I have his discharge papers ready. You can pick them up from reception.'

'Who's with him right now? Is it Thompson?' I didn't need an answer. A smell of mildew and cats lingered in the corridor. It could only be one person.

'She turned up an hour ago,' Jack whispered. 'They're having the most terrible row.'

I listened at the door. 'That's not a row. That's a conversation.'

I pushed the door ajar, shocked to see Carl out of bed and standing, taller now than his shrunken mother, rocking back on his heels, his hands in his dressing-gown pockets, emphasising his point. 'I am not denying your eminent career as a biologist, Mother, but I hardly need to point out that the brain is not your area of expertise, whereas it is mine. At least it will be.'

Beatrice turned at the rattle of the door handle. 'Oh, it's you. I wondered when you'd show up. My son has been telling me about his ridiculous idea of creating a mobile phone that picks up electrical activity from the brain. Total nonsense of course.'

'I thought it sounded like a good idea,' I replied, watching Carl's reaction. 'Think what it could do for people who can't speak.'

'We're light years away from having the capability to harness brain activity in this way and from what I can see, he hasn't got light years ahead of him.'

Carl slumped onto the bed. 'Thanks, Mother.'

He turned to me. 'You shouldn't have invited her.'

I hated Beatrice. Her need to be right, to always be the best, had once again trumped any miserable shoots of parental concern that had brought her here.

'I didn't...' I let my voice trail away.

'I think Carl can go home,' I said to Beatrice. 'Let's pack his case. I can drop you off at the station.'

'The station!' she snorted. 'I didn't come all this way to spend one hour with my son. I'm staying until Monday.'

Beatrice insisted on sitting in the front passenger seat because of 'her leg', although I hadn't noticed anything wrong with it. Carl had to squeeze into the back. He had never been a passenger in my car and only ever sat in the back of his own when driven by his chauffeur. This new experience was compounded by several others: Madeleine tapping on the window and waving, and Tom climbing into the back seat, shoving his rucksack against his father's elbow as he adjusted his seat belt.

'Wow, quite a crew,' Tom commented. 'Where did you pick up this lot, Mum?'

Beatrice reprimanded Tom, without turning around. 'Hello, Grandmother, I'm so pleased to see you again.' I glanced in the driving mirror and saw Tom hold his fingers over his nose like a clothes peg. I heard Carl chuckle, and I laughed too.

'What's so funny?' Beatrice asked.

'We don't ever do things like this, drive around like an ordinary family. It feels so different, I just felt like laughing.' In the driving mirror, Tom was making winding gestures at my reflection. 'Have you and Carl ever been in a car together before?'

Beatrice tutted. 'You always were a strange girl.'

Tom helped his father up the steps, while I carried all the bags into the house.

'Look after your grandmother,' I said to Tom, 'while I take Dad up to his room.' I didn't wait for an answer, but helped Carl make a slow climb up two flights, both feet on every step, to his suite of rooms. Pale and struggling for breath, he collapsed into bed and I tucked his pillows at his back so that he could sit up.

'I'll get rid of her as soon as I can,' I said, trying to reassure us both.

He grasped my arm. 'How has my mother met Tom?'

I stared at my arm, where Carl's thin fingers gripped my sleeve and he let his hand drop. 'I took him to see her last week. There hasn't been an opportunity to tell you. You did ask me to let her know.'

Carl shook his head. 'I meant a text or something. Now look what you've started. When were you going to tell me?'

'I wasn't... shall I insist she leaves?'

'She can stay if she wants but don't let her anywhere near me. Since Tom found her so amusing in the car, she might be a distraction for him.'

I knew better than to argue and put on music, setting a drink on the table by Carl's pillow and followed his whispered instructions to organise the room so that he could use his laptop. Only one thought dominated as I performed these routine and familiar tasks; how on earth was my night in London going to survive this unwanted invasion?

I glanced at my watch. 'I'd better go and see how they're getting on, they've been alone for over half an hour.'

Carl nodded but he was already working and didn't look up when he said, 'Where's my mobile?'

It lay at his elbow, hidden by a fold of pillow. I scooped it into the sleeve of my sweater and said, 'I've no idea. If I find it, I'll set it to charge.'

Beatrice sat next to Tom at the table in the conservatory. He had made tea, leaving teabags in the mugs. They had both squeezed these out and slopped them across the polished surface. Tom's school workbooks were spread between them and Honey sat with her chin in Beatrice's groin, her nose twitching to better catch the delicious scents of unwashed body and cats.

'Hi, how are you two getting on?' I asked, forcing my voice to sound busy and cheerful.

'This boy has either been born stupid or you two have made him stupid by sending him to that ridiculous school. You're well rid of that place. It looks like I'm going to have to teach him myself.'

I sat down opposite. 'Well, Tom, perhaps you have your home tutor after all.'

He grimaced at me, giving his head a slight shake but I ignored him. 'I'll leave you two to get on with whatever it is you're doing. I need to think about dinner.'

In the kitchen, I checked Carl's phone. The battery was flat, as I suspected. I pushed it deep into a jar of rice, hiding this at the back of a cupboard, then pressed my forehead against the cupboard door. *What should I do about tomorrow night?*

TWENTY-TWO
SATURDAY 27TH SEPTEMBER

The house was silent, everyone apart from me in their bedrooms. Beatrice was unlikely to sleep late and would wake soon but Tom had hours ahead of him. In the middle of the night, I had crept downstairs to look again at my sister's unanswered email. All evening, in front of Tom and Beatrice, I had pretended that having my terminally ill husband sent home from hospital, along with his estranged mother, was entirely normal and I would cope. But at three in the morning, in the winking blue light, shock at my situation finally released my dry lips from the rictus grin they had assumed and my eyes blurred with tears as I reread Hazel's welcoming, friendly words.

I woke in the office, my head on the desk, my neck stiff and aching. Instead of packing for London and anticipating Fran's arrival, I had to decide whether to go to London at all. Exhaustion chipped away at my confidence, and by seven, I had resolved not to go. If anything bad happened in my absence, I would never forgive myself. There was no choice, I would stay.

My phone buzzed, making me startle. It was Dan.

'Why are you ringing?' I whispered. 'Is it safe?'

'Nothing serious. She's had to go to her mother's and has

taken the girls, because I'm at a conference this weekend.' I heard speech marks around the word conference. 'I wanted to hear your voice, check everything is still okay.'

'It couldn't be worse. Carl is here, sent home from hospital without warning and his mother has turned up. I can't leave Tom in the care of those two, and Fran of course. Should we postpone?'

I held my breath through Dan's silence. 'Postpone until when?' he said at last. 'It's great Carl's mother is with you. If she wasn't there, you might have a point. You couldn't leave a teenage boy and a barely adult girl alone with their very sick father. But there's another adult at home, a competent adult.'

'You think we should still go?'

'Of course! Give his mother a chance to be the parent she's singularly failed to be, so far.'

'But what about Fran?' I argued. 'She's never met Beatrice. Perhaps I should ring her... ask her not to come.'

Dan lowered his voice, sounding deep with reassurance. 'Leave everything as it is, Alice. You said Fran was really coming to see that nurse. It will feel a lot safer, surely, with a proper adult in the house?'

'Hmmm,' I said. 'You haven't met her. But you're right. I couldn't navigate my way through this... I'm too tired... but everything you've said makes sense. I'll see you this afternoon, at the station, exactly as we planned.'

Carl was still asleep in his bedroom when I took him some breakfast. He rarely ate in the morning but the gesture mattered. I left the tray at his bedside, hoping that he might, at least, swallow some orange juice. Downstairs, Beatrice was in the kitchen, fully dressed. Taking a deep breath, I spoke to her back as she washed last night's dishes at the sink rather than putting them in the dishwasher. I grimaced behind her as she lifted Honey's bowl from the floor and tossed it into the sink with the breakfast things. 'I'm going to London today, for the night. Fran will be here. You haven't met her yet but I'm sure that between the three of you, you can look after Carl.'

'You should stay here to look after your husband,' Beatrice replied, dropping a bowl covered in suds onto the draining rack. 'Not go swanning off to London.'

'I didn't think Carl would be home this weekend,' I blustered. 'I've made plans I can't cancel. He should be fine with two adults here, especially his mother. I'll write out a list of instructions for you.' Despite the years of carers and the nursing he'd needed in hospital, I'd done my share of caring for Carl. I knew what was needed. It was only for one night... they would manage.

Beatrice reached for a tea towel and began to scrub at the bowls, half turning towards me. 'I suppose I can always ring the hospital if I need help.'

'No you can't, he's not a patient there now. We can't afford it. If there's a problem ring me or the GP out of hours service, not that they know anything about him. I'll take Carl to the practice on Monday.'

Beatrice lifted a mug and poked the towel inside. 'So you have got money problems after all,' she crowed, victorious in being right.

'It seems we have, but I'm not certain of the degree. Carl's business partner knows the detail, but he must not see Carl while I'm away. His name is Oliver Thompson and he might turn up. Tom knows how to open and lock the gates from inside the house so you must keep an eye him and make sure he doesn't let Oliver in.'

I watched Beatrice clear the rack, wondering if I could find another task for her in a different part of the house so that I could put everything back in the dishwasher.

'Why are you here?' I asked. 'After all this time, why have you come?'

She hung the mugs on the hooks underneath the cupboards, taking care that each faced the same way. I was reminded of Carl. 'I like your boy. I liked him the first time we met. It's too late for Carl. I didn't feel the same about him and I regret that, but it's not too late for my grandson. Now, if you'll excuse me I'll take the dog out, since you haven't bothered this morning. You get that boy out of bed and his lessons will start as soon as I'm back.'

After lunch, we all drove to see Madeleine. Tom was keen to escape from Beatrice's probing at his lack of basic education and she seemed equally keen to ask a vet for free advice about one of her cats. Madeleine, generous and hospitable, gave Carl's mother a tour of the practice and some samples of worming tablets.

'How are you, when's the op?' Madeleine whispered while Beatrice was distracted by the misery of caged, post-operative cats.

I nodded towards my mother-in-law. 'I haven't said anything to her because I want her to go home but it's all happening next week.'

'You know that Tom can spend as much time here as he wants. He's very willing and he loves animals. How is Carl?'

'Unexpectedly back home but very frail. He keeps out of the way, right at the top of the house.'

'How on earth will you manage next week, and afterwards?'

'We'll sort something out. Ella will be home and who knows, Beatrice might still be with us.'

'Let me know what I can do... I want to help.'

'Thanks, but keeping Tom occupied is more than enough.'

At home, I encouraged Honey to make the climb with me to Carl's attic rooms. We waited outside the door, both of us alert, Honey's head to one side and her ears forward as if the simple act of listening harder might make hearing possible. I picked up the familiar sound of the Smiths through the heavy door and tapped, pushing my way in without expecting a reply. Honey frisked towards Carl, working at his desk and ran a circuit of his study, exploring the base of the skirting board with her nose.

Carl had his back to me, facing one of his computers. I sat on the edge of his day bed, making furrows in the velvet upholstery with my fingers.

He spoke without turning around. 'And you've brought the dog up here because...?'

I ignored his question. 'Your mother's having a rest. I'm wondering if you're planning to join the others for dinner tonight. Fran will be here.'

Honey had already found Carl's unfinished lunch and I lifted the tray from the floor onto my knee.

'When is she going? My mother I mean.'

'I thought you felt she should stay.'

He sighed, impatient. 'I said I thought she was interesting for Tom, I didn't say I liked having her here. He doesn't have a relationship with her. To him, she's no more than an amusing specimen. As far as I'm concerned she can stay but I won't have anything to do with her.'

'I think she's going on Monday. Her cats are only being fed by a neighbour until then.'

I decided to say nothing about London, the fewer words spoken, the less chance of being caught in a lie. Hidden up here, perhaps he need never know.

'Carl... Oliver says we're in trouble financially.'

He spun around on his office chair. 'No more or less than anyone else, unless Oliver's been playing fast and loose with company funds.' He sniggered as if this was amusing, as if it wasn't a serious possibility. 'Where is he anyway?'

'I've asked him to stay away until you're well enough to see him.'

'I'm well enough now.'

'You're not. The hospital said you shouldn't have visitors.'

'Well, where's my bloody phone? If I could find it, I could speak to him.'

I pretended to scan the room. 'We must have left it at the hospital. I'll track it down. It's only a matter of hours since you recovered enough to sit up and talk. Stress might trigger another collapse... the business can wait.'

I swallowed. My trip couldn't be kept a secret. 'You'll be alone with Fran, Tom, and your mother tonight because I'll be in London. I've said Oliver's not to visit. Your mother's been instructed not to open the gates and I'll speak to Tom.'

Carl grinned, defiant, but the smile didn't reach his eyes. 'If he turns up, I can open the gates for him.'

'Don't, Carl, don't open them for anyone. I've spoken to Oliver and I think we're very, very short of money. We couldn't pay the hospital fees and he's talking about selling the girls' flats. There's a possibility Claudio might roll up as well, because he's not getting paid either. We mustn't involve your mother, Tom or Fran in our problems or put them at risk. Keep the house locked up and wait until I'm home. We can see Oliver together.'

Carl narrowed his eyes. 'You've never had any faith in Oliver. You have to learn to be more trusting.'

The audacity of this took my breath away, but I couldn't risk an argument. 'In this instance,' I said, 'I think my mistrust has been well placed. You must promise me you won't see him until I'm back.'

'I can't promise that. Anyway, remind me why you're going to London?' Carl frowned at me over the top of his glasses.

Honey rested her chin on his leg and wagged her tail, hoping he might stroke her head.

'I'm having surgery next week. It's going to be pretty tough and I'll be out of action for a while. I wanted some time on my own; to stay in a good hotel, go shopping and there's a new production of *Madame Butterfly* at the Royal Opera House. If I don't see it this weekend then–'

'I thought we were short of money,' he interrupted.

'*We* are but I'm not... at least not immediately. The school paid back the rest of the year's fees and they're in my account.'

He blew on his lenses, holding them up to catch light from the single attic window. Honey left his side and leaned against my knee, panting.

'Oh well, as long as you're okay. Never mind the rest of us.'

I pressed my spine into the chair and stared at the pictures jumping across the screen of Carl's muted television. Words tracked below the images, telling us the mass selling of HBOS shares had slowed. This is too difficult, I thought. While we're collapsing, so is the rest of the world. I can't manage this, so many players, so many factors. It's beyond my control.

Aloud I said, 'Carl, do what you like but don't cause any distress to your mother or your children. I'm not okay, remember? I'm having radical cancer surgery next week and I intend to go to London and spend a little money. You will be safe and you will be well looked after. I don't need either your agreement or your consent.'

The next step in executing my plan, the one I most dreaded, was to speak to Tom. He was in his bedroom, lying on the bed, listening to music through earphones. He saw me enter and removed his headphones, swinging his legs over the side of the bed to make space for me to sit down.

'You know Fran is staying overnight,' I said. 'I'm not sure if I made it clear to you that she's coming because I'm staying the night in London. I'm going to see an opera.'

Tom gave me a formal, bright smile. 'That's fine, Mum. I hope you have a good time. Thanks for telling me.'

I hesitated. This wasn't what I had expected from my son, my worst critic. 'Beatrice is here, thank goodness, so your dad will be looked after. If Oliver texts you and asks to visit, please say no and don't let Claudio in. It's not fair on Fran or Beatrice to have to deal with visitors or face your father's dealer. I'll be back tomorrow.'

'Don't worry, I'll behave myself,' Tom said, sounding twenty years old rather than fifteen.

I squeezed his knee and waited. Tom kept his gaze steady, his pleasant smile fixed. This wasn't right. I glanced at my watch, realising I had to leave. At the door, I looked back at him, already lost in his music, his foot tapping in time to the beat. He saw me hesitate, gave me a reassuring grin and blew me a kiss.

Tom was performing but there was no time left to interrogate him. I could only hope that whatever was on his mind, whatever scheme lay behind his fake smile and false words, would be no worse than typical adolescent misbehaviour. Perhaps Carl was right, I had to learn to trust.

TWENTY-THREE
SATURDAY 27TH SEPTEMBER

There is a point below Dan's ear, about an inch below his earlobe, where I can breathe in the salted almond smell of his body. I leaned over, inhaling deeply, running my hands across his back and over the wide sweep of his belly. Dan rolled over to face me and resting on his elbow, touched my cheekbones, the bridge of my nose and traced the outline of my lips with the tips of his fingers. He kissed my neck, then my breasts and our hands travelled through the familiar mounds and creases of each other's bodies. Our breathing quickened, and my world narrowed to the sensation of Dan's touch. We moved together, kissing mouths, necks, earlobes until there was only hard, practised rhythm. Dan held his breath, stilled, and sighed. His weight settled over me and we stroked and whispered words of love as if we might never hear them again.

I woke from a sleep that was deep enough for dreams but light enough to make me aware I was dreaming. I had forgotten to meet my mother. Where were we going? Remembering that she was dead was reassuring, not sad. I hadn't let her down after all. I moved my head back to look at Dan's face. From this distance, the lines on either side of his mouth, the grey hairs in his eyebrows, the mole on his left cheek, just below his eye, seemed more visible than his features. It was like looking at a map instead of a photograph, his precious cartography. I lifted my head and saw our shopping bags resting haphazardly against each other on the sofa, a trail of shoes and clothes cast like stepping stones towards the bed. I knew I should get up and shake out my linen trousers but allowed the moment to pass, resting my head on the pillow and watching the folds of oatmeal-coloured fabric at the window pucker and billow as the curtains were caught and released by an updraft of warm air from the street. I heard traffic ebb and flow at lights, the orchestration broken by fractious brakes and horns. If I listened particularly carefully, I could hear voices, laughter, a shriek, a baby crying. I turned back to Dan and looked at his body, splayed out in sleep. I wanted to run my hand through the soft, grizzled fur across his chest but instead, I closed my eyes and thought about the precious gift of afternoon sleep, allowing the sounds of his breathing to pull me back towards him.

Before Dan woke, I slipped into the bathroom and ran a deep bath, luxuriating in my choice of lime and bergamot bath oil. The sound of rushing taps must have roused Dan because he pushed backwards through the bathroom door, his body wrapped in a white towel, holding two glasses of champagne. He placed my glass on the edge of the bath and as he stood up, the towel slowly unravelled and fell to the floor.

'Damn, so much for my romantic entrance.' Dan sat, naked, at the tap end and drank his champagne. 'Do you want me to wash your back?' I nodded and leaned forward with my forehead on my knees while Dan soaped me, lifting my hair away from my neck.

He held my hand as I climbed out of the tub and wrapped a clean, warm towel around me, pulling my body towards him. I closed my eyes as he lifted me to the bed and felt him kiss my face and dry the ends of my hair. He peeled the towel away and I felt the touch of cool hands as he worked his way down my body, stroking droplets of water from my skin.

Our taxi dropped us in Covent Garden an hour before the start of the opera. I hooked my arm through Dan's and we forced our way through crowds who watched street performers or huddled around the cafés and bars, eating ice cream, or drinking wine.

'Look.' I tugged his elbow. A statue on a plinth had turned and winked at me. The figure rolled its eyes as a large woman hurried past and the crowd roared when she turned around and kissed the statue on the backside.

'Can we find somewhere to eat outside?' I called to Dan, over the babble of different languages. 'I'd like to watch the crowds.'

'Not likely. If we'd been here by four o'clock...'

'We had other things to do at four o'clock,' I said, scanning the tables outside an Italian café. An elderly couple signalled to us, gesturing towards two empty seats at their table.

I shouted to them, 'Are you leaving?'

They gestured again and waited for us to find our way through the wicker fence that marked the boundary of the café, ignoring the sign that said diners had to wait to be seated, apologising as we squeezed past crowded tables.

The man spoke in an American accent. 'Sit here, please, while we finish our coffee. If you two are going to the opera, you're cutting it fine.'

'Thanks for the table. I'm sure we'll make it. Could you order us a drink for the interval?' Dan turned to me and winked.

After the Americans left, we ordered wine, ravioli and salad. Our food came quickly and we ate fast, without speaking, drinking our carafe of red wine as if it were tap water. I caught Dan's eye and laughed.

'What is it?'

'I don't think he realised you were joking. His wife looked a bit shocked ... when you asked them to order us an interval drink.'

'Oh well.' He shrugged. 'I'm not going to complain if they buy us one, are you?'

Twilight faded into darkness and the candles around us trembled in their glass shades. The waiters' white shirts flitted between the hum from the tables. I felt the wine blur my senses until everything seemed wrapped in a soft mix of light, the smell of good food and conversation.

'The last time I was able to do this was in the nineteen seventies when eating outside meant a picnic in the park. Pavement cafés hadn't been invented then. Carl hated eating outdoors because of his allergies and more recently his worries about spies or some other nonsense.'

Sadness flickered across Dan's eyes and lips, and I regretted allowing our other lives to intrude. He searched inside his jacket for his wallet and threw two notes onto the saucer left discreetly at his elbow.

'You will be well again and once you are, we'll eat outside whenever you want.'

'Even if it's snowing?'

'Especially when it's snowing.' Dan smiled and I knew I was forgiven.

Our seats were at the end of a row and I shivered from the draught flowing through doors left open for the last of the audience. Dan offered me his jacket, but I shook my head and wrapped my shawl around my bare shoulders. The orchestra warmed up, its discordant sounds creating the tension of anticipation. A bell rang to chase latecomers from the bar.

'These seats must have been expensive,' I said.

Dan looked around us and above to the balcony and galleries. 'You've no idea... even worse because they were last minute. Let's not worry about it. Have you been here before?'

I turned to look up at the Wedgewood blue dome. Tiers of golden angels descended from the top, with cherubs at the highest point growing into full-breasted women just above our heads.

'We were in that box there,' I pointed. 'We brought the children to see *The Nutcracker* one Christmas. It was my idea of course, always trying to do the happy family thing.'

'We took ours to see *The Nutcracker* on ice at Nottingham Arena. The girls kept hoping the dancers would fall over.'

'I think our driver enjoyed it most. Carl fell asleep, Ella read one of her boarding school stories, Fran constantly needed the toilet and Tom kept scrambling over the seats.'

'This is my first *Madame Butterfly*. Actually, my first opera,' Dan confessed.

I put my hand on his arm. 'Ssh... it's starting.'

The stage glowed and beautiful voices swept upwards with the orchestra, trying to elevate me into the fantasy world of Butterfly and her love for the hopeless Pinkerton but my own drama kept interrupting. I worried about Oliver and his threats, I made a list for the days I would be in hospital, I wondered about Carl, Beatrice, Fran, and Tom, the strangely reconstituted family I had left behind. How were they coping? Fran had been furious with me for abandoning her with Carl and her refusal to speak to her new grandmother had not been promising. By comparison, poor Butterfly and her serious misjudgement in her choice of lover, seemed of little importance.

At the interval, we followed the crowds into the Flower Hall and in the crush, I rested my head on Dan's shoulder, fascinated by our reflection in the mirrored wall. We were together, in public. We looked like any other couple.

'Enjoying yourself?' Dan asked.

'It's wonderful but I'm distracted. I can't bear that she's going to wait for him and do nothing else with her life. I want to grab her and give her a shake. I think my impatience with Butterfly is shaking my confidence about my own future. She's running out of chances, and perhaps I am too.'

There was a tap on my shoulder and our friend from the café stood behind us. Beyond him, his wife's reflection pointed towards two glasses of wine.

We pushed back through the crowd to join her.

'Dan was teasing,' I said. 'We didn't really expect you to...'

The American man interrupted with a dismissive wave of his hand. 'Did you guys get to eat?'

I heard Dan's tone become formal and polite, much like he sounded when our paths crossed in public at the university. 'We were served very fast. The cafés around here must be used to meeting theatre deadlines. Are you enjoying your stay?'

The wife spoke. 'Americans aren't travelling because the world hates us, which makes it easier for those of us willing to take the risk. London's changed, don't you think? Do you live here?'

We shook our heads, but she carried on regardless, her husband listening intently and giving little nods of agreement. 'Nobody speaks English, everyone's in a hurry, it's so crowded. Next year we're going to Edinburgh.' She said this in the American way, as if the city's name ended in 'borrow'.

'What's happening in your financial sector?' I asked, and then worried whether I had misjudged the mood.

The man paused before replying, squeezing his eyebrows between pinched fingers.

'All I know is that the US government is bailing out

mortgage brokers who lent money to anyone who wanted it, regardless of whether they could ever pay it back, but they've allowed a major bank to collapse. It doesn't make any sense. We're concerned about our pension.'

'But they've rescued AIG,' Dan interrupted, failing to notice the Americans' discomfort. I squeezed his elbow in warning, a signal that we should leave.

He glanced at me and gave the smallest nod of understanding. 'Please excuse us,' he continued. 'My wife hasn't been well, and I think we should get back to our seats before the scrum.'

Dan swallowed the last of his wine in one deep gulp, but I left mine unfinished. We linked arms and pushed through the crowd, voices flooding around us like sounds heard underwater.

'Your wife?' I asked, as we settled into our seats.

Dan laughed. 'Sounds good, doesn't it?'

The second half felt different. My attention was gripped by Butterfly's endurance and the moments of happiness she shared with her child and servant. My hopes rose with hers as Pinkerton's ship sounded in the harbour but when he ran away, unable to face her, I despaired. I wanted to frogmarch him back and yell at him, 'Look what you've done. Look at your child. Take responsibility.'

When Butterfly handed over the boy to Pinkerton's wife, I froze in the grip of an old rage and then my body shook with sudden terror. I reached out for Dan and he grasped my hand, stroking my bare arm with his free hand. He didn't look at me, but I saw his eyes shining damp in the light reflected from the stage. The audience rose to thunder their appreciation and we stood too. Dan pulled me towards him and pressed my head against his chest with one arm, the other around my shoulders. Afterwards, we remained sitting until the theatre was almost empty, allowing everyone in the row to squeeze past without bothering to stand.

'Her love for Pinkerton stopped her from living, Dan. She was as much a prisoner of herself as of the men who controlled her. Women can be very stupid.'

Dan paused and I saw him choose not to comment. 'Are you okay to leave now?'

I nodded, wiping my eyes with the back of my hand. We gathered our things and walked out through the empty theatre into Covent Garden. The cafés were still busy, and groups of tourists and locals mingled in the lights from shops, some of which were still trading. It was soon apparent that we would not be able to find a taxi and the entrance to the Tube station seemed dangerously crowded. Dan asked if I wanted another drink, but I shook my head and suggested that we walk a little further. The streets were tangled with people's legs and feet, pub customers using the pavement as a terrace for evening drinking and all the theatres spilling out their dithering, blinking hordes at once. It was hard to keep together but I gripped Dan tightly, as he used his bulk to force a way through.

We reached Trafalgar Square and I stopped walking, tugging on Dan's arm to wait. This was a Britain I had heard about but not seen. Groups of young people filled the square and many were already drunk, even though it was not yet midnight. There were loud voices, young males threatening each other and bursting into football terrace medleys in rounds of spontaneous harmony. The girls stood apart, shrieking and giggling, struggling to hold each other upright. One girl held another's hair as she leaned over the gutter to be sick.

Dan gripped my hand, keen to hurry away.

'No, wait, Dan. I want to watch.'

'It's not a zoo, Alice.'

'The girls have almost nothing on.'

'I know. It's the same all year round, they wear next to nothing. When I see any group of teenage girls, I wonder where they've left their cardigans.'

'Have you seen anything like this before?'

'Every weekend in Leicester, when I pick the girls up from whatever club they've been to. Come on... it's not very interesting watching other people being sick, and I don't feel very safe. Let's find a taxi.'

'I feel safe with you.'

'Yes, but I don't feel safe with me.'

'You collect the girls yourself at night? You are a good dad.'

'They want to get a taxi home with their friends, but I worry one of them might be left behind or end up as the last one to be dropped off. Whatever time it is, I pick them up. It'll be different when they're at university. I won't know anything about it.'

We stood at the side of the road and waited for a taxi. 'When I was at university the streets were deserted after eleven. I remember walking back down Welford Road with Carl and Euan after we'd spent an evening at the union. There might have been a few other students but that was all. When did all this start? When was it that parents allowed children out so late and where do they get the money for all this alcohol?'

'Come on, Alice, no one can be quite so insulated from the real world. Surely, Fran and Ella went clubbing at weekends, when they lived at home?'

'I've not experienced it for myself,' I said. 'Carl insisted the girls were always picked up by our driver. They hated that, so maybe they didn't go out much. I mean, they weren't saints, but perhaps they went to friends' houses, rather than this.' I waved a hand expansively, to take in the square.

Dan held up his hand and flagged down a taxi. We sank into

the seats and held on tightly to the straps as the driver executed a sharp U-turn.

'Doesn't Tom go out on Saturday nights?'

'He can't because of the lack of security. Carl would hire bodyguards to protect him and send our driver to collect him. One of Carl's greatest fears is kidnap. It's why we chose The Mount School with its walls and gates. I thought Tom had everything he needed but I understand why he thinks he's missing out. It was good for me to see this, what other kids his age are doing at weekends.'

The taxi driver turned his head, catching the drift of our conversation. 'It's terrible, isn't it? I won't let them in my cab. They're sick or refuse to pay.'

I leaned forward. 'Do your children go out at weekends?'

He shook his head. 'We don't drink alcohol. My girls stay at home and help their mother. My sons,' he shrugged and grinned at me in the driving mirror, 'who knows?' Dan grimaced, tilting his head back towards the youths in the receding square and pressed one finger against my lips to stop us both from laughing.

I sat against the open window of our room, my knees pulled up towards my chin, wrapped in a quilt. Dan snored deeply and rhythmically from the bed. I hadn't been able to sleep, but I didn't mind. It was so long since I had shared a bed with a breathing, moving body that I loved to hear his night-time sounds. Why had we never risked this before? We hadn't even fantasised about spending a night away together. Perhaps we thought our affair would stay alive and exciting, if we avoided the inevitable domesticity of a shared hotel room, bathroom smells, dirty towels, and toothpaste. Now, this was all I wanted but the chance might never come again.

The street was quiet at last. I watched the last young girls stagger home carrying their shoes. Latecomers to our hotel, from the airport or the clubs, were tipped from taxis into the street and into the arms of night porters. The occasional police car hid moodily in a side street before pulling out like a snake. Lights were on in Buckingham Palace and I wondered if the Queen was also having a restless night. Just before three there was a pause, a complete silence, and then a solitary bird awoke to his duty to rouse us with the dawn chorus.

I tiptoed back to bed, curled against Dan's body, and shivered, pulling the quilts over us against the early morning chill. I slipped my hand over his hip and he whispered in his sleep, rolling over towards me. We kissed and moved together, slowly at first with the rhythm of night and then more urgently, as the first sunshine of the day spread its warmth across our naked feet.

TWENTY-FOUR
SUNDAY 28TH SEPTEMBER

I woke to the reassuring sound of breakfast being set out in the room next to our bedroom, hushed voices, the chink of cutlery on plates, a discreet tap on our bedroom door, the satisfying rattle of the departing trolley. I kissed Dan on the side of his mouth, then propped myself on my elbow, watching the expression on his face muddle between sleep and awareness. He opened his eyes, focusing on me.

'Breakfast,' I whispered.

We ate in silence, occasionally reading aloud to each other a few lines from the Sunday newspapers. I put down my coffee and studied him. I would happily lose the house, the business, the paraphernalia of wealth, if I could have him but what would he lose?

'Dan, there's something I have to tell you,' I said.

He frowned and folded his newspaper. 'This sounds ominous. I'm struggling to imagine how there could be anything else for me to find out.'

'I've been stupid, believing we could hide our affair from the world's biggest surveillance organisation. You know that Oliver has been tracking us... of course he has. But he's threatening to tell Carl about our affair, if I don't collude with him in some dodgy business practices.'

Dan's eyes widened. 'Am I at risk? What about my wife, the children?'

'Carl has never physically hurt anyone, at least as far as I know. He enjoys revenge but prefers to manipulate others through fear. The worst that will happen is he'll use Oliver Thompson to find a way to muddy your reputation at the university or help Sarah find out about us in the most humiliating way possible. That's bad enough, I know.'

'When did Thompson threaten you?'

'At the hospital, on Thursday. I think he's monitoring our emails but I'm not certain about texts or phone calls. I should have told you sooner but I felt we had to talk about it face to face.'

'What does he want you to do?'

'He wants me to hide money, in my bank account. I've refused. I believe we're protected for now, as long as I can prevent him talking to Carl.'

Dan swept back his hair. 'This is dreadful!' he muttered. 'Perhaps you should agree, keep him off our backs for a few days until after your surgery. You can't manage his threats when you're ill and I can't cope with the not knowing, the waiting for something awful to happen.'

'Then I'd be a criminal too. This is horrible for you, Dan, but his threats might come to nothing. The best thing is for me to speak to Carl, to tell him the truth. If there's nothing to hide, Oliver loses his control. His only power lies in our fear.'

———

We walked in the sunshine through Green Park and along Piccadilly, trying to rescue something from our irresponsible weekend. In Piccadilly Arcade I pointed out the tailor who made Carl's suits and we bought some handmade chocolates from a chocolatier for Fran and Tom. We ended up at Fortnum's. Lunch was over and afternoon tea had not yet started, so we easily found a table. I ordered cake, a large slice of buttery Victoria sponge. Cancer, like pregnancy, made dieting irrelevant but Dan, who still sat on the side of the well, patted his stomach and declined. When the cake came, Dan shared it with me. Watching him fork large pieces into his mouth, I regretted not ordering two slices.

We couldn't talk about the uncertainty, the fear, so I chattered about Beatrice and how I would make sure she left for Oxford in the morning.

'Her cats are on their own, surely she'll have to go,' I argued, even though Dan was barely listening.

He changed the subject, pressing the last of the jam and cake crumbs onto his fork.

'Have you made any progress with finding a school for Tom?'

'No, but the local authority is sending an application form. I'm not very hopeful. Have you any ideas?'

'They're obliged to provide him with an education, even though he's been in private school. There will be a place available somewhere, or perhaps a pupil referral unit. It just depends how fussy you are and how much the security thing is a serious issue and not just Carl's obsession.'

'I can't see Tom staying in another school,' I said. 'I'd get him there every day, but I think he'd just abscond. The sad thing is he had settled at The Mount and was doing quite well. The expulsion has been a huge shock, even though he pretends otherwise. He's always got away with everything, as I was reminded at the governors' meeting. I've been blinded by my own problems. I should have seen what was happening. We took The Mount for granted. I had no idea how precious that school place was.'

'We can't watch our children all the time. If they want to hide something from us they'll succeed. I haven't told you before, but Emma had a difficult time with a boy last year. She sent him some explicit photos and he shared them round the school. I only found out months later, long after she'd told her mother. Once my wife reported him, the school dealt with it. Our kids know we trust them and exploit how busy we are. That's how they hide things.'

I touched Dan's fingertips over the white tablecloth. 'You must have felt so powerless.'

'It's been made worse because I can't say anything. I can't hug her or tell her how sad I am that she thought she couldn't tell me. I'm not supposed to know... her mother promised. Sometimes I feel like a spare part in my own family.'

'Dan, I'm surprised, I had no idea you felt like this. I thought you and Sarah were brilliant at communicating.'

He paused before replying, lifting sugar cubes with a pair of silver tongs, and dropping them back into the pot. 'In a long marriage, change happens in such small steps, you almost don't notice. I'm so guilty about this affair, I don't feel able to talk to her about anything at all. I'm afraid of rowing... what might come out. It's too important that she believes everything is okay.'

I wrapped both my hands around his and he dropped the tongs. 'Perhaps we've both kept secrets for too long?' I said.

'I understand how your life has been, Alice, keeping so much hidden. Secrets affect everything, they change every single moment. I'd like to have a go at living honestly.'

I felt my insides drop. 'Does that mean we have to end? Is that what you're saying?'

'Not at all. I'm not sure what I mean. The day I found out about your diagnosis, all certainty ended. I've felt so inadequate, waiting on the sidelines, unable to help you with Tom and Carl, but Thompson's threats put me right in the thick of it. If you are planning to be honest with Carl, perhaps I should be honest with Sarah. It would be the responsible thing to do. She would be badly hurt but perhaps less than if Thompson got to her first.'

We stared at each other, both of us trying to fathom what his words meant. Once we told our partners the truth, what would come next? Did we have the strength to face the consequences?

My heart raced, joy and panic fighting for control. 'Dan, I... this is everything I wanted... everything I've hoped for, but don't rush, wait until I've told Carl.'

He looked at his watch. 'We'd better get back, our train is in an hour. After your surgery I'll try to be with you as much as I can. For now, that's the best I can promise.'

TWENTY-FIVE
SUNDAY 28TH SEPTEMBER

We were quiet on the train. I had a feeling low in my stomach that was like the last Sunday night of the school holidays and I imagined Dan was feeling something similar. We spoke in a desultory way about my operation and Dan promised again that he would see me as soon as possible afterwards. We even joked that our next meeting would be on a gynaecological ward. Through the train window, I watched the north London suburbs drift into Midlands towns and fields and wondered about our future. In six months, would we be back to walks and pubs, with occasional hotel rooms, or was there a chance we would be together?

It took a few minutes to recognise my own ringtone and I scrabbled to find my phone in my bag. The voice sounded breathless, frantic. It was Fran.

'Mum, are you nearly home? Something awful has happened.'

A cold hand gripped the nape of my neck. 'Tell me, Fran... quickly.'

'Carl went mad... an ambulance is here and the police. He slashed Beatrice. She's not badly hurt but he won't allow her anywhere near him. He's getting so worked up that the medics need me in the ambulance too. I'm afraid I can't find Honey. I have to leave right now. I'm so sorry.'

'Where are they taking him?'

'I'm not sure. The Royal Infirmary, I think. The police are taking Beatrice to casualty. She needs her arm checked out.'

There was one person Fran hadn't mentioned. 'Where's Tom?' I asked.

I heard her sharp intake of breath. 'I'm really sorry, Mum. I slept over at Jack's last night. Tom said he would be fine with Beatrice. I got back about an hour ago to find this... this chaos. I've only just checked his room. Beatrice says he went upstairs when she asked him but it looks as though he didn't sleep in his bed. I'm so sorry, Mum.'

Fran started to sob in deep shuddering breaths. 'I was terrified. Carl was standing in the kitchen with a knife, ranting. When I ran up to Tom's room, I thought I'd find a body.'

'Have you phoned Tom's friends?'

'I haven't had time. I have to go with the ambulance, right now.'

'Oh, my poor girl. Keep in touch. I'll go straight home, unless I hear from you that I'm needed somewhere else. I'm so sorry too. I love you.' There was nothing else I could do or say, trapped on a slow Sunday train.

Dan looked at me quizzically, but I needed a few minutes to rein in my panic. I leaned back in my seat, pushed my fists against the table between us, swallowing down my nausea.

Dan listened, his heavy eyebrows weighed down by his frown, as I relayed the few details I had.

'I should never have left them alone with Carl. Fran thinks Tom might have been out all night. When she arrived home, Carl had just attacked Beatrice and Tom was missing. The poor girl thought Carl might have killed him.'

Dan looked puzzled. 'Where was she... I mean, where had she come back from?'

I banged my open palm on the table. 'She spent last night with Jack. I trusted her, Dan. I trusted Jack too.'

We stopped in Oakham. The platform was empty but nevertheless, the train waited for ten minutes, making a strange ticking sound that ratcheted up my anxiety.

'This isn't Fran's fault,' Dan said, maintaining a frustrating calm. 'Tom has let you down too. Try not to be too hard on her, she's had a dreadful shock. And what about Beatrice, what about her responsibility?'

I pressed my hands flat onto the table to steady them, my lips turning down and trembling as I spoke. 'If she'd made even half an attempt to raise her own son, she would have known to check on Tom before she went to bed. And where is Honey? What a mess this is... I should never have left them.'

'Carl is ill, he's delusional. No one is to blame here, least of all you.'

'Of course he's to blame,' I snapped, infuriated by Dan's innocent and quite reasonable comment. 'Carl's not an ordinary mental health patient. He's an addict. He had choices. My son is missing and he's an addict too.'

I watched Dan struggle, finding himself at the core of my anger. His eyes narrowed, darkened, and then grew soft. I hated him for being so fair and searched for any blame I could direct at him, wanting to provoke him to be angry with me, so that I could feel less anger for myself.

I stared out of the window at the empty car park of Melton Mowbray station, my chin resting on my fist, struggling to control heartbeats that drummed and leaped at random in my chest.

Dan reached for my hand and pulled it towards him. 'I'm sorry, this is the last thing you need. Talk to me about Tom being an addict. You haven't said that before. I thought he just used some cannabis, which is fairly typical for his age, isn't it?'

'It's a feeling I have. I hope I'm wrong. He reminds me so much of Carl when we first met, and he was only a few years older than Tom. There's a determination or neediness about his use. It's different from the take it or leave it attitude of most kids.'

Dan continued his search for a rational explanation. 'So why wouldn't he just stay at home and get stoned? You've said before that Carl's not that thorough about locking up his stuff and Tom knew Fran wasn't coming back. It doesn't make sense that he's run away.'

'He's so angry, it would be his way of punishing us all. His school has thrown him out, his father didn't fight for him and I'm preoccupied with my own health. Or maybe I'm reading too much into it. Perhaps he took his chance for a night out, sleeping on a friend's floor. Actually, I'm relieved he's not there. He knows nothing about what's happened and didn't witness his father cut his grandmother. I want to get home. I need to find Honey before he turns up... clear up blood, if there is any.'

'I'll come with you,' Dan said. 'I can text Sarah and say the train is delayed.'

When I refused, his expressive features struggled between disappointment and relief. I had to manage this alone.

Standing in the cool, dark entrance I could almost touch the emptiness and silence. I put down my bag and looked into the rooms that led off the hall, pushing against each door and waiting for it to swing ajar before I took a few steps forward, as if someone might be behind, hiding from me. The kitchen door was open by just a few inches. I stepped forward and saw that the floor was streaked with blood and a knife lay on its side, like a gash, on the granite counter.

'Honey... Tom?' I called out, seeing that the door to the boot room and the garden door beyond were both ajar. Then I heard a sound, a click from the gate that led to the woods. I leaned against the table, uncertain whether my shaking legs would support me. A slow claw of fear climbed up my spine. Who was this?

The outside door slammed shut. I grabbed the knife and called out, 'Don't come in here!'

'What the fuck!' Tom stared at the knife and then at me. 'Mum, what's happened? Where is everyone? Put that thing down.'

It was only an inoffensive bread knife, one we both recognised from the kitchen drawer, now rendered harmless by being placed back on the counter.

'Dad's been taken to hospital,' I said, wiping blood from my hands onto my trousers. 'Fran's with him but I've not heard yet if he's been admitted. Beatrice had to go to casualty because he slashed her arm.'

Tom glanced at the knife on the counter. 'With that?'

We both looked at the weapon, now lying at an angle to the sticky, dark red smear left behind on the worktop. Tom stepped over the blood on the floor tiles and walked backwards out of the kitchen. I followed him through the open front door to where he sat outside on the bottom step, his head on his arms. We touched heads and I stretched an arm around his back.

'Let's look for Honey,' I whispered. 'Fran says she's missing.'

We found her under the garden shed, in the dug-out hollow where a vixen had raised her cubs in the summer. She smelt my outstretched hand, and crawled out towards me on her belly, whimpering.

'Look after her,' I said to Tom. 'She needs comfort. Wait there and I'll bring her some food and water.'

When I returned, Tom was sitting upright on the grass cradling the dog, his face flushed and eyes red. He raised his head and looked at me. 'Mum, you weren't here.'

I stared hard at my son, fighting my shame. 'And nor were you,' I said. 'Let's see to Honey and then we'll talk.'

TWENTY-SIX
SUNDAY 28TH SEPTEMBER

From the kitchen, I heard a taxi. It could only be Fran and I ran out to greet her. She pulled away from my hug and ran up the steps into the hall, almost colliding with Tom, waiting with Honey. Fran slapped him hard, across the back of the head.

'Ow,' said Tom, looking at me. 'Aren't you going to tell her off?'

'No, I'm not, you owe her an apology for disappearing last night. It's time for an explanation. Where were you?'

Tom shrugged. 'I went out with my mates, since you weren't here and she wasn't either. Beatrice had gone to bed. It wasn't my fault Dad went crazy. Anyway, Oliver brought me home.'

Of course, someone had delivered him. How else could he have appeared like magic through the garden gate? Oliver would have known for sure I'd been away with Dan. How could I have risked so much for one selfish night?

I shouted at Tom, angry as much with myself as with him. 'Did you have to involve Oliver, of all people?'

Fran interrupted, her tone cold and businesslike. 'Mum, it doesn't matter who brought him home, he's safe, isn't he? Carl's being transferred to the Gables Mental Health Unit and he needs some of his things.'

She held out a piece of paper. 'We have to get this stuff over to him and rescue Beatrice from the LRI. She texted me about ten minutes ago. They've bandaged her up and she's ready to come home.'

In my fury, I had forgotten about Beatrice, abandoned at the hospital. Together, Fran and I hurried up to Carl's room and at the door, she reached for my hand. Immediately, I understood. For her, this was a forbidden and secret place. Once we were inside, it was obvious that someone had prised open the cabinets. I sat down on Carl's day bed, drawing my hands down my cheeks, guessing at what had happened. Fran sat next to me, very close and still. I watched her eyes flicker across the desk and the filing cabinets, from the armchairs to the music centre.

'What's the matter, Fran?'

'I expected some awful lair but it's ordinary, it's just a study.'

'Your dad's an addict, not a monster. This is where he works and lives... his bedroom is through there.' I nodded towards the adjoining door. 'As the meth has taken over, he's preferred to spend more and more time alone. It's just his private space. There aren't any horrors except in Carl's mind.'

'But we were always banned from here. There was horrible music and when he came out he was sometimes so weird. In my mind it was like some evil cesspit. I was afraid of it and I didn't even want to pass the bottom of the stairs. I've had nightmares about this room since I was little.'

'Fran,' I pulled her to me, 'I've let you down.' I gestured around the room. 'I didn't see how all this was affecting you. I should never have tried to keep everything hidden.'

Fran started to cry. 'What about Tom? That's my fault.'

I put my hands on her shoulders and looked hard into her eyes. 'I think Tom let himself in here with a key, after Carl went to bed. He must have had one copied. He was waiting for his chance and you gave him that chance, that's all. I'm sorry I didn't warn you how much of a risk Tom was. I don't think I realised it myself. I'll check the cabinets and see what's been taken. Carl woke to find that someone had been in his room. It's his worst nightmare, to have his secrets stolen. He would have blamed Beatrice.'

'Jack's worried sick. He thinks you'll complain to the hospital.'

'Carl is no longer Jack's patient. You shouldn't have stayed out overnight, but Tom was left with his grandmother, a responsible adult.' I paraphrased Dan, silently thanking him for always trying to be fair.

'But, Mum... poor Honey.'

'Yes, she must have been very frightened, but she's okay. All of this might have happened even if you'd been here. It's not your fault.'

Fran went to her room to telephone Jack and I searched the cabinets. All of the drugs were gone, the solid meth for smoking, the cocaine, and the cannabis.

Fran called out to me. I heard it too, the whine of our electronic gates. It could only be Oliver. Why hadn't I locked them? I tiptoed down to the drawing room, to keep hidden and pulled the heavy drapes away from the window to watch him arrive. I breathed in dust from the folds, listening to the gates close and the crunch of car tyres on gravel. Oliver emerged from his car, pulling up his trousers from where they had slipped below his belly, his eyes darting as if he guessed someone was spying on him.

'Fran! Tom,' I yelled. 'Wait for me in the drawing room. Now!'

I held the door open for Oliver and indicated the formal, rarely used room where Fran and Tom were already seated.

Tom's face was speckled with white blotches that made his freckles stand out. Fran sat on the other side of the room, chewing on her lip. Only Oliver looked comfortable, his legs spread wide as he filled his armchair, his arms folded across his stomach.

Everyone avoided the sofas. I sat in a fourth vacant chair, and we looked at each other across the coffee table, all except Fran, who stared through the window. In the heavy pause, I noticed the browning flowers on the table in the bay window, their stems left to rot in shallow water. There was a thin film of dust across my side table.

'If you've come to see Carl, I'm afraid you've wasted your time,' I said. 'He's been admitted to a psychiatric unit. Someone broke into his cabinets and the discovery must have triggered a paranoid state. I'm afraid he attacked his mother. We all have to leave for the hospital shortly. I'm sure you'll want me to inform the police, in case any company documents were stolen.'

I turned to Tom and held out my hand. 'And you can give me the key to Dad's study, right now.'

'Come on, Alice,' Oliver interrupted. 'There's no need for the police. No real harm's been done. Tell you what, why don't you make us all a cup of tea.'

'I'll do no such thing. Tom, go up to your room. If you need a drink, Oliver, there's tap water in the kitchen. Help yourself.'

Tom hesitated, looking between Oliver and me. Fran said, 'Do what Mum says or I'll hit you again.'

'Piss off,' Tom said to her. As he strode past my chair, I stretched out my hand.

'The key please, Tom.' He reached into his jeans pocket and pulled out a key for Carl's study. He laid it with excessive care onto my outstretched palm, then slammed the door behind him.

'Fran, could you leave us now, I need to talk to Oliver alone.'

She hesitated. 'Don't forget about Beatrice.'

'This won't take a minute,' I said.

We sat in silence until I heard Fran's footsteps outside, scraping on the gravel below the window.

'Leave my family alone, Oliver. I believe you asked Tom to find something you needed from Carl's study. What did you give him in return?'

Oliver looked around the room with ill-disguised propriety. 'Just as well I was around, my dear, ungrateful, girl. You were off in London, shagging Dan Lewis and Fran was shagging that skinny nurse from the hospital. Who was here for Tom apart from a madwoman? I admire the boy for ringing me. He'd got out of his depth with local dealers and I was able to bring in a few heavies to rescue him. I've told him he can call me any time. Tom needs a bit of guidance, a man around the place.'

'I said leave the family to me. Perhaps Tom needed to learn a lesson. He thinks he's invincible and you've just bailed him out.'

'Alice,' Oliver said patiently, 'the lesson Tom was about to learn would have been his final one. The boy thinks he can pass off a few ounces of draw at school and *wow!* he's a dealer. It didn't go down well with the local scum, I can assure you. You have your son back thanks to me. I reckoned you could do without a murder this week, on top of everything else.'

Oliver raised a plump hand to stop my protest. 'Tom's told me everything. You've got cancer and Carl's dying. The boy had nowhere to turn. A cry for help, Alice, and no one listening, not even his mother.'

I knew I had to pretend to show appreciation but the words stuck in my throat. I hesitated and swallowed, disgust mingled with shame.

'Thank you... I'm grateful to you for helping Tom. Now please, leave my family alone.'

Oliver cleared his throat. 'You think Dan Lewis will stick

with you once you're sick? Even if he does, he won't fit in. He's not one of us, he'll be out of his depth. You need me. I know the business and I'll be there for the boy. We'd make a good team. Get rid of Lewis, as soon as you can.'

'What are you talking about, Oliver?'

For the first time ever, I saw Oliver look sheepish and craven, his public school bravado seeping away. 'Just a plan for the future, one that makes a lot of sense. Come on, Carl's not going to last that long. If I tell him about you and Lewis, his lawyers will make you fight for every penny. And don't assume you'll have access to Tom. Frankly, even if you survive your cancer, you'll be dead of old age well before your payout is settled in the courts.'

Oliver leaned towards me and winked. 'Think about what side your bread's buttered on. Choose the winning side.'

I couldn't keep the incredulity from my voice. 'You are the winning side?'

Oliver loosened his tie. The room was hot and airless and smelt of dust from ash in the uncleared grate. 'In Carl's present state of mind he might believe that Dan Lewis is more of a risk than he can tolerate. He might think that Lewis knows too much about the business. You and I would realise that's nonsense, but he doesn't always see things rationally. He might ask me to intervene and I always follow Carl's instructions, to the letter.'

This was so outrageous, I almost laughed. 'Are you actually threatening Dan?'

'Good heavens, no. What an imagination you have... you could have written a novel, several in fact, with all the time you've wasted over the years. But I can't be responsible for Carl's actions once he finds out.'

I flushed with anger, but my best strategy was to play for more time.

My tight lips grimaced into a parody of a smile. 'I'm

genuinely grateful to you for rescuing Tom but I think you're being less than honest with me. This isn't about me or Tom or Dan, it's about you and the business. I think you're in serious trouble and you're trying to find a way out, though why I'm your way out escapes me.'

Oliver tried to interrupt but it was my turn to raise a hand. 'What you must realise is that Carl doesn't want to see you at the moment. He's really very ill and all he wants is time to focus on his ideas. If I find out that you've tried to whisper a word to Carl about me or Dan, then I will alert Carl that on your watch, the precious business he formed with Euan has been sacrificed. You'll be frozen out forever. I could do that tonight, if necessary. Oliver, you need me, much more than I need you. Do we understand each other?'

TWENTY-SEVEN
MONDAY 29TH SEPTEMBER

Beatrice sat at one end of the kitchen table, her large hands curled around a mug of tea and her frayed overnight bag slumped against the table leg. The bandage on her wrist poked out from under her sleeve. Her hair was pulled into a tight French roll and either clean clothes or the lift given to her features by her scraped-back hair, made her look more like the woman I remembered. I was still in my dressing gown, ragged from the night before. I poured another mug of strong, thick tea from the pot and sat facing her, at the other end of the table.

'So, you're going home today after all?' I spoke at last.

'I need a lift to the station, that's if you're not too busy meeting people in London.'

I bit my lip. It wasn't the moment to sound ungracious. 'I'll drop you off after we've been to see Carl. Thank you for everything you did for him yesterday.'

'He tried to kill me.'

'I understand,' I said. 'It must have been terrifying. Tell me what happened.'

'He accused me of stealing his mobile phone... believed I'd

been in his room, searching through his things. He was prowling the house with a knife, looking for me. I was standing right here, he accused me, then the dog went for him. That's what happened.'

It made sense. Carl had been violated in his place of sanctuary and of course, he would have blamed the stranger in the house, the woman who had always betrayed him. Thank goodness for Honey.

I glanced at the jar where Carl's phone was hidden. 'It wasn't a personal attack,' I said. 'You were in the way, caught up in something that existed only in his mind.'

'It's a pity he didn't turn the knife on himself,' Beatrice hissed.

I stopped myself from making the obvious but incredibly hurtful reply. My phone vibrated against the skin of my thigh, deep inside the pocket of my dressing gown. Dan was trying to contact me. 'If you'll excuse me, I need to dress.'

'If you'll excuse me,' Beatrice mocked me, 'your family is out of control. Carl was no catch, but I expected better of you. At least you could have tried to be a good mother. God knows, you were fit for little else.'

I pressed my knuckles against the table, pushing myself to stand. 'And you are a fit judge of who is a good mother and who isn't?'

As I reached the door, her parting words hit me hard between the shoulder blades. 'Your eldest daughter. She's the one who started all this. I don't suppose you've told her, have you?'

I turned towards Beatrice, allowing my dressing gown to fall open. 'No, I haven't... not yet. And it's not your duty to do so either.'

I heard the front door slam. Tom shouted from the hall. 'Mum?'

I continued to stare at Beatrice but called out, 'We're in here.'

He carried the mushroom smell of an autumn morning into the kitchen and released Honey from her lead. She wagged her tail and barked when she scented that her favourite person, Beatrice, was still with us.

My phone vibrated again. 'I'm embarrassed I'm still in my pyjamas,' I said. 'I'm going to dress. I'll leave you two to talk. You have plenty to say to each other, I'm sure. Tom, I'm afraid Beatrice is very upset and is going home today.'

Once I had dressed and spoken to Dan, reassuring him that we had all survived the night and Carl was safely in psychiatric care, I crept down and listened outside the open kitchen door. Beatrice and Tom seemed to be deep in debate about the life-enhancing properties of psychedelic drugs. Of course, Beatrice had all the facts but Tom, to his credit, wasn't interrupting. I relaxed. I had forgotten how suddenly Beatrice's anger was drawn but how quickly the rage passed. Once it was over, she would have forgotten our row almost immediately, especially the hurtful things she had said.

Through the open door of the conservatory, I walked towards the orchard, the wet, long grass darkening the bottom of my jeans. Spider webs were strung across every low branch, droplets of shimmering dew dancing along each thread. Despite the heat, autumn was underway. Nothing stayed the same.

I drove Beatrice to see Carl, leaving Fran and Tom, almost friends again, watching old episodes of *South Park*.

'I'm sorry it turned out so badly,' I said, after twenty minutes of silence.

Beatrice snorted. I wasn't sure whether this meant assent,

derision, or mockery but I pressed on. 'We're pleased, especially the children, to have made some contact with you at last.'

'Tom told me you're having surgery for cervical cancer on Friday,' she said. 'Things are going to get worse for you, not better. I think you need me around, whether you like it or not.'

'Tom told you that?'

'Don't blame him. I asked why Ella was coming back on Thursday. Frankly, he was surprised I didn't already know. You keep too many secrets, Alice. People can't help you. You should have been in touch with me a long time ago, you knew how to find me.'

'And you knew where we were. There was nothing to stop you contacting us.'

'I thought you must be doing fine. After I didn't show up for your wedding, the first contact had to come from you. Since I heard nothing, it meant you were bearing a grudge, even though I'd paid for the darn thing. Besides, Carl was never going to do it.'

We reached the suburbs of Leicester and Beatrice seemed distracted by the shops and houses and other people busy with their lives. There was so much I wanted to say; to defend myself, to be angry with her but there was too little time. I had to get it right.

'Yes, we were very angry and hurt... we chose not to speak to you for a long time. Once Carl's addiction took hold, I believed that contact from you would only make things worse. It might have been harmful to him and us. I think my judgement was sound on that one.'

Beatrice thought for a few moments. 'You're probably right. Yesterday's events would support your case.'

'I struggled so hard to keep everything going. If I'd thought you'd have helped me of course I'd have contacted you. A grandmother for the children would have been fantastic.'

It was as if I hadn't spoken. 'Truth is always best,' she continued. 'I haven't tried to pretend, like you, so I come across as blunt, hurtful even. You should have stopped hiding his addiction, got some help. You must talk to Ella before too long about her father, her real father. I wasn't truthful about my absence from your wedding, and I'm sorry for that. I couldn't be sure whose child you were carrying, yet it was my son you were committing to family life. He's been a bad father and husband but what you did to him wasn't fair.'

'I loved him, Beatrice, and there was every chance the child was his. We never spoke about it, but after Ella's birth, I think he knew. I believed we could be happy... the four of us.'

We found the unit, a Victorian house stranded amongst ragged Portakabins, the outer shanty town of a modern hospital. Beatrice sat in the car, staring ahead while I fed the parking machine. How long we would stay was anyone's guess. With Beatrice here, it might only be a few minutes.

We walked with the nurse into Carl's room. His back was to me, hunched over a desk, working on his laptop. The sharp angles of his shoulder blades pushed through the folds of his sweater. I called hello and bent to kiss him. His hair was newly washed and smelled of fresh-cut hay. I rested my hand on his shoulder but withdrew it quickly. He was so thin, it felt like a newel post.

'Carl, your mother's here. Is it okay if she stays?'

He didn't turn around. 'If she must.'

'Where did the laptop come from?' I sat down next to him and leaned across to look at the screen, while Beatrice shuffled onto his bed.

Carl carried on working, frowning as he tapped at the keys. 'Fran brought it yesterday with my things. I haven't been able to use it until now. I thought I'd make a start on some work. Have you found my mobile?'

I ignored his question. 'You hurt your mother,' I said, 'but it wasn't Beatrice who was in your room. That was Tom.'

'The dog bit me,' he complained, turning around, and pulling up his sleeve. I could see the teeth marks, just below his elbow. He looked up at me from our mutual study of the bite and I was reminded of Tom, expecting help from me when Fran hit him.

I glanced across at Beatrice, seeing her roll her eyes. 'Your mother believes Honey was trying to protect her.'

'I don't recall trying to kill my mother,' Carl turned his chair to face us both, as if it were an interview, 'although who could blame me? If you're right, the dog not only saved my mother but saved me from a murder charge. From my point of view, that's a stroke of luck.'

'You had a knife this long.' Beatrice held up both hands. 'You meant to seriously hurt someone.'

Carl folded his arms tightly across his chest. 'I've told you, I don't remember anything.'

'The dog acted as she did because she was frightened and threatened by you,' Beatrice continued.

'A dog isn't capable of such sophisticated emotion,' Carl interrupted. 'She threw affection over you in the same way she does to everyone else. Her defence of you,' he tossed a hand in his mother's direction, 'simply reflects the indiscriminate nature of her responses. She behaved through instinct, not reason.'

'You're not sorry,' I interrupted.

'I know what you're both trying to do. You want me to cry and beg your forgiveness. Of course, I regret what happened, but I don't recall a single thing about it. This is the first time I've made sense in days. I'd like to hold on to what's left of my mind on the rare occasions it surfaces. Alice, I appreciate you're ill too, but I'd say I'm worse off, wouldn't you?'

I held my breath, said nothing. I wanted to see humility, I wanted to hear his contrition, but I would get neither.

'Beatrice is going home today, as she has to see to her cats,' I changed the subject, 'but we've agreed we'll try to see more of each other.'

'That would be a mistake,' Carl said, turning back to his keyboard. His typing became more frantic.

'Beatrice, we shouldn't keep any more secrets. Tell Carl that his father is still alive.' I waited for her response. Carl's hands were still. He stared at the screen, and Beatrice scowled at me.

I ploughed on. 'We have his name and address. Tom looked him up on the internet. Do you want me to contact him?'

Carl folded his arms, tucking his hands right into his armpits and resting his chin on his chest. I felt the memory of love.

'I already know... tracked him down years ago,' Carl whispered. 'Surveillance is my business, remember?'

'I was nineteen years old. I did my best...' Beatrice interrupted.

'Carl, why didn't you tell me you'd found him?'

He shrugged. 'There was no point. You'd have got all excited and wanted to meet him. I don't and that's all there is to say.'

'But why don't you want to get in touch? He might be pleased to know you and he's a biologist like Beatrice, so he might be able to help with this.' I pointed to the screen as if I knew what it was about.

'He was my tutor, do you know that?' Beatrice added.

'Shut up, Ma.' Carl spat the words at her without taking his eyes from the screen.

'Alice, don't be stupid, he can't help *me*. He's a retired old fool. I'm in contact with the only people who matter, those already making headway in this field. They're close to creating a headset which converts electrical activity in the brain to signals on a phone and can see a way to using the tech to play games or control devices, much like a music system. They think we can collaborate.'

Carl sighed and turned to look at me over the top of his frameless glasses. 'I'm rather busy and I'd like to get on with this while I'm well, if you don't mind. I haven't got much time, so would you both just leave me alone to work.'

I drove Beatrice to the station in silence. We pulled into the bay where passengers could be dropped off but she kept her face turned away and her hands worked the straps of her bag. She opened the passenger door and swung one leg over the rim, but turned back to me, as if a new idea had just occurred to her. 'The boy should come to me before it's too late. Think about it.'

'No, thank you, Beatrice,' I said in our new spirit of honesty. 'However much I wanted a weekend in London, I shouldn't have trusted my family to your care. How could I ask you to look after your grandson when your own son, the one you raised, was driven mad by your presence. I've made other plans for Tom, but you will see us all again, I promise. Ella will keep in touch with you after my operation.'

TWENTY-EIGHT
TUESDAY 30TH SEPTEMBER

The consulting room at the psychiatric hospital had the tidy, impersonal feel of a shared space. I had an early morning appointment with Mike Pritchard, who had agreed to remain as Carl's NHS consultant. I sat down at a table intended for meetings, avoiding the more intimate chairs around a low table. While a nurse searched for Carl's notes, Mike and I talked about the continuous heatwave that was the torrid backdrop to my unravelling life. From the window, the grass surrounding the unit was burnt dry, the trees grey and fatigued. A bee droned in the bushes below the open window, the note dipping and rising as if she had found something of interest. Mike told me that he was flying to his villa in Florida on Saturday and I had an image of myself on Saturday, lying in a hospital bed, attached to tubes and wires.

'This is quite a setback,' Mike said, 'but actually nothing too much to worry about from a mental health perspective?' He addressed this question to the nurse.

'Mr Williams is much better today,' she replied. 'He knows what he's done, and he seems quite rational, although he remembers little about the actual events.'

Mike turned towards me. 'Remind me, how long has the binge and crash pattern of his meth use been happening? I mean injecting meth every few hours, over several days, to try to hold the high, then losing consciousness?'

'He's always done the first bit, the binging, ever since I've known him, although I'm not sure what he was using then. You see, he works day and night, for weeks at a time. He has to stay awake because he's afraid of losing the vision. It's so blindingly pure and clear for him and this way of life, it actually used to help him perform... to meet targets.'

'But when did the crashes start... regularly, I mean?'

'About two years ago, I think. That's when I had to start caring for him as if he were an invalid. He had crashes before, but they were more like days of normal sleep. I haven't done a good job, have I?'

Mike stared, puzzled by my question but when he spoke, he cleared his throat, his voice softer and deeper.

'You've done very well. Looking after people when they're ill isn't easy but the families of crystal meth addicts struggle more than most. It's hard to let go of the conviction that the patient could have made a different choice. The death rate during the crash phase is high and they're not all accidental. It's an easy death and it's forgivable to let it happen.'

I looked at the floor. A cleaner was vacuuming the carpet outside, droning in competition with the bee.

Mike spoke again. 'This wasn't your fault, you didn't make it happen.' He paused, waiting while I swallowed some water. 'What has he used to manage the paranoia and aggression during the withdrawal phase, before he crashes?'

I listed Carl's props. 'Alcohol, cannabis, heroin, loud music, excessive working... he's tried everything. Sex might once have helped. He's tried rehab several times but without the crystal meth, he loses the ideas. For Carl, being sober isn't worth it.'

Another silence. The cleaner was working further down the hall.

Mike carried on. 'Addiction is very, very hard for family life. As I've said, methamphetamine addiction is one of the worst. You've coped well. No one could have expected anything more. And no one could have anticipated what happened at the weekend.'

I shrugged. I had layers of guilt and regret that Mike would never understand but this wasn't about me. I would have to deal with those myself, in my own time.

'Okay, so what's the plan?' I said, trying to sound more confident.

'We have to stop the binge and crash pattern if he's to live even another three months. He's at high risk of a stroke. Medically we'll manage that by ensuring his use is controlled. At the moment he's getting the meth through a drip and that may need to continue. As for his mental health, my colleagues in psychiatry will need to assess him.'

'What if he doesn't co-operate with your plan?'

'We can't force treatment onto patients. For now, the important thing is that we'll keep him here until after your surgery. Once he's ready to leave hospital, we'll talk about longer-term care options. After Sunday's episode we need to know he's not a threat and you need to feel safe. Do you have any idea what the trigger was?'

I searched in my bag for a tissue and the nurse passed me a box from her end of the table. Tissues and hospitals, I thought but said, 'I should have been there. His mother was staying with us and I know that doesn't sound like a threat, but they're estranged. She wasn't a good parent and when someone broke into his room through the night, his paranoia settled on her. The dog bit him... that didn't help. He seems to think he's the victim.'

Mike tried to reassure me. 'If you'd been there, it still might have happened. It was a series of circumstances no one could have predicted. But now it has, Carl will need monitoring day and night and that will be a permanent arrangement.'

Without another word, we began to make the small movements that signalled the end of the meeting. Mike shuffled Carl's notes together and passed the folder to the nurse. As I stood, I felt my damp trousers cling to my thighs and used my fingers to pull the fabric away.

Mike seemed uncomfortable, touching his nose with the edge of his thumbnail, looking at the door rather than at me. 'Just one more thing. I saw in the notes that you don't want Oliver Thompson to visit Carl.'

'I think it would make Carl more agitated. The business is in trouble as you know. I've hidden his mobile phone, so they can't speak.'

'That's fine but if Carl asks to see him, there's little we can do.'

'I want you to let me know first.'

'We'll try, but you're going to be quite poorly for a few days. Our staff might not be able to reach you. Also, we might find ourselves in a situation where Carl is becoming more agitated because we're not letting him see Thompson. You can see my dilemma. We can't make any promises. The nurse on duty will decide, based on what's right for everyone at the time.'

'Speak to my daughter Ella. She'll be at home with me for a week after the surgery,' I said. 'You can at least do that.'

'We'll certainly try but there are no guarantees.' He looked at his watch. 'I believe Carl is waiting for you, so we mustn't keep him any longer.'

I would have preferred to walk out of the hospital, see Fran before she left and keep Tom company, but if the hospital couldn't promise to keep Oliver away, there were things I needed to say before it was too late.

'Did you know that Tom ran away on Saturday night?' I told Carl. 'He was trying to sell drugs on the streets, drugs he'd taken from your room. Tom broke into your cabinets. I think Oliver had asked him to find a document.'

Carl hesitated, finishing his line of typing before turning to face me. I had his full attention. 'And where were you,' he said, 'when all this breaking and entering was going on?'

We had a fragile moment of connection. I couldn't waste it. 'I told you, I'd arranged a weekend away. Carl, how much do you trust Oliver?'

Carl frowned. 'I don't like him, but I trust him. What are you getting at?'

'Oliver has been threatening me. He even tried to persuade me to hide money. He says he wants to visit you, but it's not about you, or the business, it's more about controlling me. The last thing he actually wants is to see you, because then he'd have to confess to the dire state of the business. He must be desperate because he's trying to build some sort of relationship with Tom. It was Oliver who brought Tom home on Sunday. I'm glad Tom rang him, the alternative doesn't bear thinking about, but I'm not happy about his influence on me or the family.'

Carl thought for a few moments, his head lowered, the skin on his scalp visible through threads of his hair. 'Why is he threatening you?' he said.

I swallowed and took a deep breath. 'I have a lover. His name is Dan Lewis. We've been together for five years. Oliver thinks he can use this information against me, and perhaps against Dan, to secure his financial future.'

Carl turned to stroke the computer keys with his fingertips, making small, circular movements. I waited for some response but he spun his chair back to face me and took both my hands in his, turning them over, before passing them back. His wrists looked so thin, poking out from under his sweatshirt.

'I tried to use CU.com to help bring peace and security to the world. We weren't always honest or ethical but the ends sometimes have to justify the means. As you have discovered, I can track any individual, anywhere, anytime. I promised myself not to use surveillance on you but when I started to lose control of everything, including you, I had to know. It was only for a short while but I was able to access the computer in David Adams' office at the university. I already know about you and Dan Lewis. I've always known.'

My breath streamed from me in an audible gasp. I stared at Carl, my mouth open. 'You know?' I stammered.

Carl's lip twisted into a sneer. 'It was typical of you, Alice, with your small-minded sense of your own importance, to imagine I would react like some sort of avenging angel. Your tedious little affair was unimportant, as long as you didn't try to leave me... as long as you stayed. You were mine, not his. Now, I have no choice but to leave you. Revenge is meaningless... in the time I have left, I must finish this project, not think about you or the business. What you do with your life, once I'm gone, is up to you. Leave me now and tell Oliver Thompson to stay away too. I want nothing more to do with him. Tom should know I'm okay about the break-in, but don't try to make him visit me... or the girls.'

TWENTY-NINE

TUESDAY 30TH SEPTEMBER

At home, Tom was swimming, so I made us both a cold drink and waited for him underneath the sunshade beside the pool. I looked around for Honey and saw her panting in the shade of bushes at the edge of the lawn.

Tom noticed me and swam to the poolside, blowing water from his nostrils into his fingers.

'Where were you?' he called.

'I left a note in the kitchen. I've been to the hospital to see Dad and talk to his doctor.'

'Ella's been on the phone,' he said. 'We were making plans for when you go into hospital. She's coming home on Thursday.'

Tom climbed out of the pool, his skin sparkling as water streamed from his body. We sat in silence and finished our drinks. I tried to find the courage to speak, to tell him of the decision I had made. From the woods beyond the wall, I heard a woodpecker tapping for insects in the bark of a dead tree.

'How is he?' Tom asked.

I started to tell him about the meeting, but he seemed engrossed in picking dead skin from the soles of his feet.

'Don't you want to hear about Carl?'

'I only asked out of politeness. I really don't give a shit.'

'For many years he was amazing with you,' I defended his father. 'I know he sometimes scared you, but it was the addiction, not him.'

'He doesn't care about me. He fought for Fran's school place but didn't do anything to stop the school from chucking me out.'

I saw my chance. 'Actually, that was Oliver's decision. Dad was too ill, remember? Oliver makes all the decisions about the company's money. Anyway, it wouldn't have made any difference. They didn't want Fran back because she only passed one GCSE and they thought she'd bring the school down the league tables. She wasn't selling drugs.'

Tom's eyes lost their focus and his mouth curled into a half smile. 'Well, you can't trust anyone, can you?'

I smoothed the drops on his arm and smelt chlorine from the tips of my fingers.

'You can trust me, Tom, which is why I'm sending you to Australia until I've found you a place at another school. If I can find you a flight, I want you to leave tonight.'

'What?' Tom sat up, shading his eyes so he could better see my face.

'Your Aunt Hazel lives in Queensland, right by the beach, and they're just going into summer. All the locals surf and have barbecues. They have a grandson who's thirteen. He'll show you around, help you make friends.'

'Because I broke into Dad's study?' he argued. 'This is way too much. I've never met this woman. What has she got to do with me?'

I tried to keep my voice steady, as if this trip to Australia was a simple and reasonable request. 'Not just because you broke into the study. You stole drugs and were trying to sell them on the street. We have an awful time ahead of us. I'll have treatment after the operation which will probably make me tired and sick and Dad isn't going to improve. As he deteriorates, he might come home for end-of-life care and there'll be nurses visiting all the time. Our house will feel like a hospital. In Australia you'll be able to hang around with ordinary kids and go to school. You might even get a girlfriend.'

Tom went back to picking his feet, drawing them up towards his bottom and resting his chin on his knees, his face turned away.

'You won't bring me back,' he spoke to his toes. 'You just want me out of the way.'

'Of course, we'll bring you back,' I said. 'I'm sure this is the best thing for you. I'll find a school place for you to start after Christmas and you'll be home as soon as things are more settled.'

Tom looked up, his eyes glassy with unshed tears. 'You don't know anything about me, do you? You're my family, not Hazel or Beatrice or any of those other wankers. I want to be here when you're sick. I want to be with Dad before he dies. Ella and Fran get to be here, but I get pushed out. It's like you all hide stuff from me, the three of you but I'm the only one,' his voice rose, 'the only one who really knows what's going on around here.'

Tom cried long shuddering breaths into his folded arms, which slowed as I rubbed my hand across his back. This was too difficult, I thought, too hard for us both. I put my arms tightly around him and buried my face into the wet hair on the back of his neck.

We stayed close for another few minutes then Tom unfurled himself and picked up his towel. 'I'm going inside to listen to some music. Is there any food? I mean, like, are you ever making lunch?'

Tom packed without argument and in the taxi sat in the front with the driver, courteously answering any questions but otherwise silent. In the airport forecourt we met Fran and Ella and he waited in line to check in his luggage, pale but calm, his sisters on either side. I sat nearby, the weight from my insides dragging at my groin, watching their slow progress towards the desk. The airport boomed around me. Apart from my disastrous night in London, I had never been seperated from Tom but he had to leave me. I could no longer shield him from harm.

Tom reached the desk and showed his passport, and I wondered whether he had accepted the sense of my decision. I hoped he recognised, or would in time, my resolve to catch hold of him and put things right. Once his luggage was checked in, he ran across the concourse to say farewell, dodging between large families trailing suitcases. I placed my hands on his shoulders and looked into his blue eyes, telling him I loved him, how much I would miss him. There was an expression on his face I didn't understand, a fleeting amusement, a mocking smile, but the strange moment was lost in our deep hug. I breathed in his familiar boy smell, enough to hold in my memory until he returned.

Tom walked back towards the security gate with his sisters. The girls fussed with his hair and clothes and at the point where he was almost lost to us, he turned back to look at me. He didn't wave or smile but stood quite still and stared. I lifted my hand, uncertain, but he turned away and was gone.

Fran and Ella needed to leave but I begged them to stay at the airport, until Tom's flight left. His final look had left a small, nagging uncertainty that I didn't share. Instead, I pleaded a mother's grief. They agreed to have a meal with me in the concourse and we ate salad in a gloomy café that seemed like a cavern, chopped out from the walls of the terminal building.

The girls spoke quietly at first, about Tom and Australia, questioning my impulsive decision.

'After Sunday's escapade, I had to take some action,' I explained. 'I can't watch him, not while I'm recovering.'

'But why Australia?' Fran argued. 'It's so far away. It's like he's being punished for what he did... sent away from his home.'

'What did Carl say?' Ella asked.

'I haven't told him,' I admitted. 'When I visited yesterday, he sent me packing.'

'You haven't told him!' Ella gasped.

I put my hand on her arm. 'Shush, I heard something... I think it's about Tom.' The announcement, barely audible in the café, was being repeated. Ella pushed her way between the tables and out into the concourse. I picked up our bags and followed with Fran holding my arm.

Ella caught at my elbow, as if she was afraid I might fall. 'Tom's not on board the flight and it's leaving in ten minutes. That was the last call.'

We stood, confused and unsure, looking around as if we might spot him. He would jump out from behind someone's suitcases, shout 'fooled you!' and we would be furious but so relieved. Fran ran across to the check-in and was directed to the airline's information desk.

Minutes were lost as we pushed between trolleys stacked high with suitcases and small children struggling to keep up with their families. We stopped to argue about the name of the coffee shop where we had been told to take a left turn, but Ella was determined we had been told to take a right.

'I'm Tom Williams' mother,' I struggled for breath at the desk. 'You've just announced that he's missing. How could he have disappeared? We saw him to the departure gate.'

Without looking up, the young woman tapped at her keyboard and found his details on her screen. 'He's fifteen, right? We advise that minors travel with an adult. I can show you the details on the booking form.'

'For goodness' sake,' I snapped. 'This isn't about whether this is your responsibility or mine. He's not on board. What are we supposed to do?'

Her face remained blank. Our problem would be dealt with in accordance with the airline's procedures, we were told. 'The doors close in five minutes. If he hasn't embarked by then, the flight will leave without him.'

'But how do we find him? He could be anywhere.'

She passed over a card. 'We will call for him until the doors close. If he doesn't turn up, then you'll need to speak to airport security. Here's their number.'

We huddled together, arguing.

'Let's call security now,' Ella insisted.

Fran scanned the crowds. 'No,' she said, 'we have to wait in case he turns up.'

'There's a chance he's been distracted,' I added. 'Perhaps he was in the toilet or playing a game on one of those machines. There's still time for him to hear his name and run to the gate. It might be okay.'

We watched the seconds on the departures screen flicker into minutes. The flight gate closed. I looked across at the woman at the information desk and she shrugged, shaking her head.

The security officer sighed, and focused his pale eyes upon me, resting his unshaved chin on his steepled fingers, reliving the trauma of recent encounters with his own children.

'Teenagers run away,' he explained. 'You've said yourself that your son didn't want to go to Australia. My bet is he'll turn up soon enough. In fact, you'll probably find him sitting on the front doorstep at home. With youngsters it's all about making a point. I know how their minds work. Has he got enough money to get home?'

'But how could he have got back through security?' I argued.

'He's a kid. They don't get watched so closely, people assume they're with an adult.'

The man was trying to help but he was also seeking a quiet life, an easy passage towards the end of his shift. He wasn't going to try too hard at ten to nine on a Tuesday night, even for three distraught women.

'I'm sorry I haven't made myself clear. It's Tom Williams that's missing. His father owns CU.com. This might be a kidnap.' I didn't believe in the threat of kidnap and I hated the words as soon as they were out of my mouth, regretting that I had stooped to using Carl's delusional fears to make something happen.

'That's ridiculous,' Ella announced but it was too late, the words had been spoken and actions had to follow.

Around midnight, Ella begged for our release from the windowless room where we waited, seated in a line on a row of orange, plastic chairs, bolted to the floor. She pleaded my health, her patients in the morning. Hours of marking time had been interrupted only by brief flurries of activity. Each time the door opened my stomach contracted. Was there news or a sighting? All that was ever required was more information. Who are his friends? Has this happened before? Does he use social media? Raised eyebrows and glances between the police officers, questioning my judgement in sending Tom, a child at apparent risk of kidnap, alone on a flight to Australia. These veiled accusations were quickly replaced by scepticism, as the truth emerged about Tom's recent behaviour.

Fran offered to come home with me, but I wanted to be

alone, to stand in the hallway of our house and feel Tom's absence. Throughout the night drive to Leicester, I stared into cars that passed my taxi on the motorway, catching blurred images of pale faces and at dark silhouettes of trees and bushes lining the verges. Beyond the motorway, rows of houses had upstairs windows still alight, where strangers passed sleepless, empty hours until dawn.

I sent Dan a text but knew he wouldn't receive it until morning. There were many from him, growing increasingly frantic at my silence. I thought of my son, only fifteen years old, a protected, inexperienced child, out there somewhere, alone in that darkness. What were the awful statistics I had read? That a teenager would be spotted and picked up within twenty minutes by people who would exploit them. 'Please keep him from harm,' I whispered.

Home felt like a cold, silent shell. Honey waited in the kitchen and I knelt to wake her by burying my face in her ears, smelling her warm, dusty fur. I used the kitchen table to pull myself to stand, feeling a tug in my womb and hesitated before gathering enough strength to bend down again with fresh food and water. I sent an email to my sister, giving a garbled account of what had happened, promising to let her know if there was news before trailing upstairs to Tom's bedroom. I searched every drawer, every cupboard, every box for clues but found nothing, not even any drugs.

In my own room, I pulled off my clothes and looked at myself in the full-length mirror, a small woman, with a neat waist, but always a bit too heavy in the hips and thighs. I stroked my belly, as if I could ease away what was inside. Which of these stretch marks were Tom's?

In the bathroom, I ran a deep, scented bath and rhythmically stroked the warm water as it filled, building the bubbles into peaks. I lowered myself through the chill of the froth to the hot water beneath and felt the enveloping prickle of warmth spread from my toes to my back. I lowered my head below the water, allowing my hair to spread around my shoulders, opening my eyes to see the bubbles, like clouds, floating above me. I sat bolt upright, water cascading onto the tiles, froth popping on my bare shoulders. I lowered my forehead onto my bent knees and started to sob, my legs and arms shaking with fear. *Tom was missing and it was all my fault.*

THIRTY
WEDNESDAY 1ST OCTOBER

Through the night, I lay awake, straining to listen above the soft night sounds of the empty house. Blood rushed past my ears and my chest clutched at my palpitating heart. Grey dawn filtered through the pale curtains, as a single, persistent bird began his rhythmic call to start the dawn chorus. The telephone rang.

Before I lifted the receiver, I let it ring three times, trying to hold back the moment when I might hear something unbearable about Tom. It was the local police, waiting outside the gates and they had news. I could not avoid catching sight of myself in the hall mirror, but my bed-streaked face and tousled hair were of no consequence. I pressed the keypad to let them through.

Two male police officers filled the hall with a chorus of crackling radios. We sat at the table in the kitchen and I made instant coffee. Honey wagged her tail but decided to stay in her basket, not recognising the sound or smell of these strangers. There were no pleasantries, just efficiency and procedure. I thought both men looked tired.

'Is this Tom?' I was passed a grainy black-and-white photograph and saw my son striding across the airport concourse, his bag slung over his shoulder. Behind him I noticed the logo of the airline and the blurred outline of the girl at the information desk. He must have passed within feet of us. I couldn't trust myself to speak.

'And these?' Again and again, I was shown photographs of Tom's confident and purposeful progress through the arrivals hall, each step caught on a camera almost certainly supplied by CU.com.

'And do you know this man?' Tom's back was to me, facing a large man whose round face was blurred and smudged. The man rested an arm on Tom's shoulder.

'It's...' My voice cracked, and I had to clear my throat to try again. 'It's Oliver Thompson. He works for my husband. I can give you his telephone number and address.'

'It appears that Tom left the airport voluntarily, Mrs Williams.'

We study a final picture of a smiling Tom passing through a door held open for him by Oliver. I should have felt relief but instead, I felt hollow. 'You're right, Tom has gone with Oliver by choice, in fact he probably arranged it.'

I rested my forehead in my hands, then swept my hair away from my face, tossing my head back as I smoothed the hair into the nape. I remained like this for a few moments, eyes closed, my hands resting on the back of my neck. I had never felt so weary.

The second policeman spoke. 'We think we know where he is, and the Met will pick him up shortly, we just had to check we have the right boy. We'll have to ask him some questions and he needs an adult with him. If he doesn't want that to be a family member, as most runaways don't, we'll have to wait for a duty social worker. If he's safe and well, there's nothing more for us to do.'

'You're lucky. Not all of these cases turn out so well,' his colleague added. 'If he doesn't want to come home then you'll need to suggest someone he could live with, though perhaps not in Australia. I have to warn you that issues have arisen in this case which we'll need to discuss with our child protection officer, but there won't be any immediate contact from them.'

'You'll let me know when you've spoken to Tom?'

'Of course,' he agreed. The photographs were carefully slipped into a brown envelope. The men rose, draining their coffee mugs. One of them rinsed his and placed it on the draining rack. 'Just to let you know,' he said. 'Two other officers are talking to the boy's father, in case he's involved in any way.'

I watched them leave, pulling my dressing gown around my waist. Mist rose from the fields beyond the wall, the sun already distinct as a pale orb. More had been expected from me. I must have seemed cold, indifferent. I sat down on the top step, feeling the deep chill from the stone seep through my night things. Honey had followed me outside and I leaned my head against her. The exhaustion of the night tore at my eyes and dragged at the base of my skull. They had found my child, he was not at risk. Surely that was all that mattered? But it felt as if Tom were truly lost. He'd made his choice, rejecting us in favour of Oliver, a man he hardly knew.

Dan had woken in the night and responded to my late night text with an early one of his own. He asked to come and see me at home, since I was on my own, and I texted back to say that of course he should come. It was still only six in the morning, but I sent the girls a text to say that the police had found their brother.

In Tom's room, I picked up the clothes tossed onto the floor and stripped his bed, pushing his soiled bedding into my face. If he was brought home today, I couldn't face him on my own but there was one person who might help.

The phone rang and rang and finally Beatrice answered.

'Hello?' Her voice sounded fragile and querulous, much like mine had earlier.

'Beatrice, it's...'

'Is it Carl?'

I stumbled over the words. 'Tom ran away again... last night. We tried to put him on a flight, a flight to Australia.'

'He should have come to me.'

'You were right, I'm sorry. It seemed like a fantastic opportunity for him.'

'But it wasn't what he wanted. He needed to be with his family.'

I pressed the bridge of my nose with my fingertips. 'Can you come back? Tom might be home this afternoon. He likes you.'

There was a silence filled by the sound of her breathing. Finally she said, 'Someone will have to pick me up from the station. I'll be with you by midday.'

To wait for Dan, I walked through the wood with Honey, following the same path I had taken only a few weeks before. The leaves still clinging to branches were curled and shrivelled, the path crunched beneath my feet, littered with dry twigs and stones. I sat on a log and heard a scratching noise behind me, but it was only a bird searching for insects. Since Carl's attack on Beatrice, Honey was unwilling to leave my side and we huddled together, neither of us sure what might come next. My fears about Tom's disappearance had been replaced by anxiety about his return.

My mobile rang, and I stood to ease it from my pocket. It was Madeleine.

'Is Tom coming in today?' she barked.

'Oh, Madeleine, I'm sorry he didn't show up yesterday. It's my fault, I forgot to let you know, he was meant to be on his way to Australia.'

She heard the story without interruption, the only clue she

was still listening, a sharp intake of breath over Tom's escape from the airport.

'You couldn't make up your life, could you, Alice?' she said. 'Look, get through your surgery on Friday and I'll do whatever I can for Tom, you can count on me. Well done for getting that old bat on board, it's time she faced up to her responsibilities.'

I squeezed my mobile back into my jeans pocket and walked back along the path with Honey to let Dan through the gates. He'd never been to my home and even today, with everyone gone, it still felt as if we were taking a risk. I had been to his house only once, when Sarah and the girls were away, but we hadn't stayed long. The Dan I knew had seemed out of place, as if the furniture, photographs, and ornaments were not his but belonged to someone else entirely, the unit made up of Dan and Sarah. We had both felt like trespassers.

Dan's eyes travelled across the house and its grounds as he climbed the front steps, but he said nothing. He knew it meant little to me but would avoid any comments for fear of sounding envious or critical. After a brief touch of his cheek with my lips, I moved away from him towards the kitchen, where I filled the kettle. He followed me and from behind, folded his arms around my waist and kissed my neck. I turned, and he enclosed me in his arms, his chin resting on my head.

'I've been so worried about you,' he said. 'I can't believe everything that's happened. Thank goodness Tom has been found.'

I rested my cheek against his chest. 'He ought to be with me, not Oliver. I can't understand why he involved him. He knows that Oliver's motives aren't sound. Why did he do it?'

The range clock gave out a low, continuous buzz. Dan's chin

scratched against my scalp as he moved his head. 'Once all this is over,' he whispered, 'what if you both live with me? I could try to be a father to him, although I'm sure I'd be hopeless.'

He stopped talking and looked across at Honey, settled in her basket. 'And she can come too.'

I took his hand and moved us both over to sit at the table. 'That's what I want too,' I said. 'Very much.'

Dan kept his head down, his eyes averted. 'The thing is, I can't promise when it will happen, and I feel ashamed that I can't. You've been manipulated by that bastard Oliver Thompson, you're ill, your husband is dying... what's going to happen next? Until I'm free, I'm powerless to help you.'

Dan's eyes were rimmed with pink. 'My marriage is over,' he continued. 'I want to be with you for the rest of my life but first I must make sure that Sarah and the girls are okay. You have to trust me.'

I leaned forward and touched his arm, smelling his familiar scent of soap and tobacco. 'Knowing that you want me, that we'll be together, is everything I could have hoped for. I've told Carl about us and he doesn't care. I can't promise that Oliver won't try to exert some revenge on you through Sarah, but I think it's unlikely. He's not interested in you beyond trying to manipulate me. Right now, he'll be busy explaining to the police his role in assisting a minor to run away.'

'But I have to leave you... leave you to get through the next few days on your own.'

'I'm not alone. I have my daughters, my mother-in-law, my friend Madeleine, and most of all I have you. Perhaps I'll have Tom back too, if he'll forgive me.'

Dan stood to leave and we kissed again. His eyes were framed by deep lines and shadows and I thought he moved more stiffly than before. I waited on the steps to watch him drive away and it was only when the gates closed behind him, I realised that I didn't know for sure when I would see him again.

A second call came from the police at midday, as I waited at the station for Beatrice. 'Mrs Williams?' I recognised the voice. 'I'm afraid there's disappointing news. Tom was staying at the Thompsons', but he's gone and quite a few expensive items have been taken from their house. We'll keep looking for him but he's not just a runaway, Mr and Mrs Thompson are pressing charges.'

'But haven't they done something wrong here?' I argued.

'Mr Thompson says that Tom phoned him and asked to be picked up from the airport. He's also told us a bit more about Tom trying to sell drugs and the availability of Class A substances in your home. You haven't been completely honest with us. Our child protection team will have to pursue this. Don't remove or hide anything until we visit later today. Leave everything undisturbed.'

Beatrice appeared, struggling with a large box. I ended the call and dropped my mobile into my bag.

'What on earth have you got there?' I asked, although I had already guessed, hearing scrabbling from inside.

Beatrice was ready for an argument. 'Cats... couldn't leave them, could I?'

'That's okay, we'll manage,' I said, pushing the box onto the back seat, wondering how on earth Honey would cope with two cats.

'Tom has run away again, from Oliver Thompson's house,' I said, closing the boot. 'That's the man who picked him up from the airport, Carl's business partner. Tom wasn't there when they went to interview him, and he's taken things. Oliver's told the police about Carl's drugs and they're involving a child protection officer.'

'Slow down, woman, slow down, one thing at a time,' Beatrice said. 'Tell me everything in the car. I'm worn out.'

After lunch, Beatrice went for a rest and in her absence, I tried to keep her frantic cats penned in the boot room. On no account were they to be let out, I had been warned, after I had stopped Beatrice from smearing their paws with butter scooped with her fingers from a tub left on the table. Madeleine promised to send her compliant husband with cat food and a litter tray.

The telephone rang again at three. 'Mrs Williams, we've found Tom. His father traced him...'

'Carl traced him...' I repeated.

'That's correct. He's on his way home, should be with you in an hour. He's accompanied by a social worker.'

A girl who looked younger even than Fran stood behind Tom, as I pulled the front door ajar.

Tom pushed past me and threw his backpack, carefully packed only the day before for his flight, onto the bottom stair.

He climbed two steps, then turned to face me. 'I hate you. You're a rubbish mother and I hate my fucking weirdo of a father too. I don't care if he dies. You can all die. There's no one left I can trust.'

'I tried to do what I thought was best.' I reached up to touch him, but he climbed further up, glaring down at me.

'You mean you wanted rid of me,' he sneered.

'I get things wrong,' I pleaded, 'but you can still trust me. I thought you would be happy in Australia. You're a very wealthy young man, sometimes that brings out the worst in other people. They befriend you because they want something from you.'

I saw Tom tremble and he reached for the banister. 'You

mean Oliver? I've already worked that one out for myself. I'm old enough to live on my own, so don't try and keep me here.'

'Beatrice is staying with us and she's brought her cats,' I said, but Tom gave a bark of forced laughter at this ridiculous bribe. I heard his footsteps pound on the stairs and the slam of his bedroom door.

The young woman standing silently at my side, turned to look at me with a sympathetic grimace. She introduced herself as Mia, Tom's social worker. 'Best leave him alone, he's really angry with you,' she said. 'He asked to come home, else I wouldn't have brought him, but he will need time.'

I sat on the bottom step, my arms wrapped around my knees, and she sat down next to me.

'You look so young.' I peered at her over the crook of my arm.

'I am fully qualified,' she reassured me. 'Everyone asks how old I am, which I'm sure I'll love when I'm older but it's a pain right now.'

Mia told me the story, as much as she knew. 'The police found him in a hotel near Euston Station, after contact from his father.'

'But how did Carl know where he was? And what about the stuff he took from the Thompsons?'

'Everything was there. It'll all be returned. I don't think he wanted any of it. He was making a point.'

'And you're here to...'

'Check out the house for drugs, make sure you're fit to care for him, that sort of thing. Can we sit in the kitchen?' she suggested. 'I could murder a cup of tea.'

I had forgotten the cats, who had broken out of the boot room. Released from the kitchen, they scrambled between our legs, took a sharp right into the library, then raced upstairs, as if they were being chased by hounds. All the pots on the windowsill had been knocked over. Some lay on their sides, spilling their dark loam and others had toppled onto the worktop. Hundreds of cat pellets lay scattered across the floor. Honey slept on, protected from the mayhem by her deafness.

'Come on, ignore it,' Mia said, and we made tea, our feet crunching through a mulch of dried cat food. We carried mugs through to the sitting room where Mia sat with her back to the door and I sat opposite her where I could see the hall. If Tom tried to run, I would catch him. She ate her way steadily through a plate of biscuits, making notes as I spoke and looking up at me with sloping brown eyes, her intense frown encouraging me to continue.

Beatrice appeared, her hair tousled at the back like a nest. I introduced Mia as Tom's social worker.

'One of those, eh?' She snorted. 'We don't need your sort of help and anyway, what sort of life experience can you possibly have had, at your age.'

'Beatrice, you're the last person to judge,' I remonstrated. 'My mother-in-law was a teenage parent and raised Carl alone,' I explained to Mia.

'Thank you for sharing that.' Beatrice slumped onto the sofa.

'See if you can find your cats. I'm afraid they've escaped and there's a dreadful mess in the kitchen.'

We left Beatrice in the sitting room and together climbed up to the attic to check Carl's room for drugs. We decided to leave Tom alone, Mia trusting me there was nothing to find because I said I'd searched it thoroughly. Downstairs, we turned out the bag he had thrown aside but found nothing suspicious. Mia said she still had to visit the hospital to talk to Carl's doctors but would report to her manager that Tom was safe at home, as long as his father wasn't living with us. She gave me details of a substance abuse programme for teenagers and advised that, once I was recovered, I must ask our doctor to refer Tom for some trauma counselling. This very young woman, pencil thin in ripped jeans and white T-shirt, appeared to find my extraordinary life almost routine. We seemed to have a plan.

Once Mia left, I crept up to Tom's room and listened outside the door. I heard him laugh as Beatrice said, 'I wouldn't have called him Tom if I'd known about you, would I?'

An hour passed, where I waited for Tom and Beatrice, the early evening news babbling unheard on the television. At last, Tom came downstairs and curled into the opposite corner of the sofa. We watched football, avoiding each other's eyes by staring ahead at the screen. I heard Beatrice moving around in the kitchen and hoped she was cleaning up the mess.

Background roars and cheers from the match and the rhythm of the commentary meant that for now, nothing needed to be said. Finally, we spoke about the teams, whether they were well matched, who might win. Beatrice heated frozen pizza and we sat in a row in front of the television, dropping cheese and tomato sauce onto the cream, embroidered covers of the suite. The cats joined us, staring into the empty grate and occasionally startling each other with episodes of ferocious licking. Honey ambled through from the kitchen, in search of food and her ears cocked in surprise when she finally realised we had been invaded by cats. She growled, but with little enthusiasm, her nose discerning her most desirable resting place, Beatrice's lap.

I leaned over and wove my arms tightly around Tom. To my surprise, he did not pull away. 'I'm sorry. I didn't understand,' I said. 'You're not going anywhere, you're staying here with me.'

'Okay, Mum.' He extracted himself, trying not to miss a penalty. 'Don't go on about it.'

'Would you like to come with me to see Dad? He wanted you to know that he's fine about you breaking into his cabinet.'

Beatrice grunted. 'Well, I'm not sure if I'm fine about it.'

Tom stood up and yawned, scratching his head with both hands so that his unwashed hair stood on end. 'Okay then,' he said. 'Let's get moving.'

'Are you coming, Beatrice?' I asked.

'No, I'll stay here and settle these cats. That dog needs fed and I'll take her for a walk around the garden, since no one else has thought about her.'

Carl sat on a wicker chair beneath the window of a different room. His knees were pulled up to his chest and he seemed tiny and fragile, dressed in an outsized tracksuit I didn't recognise. The sun shone directly onto his face, which he kept turned away from me, and I saw that the stubble on his chin was now grey. Through the window, I could see sloping roofs covered in lumps of moss, a small bird pecking amongst them. The room was in shadow and furnished in heavy Victorian pieces that might have belonged to the original asylum. Tom opted to stay downstairs in the visitor's lounge, playing Connect Four with a patient.

'Carl,' I spoke just loud enough to let him know I was there. 'You traced Tom. Thank you.'

He turned his head to look at me, his eyes milky and unfocused. 'The police have been here too. They told me they'd found him.'

'You were brilliant. How did you do it?'

Carl shrugged and turned back to gaze out of the window. He watched the clouds as if they were the first he had seen, his eyes tracking their path as they scudded across the sky.

'It's like the story of *Babes in the Wood*, the one where the children leave a trail of breadcrumbs so that their father can find them. I simply followed Tom's electronic crumbs. Some time ago I had a device fitted into his mobile which means I can read his texts, if I can be bothered, and I always know where he is. He sent thirty texts while he was on the run and made ten phone calls. He used Oliver's credit card to pay for a room at the Euston Hilton and by the way, he telephoned your sister to let her know he wasn't coming.'

I smiled. 'That's something. At least he hasn't forgotten his manners. We can't have completely failed him.'

'I wasn't any good at it, being a father, but I was proud of them. I used to watch from my attic. I know you thought of it as a den but to me it was an eyrie, where I could soar above you all and hear your laughter.'

'Did you fit one of those devices into my phone?'

'Of course not. Without access to the phone itself, it can't be done but you never leave your hidden one lying around. You're too clever for me.' Carl followed this speech with an awkward whinny of laughter.

'Oliver couldn't have fitted one either?' I persisted.

'Why do you ask?'

'Oh, he always seems to know where I am and what I'm doing.'

'That's because I gave him access to the email account of that professor you work for. I couldn't be bothered monitoring your emails myself but I wanted to know what was happening... just in case.'

'Just in case... what?'

'In case I needed to use the information. I never encouraged Oliver to threaten you.'

'No, that was your speciality.'

Carl sighed. 'It wasn't personal. It wasn't about you. I dislike everyone, especially myself. I always have. I would have been cruel to anyone who was foolish enough to stay with me. It was your choice to stay.'

'So it's my fault. I was a fool?'

Carl stared, his pupils wide and dark. 'Let's not quarrel, Alice. Very soon, you will have the life you wanted... a life without me. There will be no money but I'm sure you don't care about that. Tom is back safely, and that's all that matters.'

'I've asked your mother to stay with us for a while. You'll be able to come home, after my surgery. Perhaps we can try to live together as a family, for as long as we can.'

Carl snorted, and I was reminded of Beatrice. 'You're a dreamer, always chasing what can't be. You can't fashion me into a husband and father... it was never possible. Let's face it, you married the wrong man. I shouldn't have married at all.'

We sat in silence and I listened to the distant sounds of the hospital. Somewhere a person screamed, and a door slammed.

I spoke quietly. 'Euan didn't want to be a husband either, or a father but I thought we were a team. I thought it would work.'

Carl groaned. 'It was a fantasy and one that belonged only to you. I'm finished, it's over... I don't want to pick over the past. To keep all of you out of danger, I'm told I have to stay on this medication, but I can't think, I can't work, I don't know who I am. Alice, I used to have ideas, I created things.'

Rage gripped my throat at his self-pitying words.

I spoke softly but made sure my words were clear and fierce. 'You've wrecked our son's future with drugs. You made a virtual prisoner of me for years and you have terrified your daughters and your mother, yet all you think about is that *you* can't work!'

Carl steepled his fingers and rubbed them across his chin. I heard the rasp, back and forth. The sun crept behind a cloud and the room darkened.

'And you're right,' I carried on, reckless now. 'Family life was never possible for us, with Euan or without him. As you so kindly pointed out, I married the wrong man, but now I've met the right one. Unlike you, we have a future... together.'

Carl closed his eyes and flapped a hand at me in a gesture of dismissal. From the open door, I glanced back at him and called out, 'Carl, I did love you once and Euan loved you too. You have been loved.'

I have no idea whether he heard me.

THIRTY-ONE

THURSDAY, 2ND OCTOBER

I woke early, trapped inside echoes of an anxious dream. I had been trying to reach someone, just around a corner. If I hurried, I could touch a shoulder and they might turn around. I ran and called out, pushing through crowds, but I was going the wrong way. Everyone seemed angry. Then I remembered I'd left a child at home, alone. A voice said, go back, stop searching.

I closed my eyes and listened to the birds, answered by the grating bellow of a cow heavy with milk. I pulled the sheets up close to my chin and drifted back towards the dream, uncertain whether it was fantasy or a real memory. The details began to fade but an urgent fear stayed with me. Tom was at home and asleep in the next room. I had no idea who I had been chasing except that they were male, and I needed to tell them something. What was it? Slowly, the certainty that it was about Carl arose from my confusion. Then I remembered it was Thursday and my operation was tomorrow.

This was my last day. I didn't expect to die, although there was always that risk, but these were my last few hours before I joined the world of the sick. I chided myself for this stupid idea, since I was already sick, but it was like the difference between having a provisional licence and being a fully-fledged driver. There was a Rubicon of sorts to cross and it would happen tomorrow. I had to see Carl again.

After my shower I looked at myself in the mirror, remembering Dan standing behind me, his chin resting on my head. I ran my hands down my hips, noticing that I had lost weight and wondered whether I should have eaten more. Women having treatment for cancer often become thin, so perhaps I should have tried to gain weight. It was too late now. I packed and dressed at the same time, remembering a few more things I needed. I would go out shopping with Tom and Beatrice, perhaps into Leicester, and I would buy some delicious food for dinner. Today felt like the end of something rotten; Dan wanted to be with me, Tom had returned and despite everything my girls chose to be with me.

When I left, Tom was still asleep and Beatrice was walking in the woods, so I stuck a note on the television letting him know where I was. I felt sure he wouldn't run, since the village had lost its bus service years ago and I knew he wouldn't walk the six miles to the city. And we had Beatrice with us, providing a bizarre and unexpected connection.

Although it was only half past nine the day was already hot, too hot for October and the ring road crowded with lorries trying to pass each other. An accident close to the city meant that the traffic slowed almost to a standstill and it was eleven by the time I reached the hospital.

The receptionist sent me straight up to see Carl and I found him alone, sitting by his bed with his laptop on his knee. He ignored me, staring at the screen and frantically tapping at the keyboard and as I looked around his room, at the obsessive organisation of his things, I guessed that another crisis was imminent.

'Carl, my operation is tomorrow so I won't be able to see you for some time. Ella will visit, and she'll bring me again as soon as I'm fit to travel.'

Carl put his laptop on the bed and began to pace. That gesture again, his hands firmly tucked into his armpits, his chin on his chest, back and forth. Finally, he stopped and looked at me as if it all made sense.

'When I'm dead you should marry Euan.'

'No, Carl, Euan is dead.'

I watched him struggle with the disappointment. 'Things aren't good... Washington Mutual has been closed down by the US regulators. I was counting on Euan to help them fix it. I forgot he was gone.'

I sighed. 'He was a good friend.'

'He was my only friend,' Carl interrupted.

'He was a good friend,' I continued. 'I'm so glad we raised his daughter. I'm planning to tell Ella tonight... who her father is. Do you want me to bring her here, so that we can do it together?'

Carl began to rock. He used one arm to circle his chest in a tight embrace, resting his other arm on it, stroking his chin with his index finger. He began to hum, random notes, like an old woman sorting laundry. When he was like this, he frightened me. I rang the bell for a nurse, but no one came. Apologising and using Tom as an excuse, I ran, searching the corridors for help. The hospital seemed abandoned.

'Carl Williams is becoming agitated,' I said to the receptionist. 'He needs to see a nurse.'

'Okay, I'll try to contact someone but there's a crisis in the Woodlands Unit. Can you stay with him until help arrives?'

'I'm afraid I can't,' I admitted, 'not after what happened last week. I'm too scared.' Realising she would have no idea what I was referring to, I added, 'He attacked his mother... with a knife.'

She interrupted me. 'It's an emergency then?'

'If it helps, yes, it is. I think it's another crash, I've seen it often.'

'It would be best if you waited, since you know what to do... I mean how to calm him or something.'

I felt my face flood with shame. 'I'm sorry, I can't... I can't do that for him, not now, not anymore, I'm so sorry.'

———

At home, I hid my guilt behind domestic tasks, chopping and stirring, while ignoring Tom's grumbling as Beatrice insisted he help put the shopping away. No one asked about Carl, not even Beatrice. It was around four o'clock when I heard Ella's car and went out to meet her, wiping my hands on a towel. We hugged awkwardly as she reached across me to hang up a new coat bought for cold weather, which surely must come. I made a tray of drinks and carried them into the conservatory where Ella joined me, leaving Tom and Beatrice to their bickering.

'How was Carl today?' she asked.

'I think he's heading for another crash. I ran away from the hospital, I'm afraid. I shouldn't have done that... left him alone in that place, to cope by himself.'

Ella pursed her lips and shrugged. 'Forget it. The staff are trained to manage crises. You had to think about yourself and make sure you weren't stressed before tomorrow.'

'Yes, but I could have...'

'Mum, I said forget about it, he'll be fine. If he wasn't, the hospital would have rung. Come on, let's walk in the garden.'

We left the conservatory and as we walked, I talked about the details of Tom's rescue from the hotel in Euston and Mia's visit.

I heard Ella slowly breathe out through her nose, like a sigh.

'What's gone wrong? Is everything so broken we need a social worker?'

'There's nothing you don't know,' I answered. 'You were brought up in this house too. Tom isn't afraid, he didn't avoid Carl, like you and Fran. I think they started to use some cannabis together, then maybe other stuff. Carl has no problem with the use of drugs, he believes he wouldn't have achieved anything without them.'

'Well that is a child protection issue.' Ella spoke with the conviction of someone who'd had training. 'But why are you worried about him running away, if all he wants is to stay at home?'

'He's lost faith in us. His father didn't try to save his place at The Mount, I said I would keep him here with me and then tried to send him to Australia, his friend Oliver is accusing him of theft. He thinks he'd be better off alone but having Beatrice here seems to settle him. She likes him, and it shows. She dislikes everyone else, so I think he feels special.'

'I'm sorry to say this,' Ella snapped, 'but children shouldn't have to live with an addict... they shouldn't be frightened. Everything was made worse by your attempts to cover it up, your pretence that nothing was wrong. We didn't know what it was we were afraid of and then we all protected Tom and look at what's happened. I'm really worried about him, but I feel angry for me and Fran... we've suffered too.'

'Ella, I tried to keep the family together. What was the alternative? I had nothing, no family, friends, money. If I'd left Carl, there was every chance he would have fought me for custody... paid the best lawyers to prove me an unfit mother. Making a case wouldn't have been difficult.'

'For Christ's sake, we became too terrified to live. Fran was so preoccupied by what she'd seen and what might happen next that she forgot how to learn. There's nothing wrong with her brain, she's as bright as I am.'

It felt as if there was a cavity in my chest.

'And what about you?' I stumbled over the words.

She hesitated, less confident now that she was talking about herself. 'I separated myself from you... from the family. My way out was to study hard, join everything that was happening at school and make loads of friends. I didn't have to spend any time at home. But now I...'

Ella began to cry. I hadn't heard this sound since she was a tiny child, and then she'd only cried in anger. I wanted to touch her. 'Now I might lose you,' she said. 'I need a family. It's like I have to start again.'

Having my guilt laid out for inspection, I wanted to argue, to explain that my chosen path was the lesser of two evils. What would their lives have been like, in the sole care of their father? But there was no need to defend myself or explain. I had a new sensation, as powerful as love but with more energy. It was a determination to change.

'We'll start again,' I begged. 'We can be a family. Everything you've said about me is true but the future will be different. You are right to feel as you do, but please stay, Ella, and be with me on Friday. I need to get well first.'

Loud hiccups of grief spilled from me. There were no thoughts, only sounds, as my daughter held me. I leaned my forehead against her chest until my breathing returned to normal, then we linked arms and walked on. In the rose garden, we threw pebbles into the pond, trailing our fingers in the water, Ella reassuring me with tales from colleagues at the hospital about recovery from cancer. In the dining room, we set the table with linen, gleaming cutlery and a silver vase of flowers dropping petals onto the tablecloth, as if we were celebrating.

I watched them eat and talk, but my mind returned to how

Carl had looked when I left him. He must be fine, or the hospital would have telephoned, I bargained, but I ought to have stayed. Tom's account of his behaviour at the Thompson's made Ella cry with laughter and Beatrice poured scorn upon every facet of Oliver's existence. I heard them, even enjoyed the words but struggled to force a smile.

After dinner, Tom went upstairs, and Ella and I walked out with Beatrice through the French windows onto the terrace. At last it was cool, and we breathed in deeply the smell of dry, parched earth. Ella leaned on the balustrade, sipping her wine, thoughtful. She had something more to say and I wondered whether Beatrice's presence would inhibit her.

'I don't know how you could have done it.'

I froze, was this about Dan? 'Done what, my darling?'

'Kept me a secret from my father's parents, from Euan's parents.'

I felt myself redden and my voice, when I found it, stammered with useless self-justification. 'It was never certain... I've never been quite sure you weren't Carl's child. Euan had little to do with his parents. Something had happened, a quarrel that was never resolved. We were his family and we thought–'

'I said you should have told her sooner,' Beatrice interrupted.

'So *she* knows.' Ella flicked a hostile glance at Beatrice. 'Everyone has been told except me.'

Her voice rose. 'Look at me, Mum, look at me, not through me or around me. How can you say you weren't certain? My height, my brown eyes, my dark hair... you're all fair and blue-eyed.'

'How long have you known?'

'All her life, most likely...'

'Shut up, Beatrice,' Ella snapped. 'It never felt right. I mean Carl has never tried to get close to me but sometimes, I saw him watching me. He's weird anyway and now we know he's an addict there is an explanation, but it made me question things when I was growing up.'

Beatrice interrupted again. 'I knew it even before the wedding.'

'I said shut up, Beatrice,' Ella shouted. 'I've had a DNA test, as have my grandparents. There's no doubt we're closely related.'

'You're right, Ella,' I said. 'Carl did know... he's always known and he's proud of you. You gave him something to live for, after Euan died.'

Ella narrowed her eyes. 'I don't believe he cares. He's not interested in us. You tried to pretend he did but it was all make-believe, all fantasy.'

'I said to her at the time it wasn't fair, what she was expecting of Carl...'

'For heaven's sake, Beatrice,' I turned on her. 'Was your way any better? Trying to go it alone, and hating your child?'

I sat down on the steps that led to the rose garden and rested my aching temples in my hands, the fingers spread wide to support the weight of my head. I could smell the heavy scent of rosehips. When I spoke, it was a whisper. 'Okay, it was a fantasy, you're right. For weeks I've thought of nothing else, how I could have managed things better. You've no idea how sharp the past becomes, when you might not have a future.'

Ella sat next to me, tucking her dress underneath her thighs. Her eyes shone in the light from the dining room windows. 'I've got two families now. I've visited my grandparents many times. I'm their only grandchild. They could have died without knowing me. That's what secrecy does.'

'Three grandparents in one month...'

This time, I ignored Beatrice. 'Yes, by not facing the truth, I kept something very precious from them, but I made a thoughtless assumption that Euan would have wanted me to keep his child away. Thank goodness they're still alive and you've met them.'

'They told me what happened with my father. Do you want to know?'

I didn't respond to Ella's question but stared at Beatrice before speaking. 'He was so bitter and funny about his parents and it all seemed terribly clever at the time. Of course, Carl was very similar. They were two lost boys, I suppose.'

Beatrice snorted, and I heard her mutter, 'Nothing lost about Carl...'

I leaned against Ella, shoulder to shoulder. 'Tell me about your grandparents... and your father's story.'

In the twilight I watched a moth dance around the security lights as Ella told me a simple and common tale of a clever, selfish child who had grown ashamed of his unglamorous parents.

'They're grateful to you by the way,' Ella added, 'for loving him, for deciding to have me, for asking them to his funeral. And they're needlessly ashamed, of course. You might think you and Carl have made a mess of things, but they've never been able to forgive themselves for allowing him to drift away. Then he died.'

'We loved him very much,' I whispered.

Ella's voice was hoarse and she didn't risk looking at me. 'Do you think he knew I was his?'

This wasn't a moment for honesty or doubt. 'Looking back,' I said, 'I'm sure he did.'

Against the cooling darkness, Ella nodded and wrapped her dress more tightly around her. 'Why did you marry Carl?' she asked. 'Couldn't you have married Euan?'

'That's the million-dollar question,' Beatrice interjected. 'Go on, Alice, tell us why. I've never understood.'

'Actually,' I glowered at Beatrice, 'that's the sort of question which doesn't have an answer, or at least there's been a different answer at different times. There was a moment on my wedding day, when Carl and I exchanged vows and I saw something on Euan's face...' My voice faded.

'Mum, what did you see?' Ella asked.

'It was nothing, probably just my imagination but I thought I saw regret. Come on, you two, let's go inside. I'm going to phone the hospital to check on Carl.'

THIRTY-TWO
FRIDAY, 3RD OCTOBER

S leep was impossible and after hours of trying I decided I no longer cared. I was going to be asleep for the whole day and hopefully most of the next, so why would one night make any difference? I had a whispered telephone conversation with Dan sometime after midnight. He was taking a great risk, telephoning from home with Sarah asleep upstairs but at the moment of the call, risk seemed fluid, something we could no longer grasp or understand. Under the covers, in the dark, I heard him speak of his love, that we belonged together. He railed against the indifference he experienced at home, made intolerable by his need to be with me.

I should have argued Sarah's case; they had a strong marriage, with just a little work they could put it right. Dismantling the human pyramid that had Dan and Sarah at its centre would require the conviction of a saint to cope with the consequences. Lying in my bed, in the netherworld of almost sleep, I knew this was the truth but instead I whispered words of encouragement. I wanted him and knew he would come.

The morning was still grey with remnants of night when I gave up and went downstairs. I sat in the library and watched the garden grow back from the shadows. Rabbits loped across the grass, sitting up to scent the air, always alert for danger. My mind felt blank, as if I had given up trying to manage a life that was as difficult to control as mercury. Today I would be ill.

At six, I heard Ella flush the toilet in her bathroom. I showered and dressed, checked my suitcase again, then looked in on Tom. He lay on his back, arms outstretched, his mouth open. I stroked back his hair and he turned over and muttered a few words that made no sense. I watched Ella eat breakfast, but we didn't speak. Her eyelids were swollen, and I guessed that she had tossed throughout the night as well.

We arrived early for my already early appointment. Ella left me at the main entrance to the hospital while she found a parking space. I walked with my small case along an endless corridor, avoiding breakfast trolleys smelling of egg and curdled milk. I waited for a lift and travelled three floors with a young doctor who carried a Bible in one pocket and a stethoscope in the other. On the ward, I was shown to my bed and was asked to undress and put on a hospital gown. I smiled shyly at another woman, already storing her few things in her bedside locker, and thought of Carl arriving at boarding school as a young child. It must have felt like this, his sense of abandonment, his old world left behind. Other women came, there were six of us in all, and our partners gradually arrived flushed from the outside, a world of traffic fumes and car parks. We nodded politely but spoke to our own families and only then in low and respectful murmurs.

A flutter of nurses at the door heralded Mr Wales's arrival, accompanied by a taller, younger man. I hardly recognised my surgeon in a dark suit with a fresh shave and brushed hair. He ought to exist only in a white coat, looking untidy and harassed.

'Mrs Williams, this is John Fleming, your anaesthetist.' We nodded to each other. Our passing acquaintance would require

John Fleming to keep me alive while Mr Wales ripped out my insides. I felt I ought to know him better.

'This is my eldest daughter, Ella.' Now we had all been introduced the party could begin.

'Ah, the new doctor.' Mr Wales put on his glasses to see her better. Ella stood up, folding her arms, her back straight, shifting her role from daughter to student.

'Interesting case,' he said. 'You won't see much of this in your working life, but they were ten a penny when I was at your stage of training. Screening has eliminated most late cancers, but your poor old mum's been unlucky. Not her fault.'

He looked at my notes, then back at Ella. 'Would you like to get scrubbed up and watch, if Mum doesn't mind?'

Ella sat down and took my hand. 'Can I, Mum? It might help you. I'll know exactly what's happened and be able to explain everything.'

These benefits seemed less obvious to me than they were to her, but I agreed. Her enthusiasm was infectious, and I felt proud for Euan's daughter, acknowledged at last.

The nurses and porters chatted as they wheeled me down to theatre. I think they talked about their break rota but already drowsy from the pre-med, I was flying on a carpet held aloft by distant voices and reassuring hands. I recognised Ella by her eyes and Mr Wales by his eyebrows, but John Fleming could have been anyone. A fuss around the back of my hand to find a vein, Ella's firm squeeze on my shoulder, the smell of sharp fear, a memory of the dentist. I tried to count to twenty. Black.

If I lie absolutely still, if I don't move, not a toe or a finger, I can stay like this forever. I am comfortable and warm, nothing hurts, nothing matters. I am swaddled, milky. My mother might come.

Ella's voice. 'I think she's still asleep. Is it usual to be asleep for so long?'

Another voice. 'If they're very tired. Has your mother had a lot on recently?'

I felt a tug on my hand. 'She's had a lot of stress, my dad's... her husband's ill and my brother's been in trouble.'

The voice again. 'Let her sleep. Why don't you go home for a bit? We'll call you when she wakes.'

Shut down, shut down.

Tom and Ella stand at the end of a long corridor. I look at them through a funnel. Concentric circles spiral down. They are tiny but in proportion.

Tom's voice. 'Hello, Mum.' I smell flowers.

Ella kisses my brow. I try to sit up, but my head is fixed. 'It's all over,' she said. 'The cancer is gone. You were brilliant.'

'I need a drink,' I whisper.

'Tom, ask the nurse... no, not that one. Go to the desk and ask for a drink. For God's sake, I'll do it. You talk to her.'

Tom's voice, whining. 'I don't know what to say. Anyway, she's asleep again. She's not listening.'

'She can hear you. Just talk.'

A smaller, cooler hand. Tom's smell. 'You okay?'

I nod. 'Mum nodded at me, Ella. I asked her a question and she nodded.'

Hard plastic in my mouth. Cool droplets drizzle down. I swallow. 'My throat hurts.' Somebody is crying. It sounds like me.

Shut down, shut down.

Carl and Euan are making love and I'm watching. I'm jealous of their tenderness. Euan's skin shines like polished beech. Carl smells of freshly sliced apple. I reach out and touch Euan's chest. He opens his eyes and smiles at me. I startle. Awake now. Someone wipes my brow and hands.

Ella's voice. 'Hello again.'

'Where's Tom?' I whisper.

'He's in the canteen. Fish and chips won I'm afraid.'

I try to stretch my lips into a smile. 'He doesn't need to stay. Neither of you need to stay. I'm not up to much.'

'We'll go once he's eaten. I visited Carl earlier and let him know that you're okay. We had a talk... about the daughter thing. Fran is coming home tomorrow. You're doing fine.'

'Thank you for staying with me.'

She kisses me, and I close my eyes. Silence.

I think it's very late because the ward is dim, and the curtains are drawn around my bed. Someone is stroking my hand. I turn my head and Dan is there. He puts a finger to his lips. My lower body is not yet mine, but I ease my torso towards him and he bends to rest his head on the pillow. Our brows touch. I sleep.

Their gentleness was a trick, a phoney war that masked the battle to come. Today was a new regime, one of tough love. The nurses were firm and doggedly cheerful as I was forced out of bed and made to walk around the ward. My internal wounds were repacked, a euphemism for torture and my dressings changed. I wanted to crawl back into my bed and disappear but was asked to sit in the chair next to my bed, shaking with pain and cold, until Mr Wales had done his ward round. Like a puppet, my arms were strung up with wires and tubes. Two bags trailed on the floor from under my grey and pink silk dressing gown, bought in Hong Kong. I watched them fill, the yellow one always winning over the brown. I didn't speak to the other women, corralled by our separate miseries. The television chattered like a parrot in the corner and I tried to watch, but the pictures made no sense. The hands of the clock moved to a different time frame. We were trapped in a parallel world.

Mr Wales frowned at me from the end of my bed and told me that the cancer had spread a little more widely than he had hoped. It had all been removed but I had lost more of my vagina than anticipated. Further tests would show whether the cancer had reached my lymphatic system. That was what mattered, he emphasised.

He seemed uncomfortable, keen to be away, as if this ward of female pain and bleeding was intolerable even to him, the surgeon who had cut us. I saw the same discomfort on the faces of the male visitors. The smell of women in distress, body effluent, breasts lolling in cheap nightdresses. This was no place for men. We wore no make-up, no lipstick and there was no bright welcome, only wild hair, and pale, unrecognisable faces.

I cried in my chair, breathless, juddering sobs and was allowed back into bed where I could be more discreet and not upset the others. I cried through Ella's visit with Fran, listening to Ella tell Fran across my recumbent body that Carl was not her father. Fran frowned but as a patient I was protected from any censure. I heard Fran say that she wished Carl wasn't her father either.

I tried to contribute. 'I should have left him, I'm so sorry.'

Ella gripped my knee and glowered at Fran. 'You did your best. You tried to keep everything together. That's more than he did.'

I was tired of hearing that I'd done my best. It sounded pathetic. I preferred Oliver's frank condemnation of my parenting. It was closer to how I felt myself.

I shook my head. 'In a family like ours, there's one who acts and one who pretends everything is normal. Both are guilty.'

The night shift. Around nine a nurse pulled the curtains around my bed and held my wrist to take my pulse.

'Your friend is outside,' she winked at me. 'I'll show him in, shall I?'

Every night Dan came, and I didn't ask how he explained his absence from home. I accepted that this was my time, not Sarah's. We spoke very little, just whispered. Dan stroked my hair, or my bare shoulder and I always slept before he left.

Each day brought new pain and more challenges from the nurses. I had to eat, I had to use the toilet on my own, I had to sit for longer in my chair, I had to walk to the day room, I had to dress, I had to wash my hair. Before I was ready, I had to go home. With disbelief I clung to the routine of the ward; home was outside, surely they couldn't send me away.

'The operation has been a success,' Ella rebuked me. 'This is the NHS and your bed is needed. If you stay any longer, you might catch something. You'll have exceptional care at home, so don't be so selfish.'

Cowed, I allowed Ella to push me in a wheelchair through my life in reverse, back down in the lift and through the long, dark corridor towards the hospital atrium. There were drifting bunches of metallic balloons held down by ribbon and bouquets of flowers in white, crimson, and yellow, wrapped in pink tissue. I could hear children crying and music from a miniature fairground ride. There was a pharmacy, coffee, newspapers and women in saris, men in shorts, other women all in black. I heard the chatter of languages I couldn't understand.

Ella weaved through the crowds and I was parked at the entrance, dazzled by the sunshine, amongst patients and staff having a smoke. A man without legs, just bandaged stumps of different lengths, drew heavily on his cigarette and winked at me. He turned his wheelchair to be more companionable, propping his cigarette between his lips, to use his hands to shift his drip closer to the chair.

'Off home, me duck?'

I nodded feeling as if my neck might snap.

'Can't go home yet, not me. Got to have the house altered. Council's made a start but could be weeks.'

I frowned with what I hoped might pass for sympathy. The sun burnt my skin and the smell of traffic exhaust was choking. Ella drew up in her car and helped me out of my wheelchair, supporting my elbow as I made tiny, geisha steps towards the passenger door.

'Good luck,' my companion called out. I waved farewell, not regally I hoped, but with compassion.

THIRTY-THREE

TUESDAY 7TH OCTOBER

Ella has allowed me to sit outside in the shade with my feet elevated on a padded garden seat, a drink and magazine by my side. The month's heatwave continues but storms are forecast. My mobile phone rests close to the magazine, so that I can reach Ella inside the house if I feel unwell. I've tried to text Dan, but my fingers don't work properly. All I can do is watch the sparse leaves above me and the occasional bird flit between the branches. Beatrice sat at my side in another garden chair, her head nodding on her chest, and Honey has squeezed into the shade underneath the seat, too hot to be outside but unwilling to waste a moment of being close to me.

A helicopter flew low over the house, its blades chopping at the electric-blue sky. I have rehearsed this moment many times, in a dream where I stand alone in a summer field, the sky a brilliant blue, the air heavy and still with just a wisp of feathered cloud. The field has been cut, so in my dream landscape, it must be August. From a distance, the sound of a small aeroplane begins to form, droning like a bee behind glass. The sound builds, and I shade my eyes to watch its progress above me. There is always a vapour trail, flowing tightly at first and then fanning out across the sky. When the plane has almost traversed my section of sky, the engine stops. The absence of sound heralds the moment the plane tumbles from the sky. A black plume of smoke rises from the earth, but there is still no sound. I always wake at this point, glad to have been dreaming.

I lifted my hand to shield my eyes and saw the company logo on the tail. There was a space and the number 1, which meant that it was Carl's private helicopter, only ever piloted by Carl himself. Today, whatever happens will not be a dream.

'Look, Beatrice.' I woke my mother-in-law. 'It's Carl... up there!'

Startled, she lifted her head and blinked, eyes darting around the garden. 'Where is he, I can't see him.'

'No, he's up there,' I repeated, pointing at the sky. 'That's his helicopter.'

Beatrice shaded her eyes. 'Must be someone else. They'd never let him out, especially not to fly.'

We tracked the helicopter thudding across the sky above our heads, thrashing the dry treetops. It circled the house twice then hovered, whipping eddies of fallen leaves and mown grass around our chairs. Once it had passed beyond the trees, the helicopter became invisible, but we could still hear the engine.

I waited, without fear, for what I knew would come next. I could see nothing beyond the high walls which enclosed the garden, so I lay quite still with my hands folded on my lap, listening for the silence.

Another fifteen minutes passed before we heard the sirens and then the phone rang. It sounded twenty times before Ella answered but I knew they wouldn't ring off. Beatrice lifted her head from her doze. 'What's happening? Why doesn't someone answer that?'

'It's okay, Ella's got it. We'll know soon.'

'Know what?'

'Beatrice, just wait.'

Fran and Tom were swimming in the outdoor pool and I could hear their voices echoing and the splash of water against tiles. I could have called them over, asked them to walk across the fields to see what was happening, but they shouldn't have to witness how the dream ends.

Ella strode towards us, frowning and handed me the receiver.

'It's the hospital, they'll only speak to you.'

The nurse sounded breathless, as if she had been running. 'We should have let you know sooner,' she apologised. 'Mr Williams checked himself out over an hour ago. Has he turned up at home?'

'No, he's not here,' I said. 'Is there any risk to us?'

'Let us know if he makes contact,' she replied. 'He hasn't taken his medication for at least twelve hours. He's not likely to be a danger but you still need to be careful. We've informed the police.' She talks on but I'm listening for other sounds.

When I told her the news, Ella sounded angry and afraid. 'He's discharged himself! That's awful... what if he does come here? We should get away.'

I shook my head. 'He won't... he's just flown over the garden in the helicopter. I think I know what he's done.'

The buzzer sounded for the gates. We froze, our eyes seeking reassurance from each other. Was I wrong to have credited Carl with a final, generous act? Ella ran inside to speak to the intercom.

'Is it the police?' Beatrice shouted, as Ella hurried back across the lawn.

'It's a motorcycle courier,' Ella said, bending at the waist and panting. 'He's waiting at the gate with an urgent letter for you, Mum. Shall I let him in?'

Ella brought the courier through the garden and he removed

his helmet, wiping his hands across his face. His red hair was wet with sweat, there were flecks of ash on his shoulders. He smelled of burning.

We heard more sirens, louder and more urgent, and Tom and Fran climbed out of the pool. They sat at our feet, wrapped in towels.

'What's happening? What's all the noise about?' Tom asked, screwing up his eyes against the sun.

'Terrible accident just up the road,' the courier said. 'A helicopter's come down in a field. The fire engines have just arrived... four of them. The police are setting up roadblocks. Don't know how I'll get back.'

I took the envelope from his hand and recognised Carl's scratchy handwriting. I placed it on the table, on top of the magazine. There was no rush.

'When did you get this?' I asked.

'Mr Williams called as soon as we opened this morning. I was at the hospital by...' he hesitated, looking at his watch, 'must have been ten o'clock.'

'Did he... did you take it from him yourself?'

'Yeah, he was in reception, waiting for me.'

I wanted to keep him here, this man who had been the last to touch Carl's living hands.

'Would you like a drink?' I asked.

Ella brought the man some iced water and we talked about different routes back to Leicester. I noticed him rub his reddened eyelids, already irritated by the smoke. 'Do you need to wash your face before you go?'

The courier shook his head and passed me his empty glass. 'I'd best get on.'

'How was Mr Williams, when you spoke to him?'

'Brilliant. Made me promise to get the letter to you by

eleven and gave me a bloody good tip. When you see him, tell him I delivered it before eleven. I'd like to keep his business.'

He pushed the helmet down on his head and adjusted the strap. 'Those poor buggers in the helicopter, makes you think, don't it?'

I heard his motorcycle roar away through the open gates and when Ella returned from checking they were secure, she stood over me, casting a shadow across my face. 'I'll ring the police and find out what's happening,' she said, passing me Carl's letter. 'We'll leave you alone for a while. Come on, you three, there's jobs to do in the house.'

Waking to another empty, fruitless day, Carl had taken control. There was no letter, only two documents. The first was a copy of a new will, signed yesterday and witnessed by a nurse. The legal firm on the letterhead was unknown to me. I scanned the document; the business was mine, to handle as I saw fit, the debts as well as the profits. Anything left from the sale of all our properties was mine too, but with small bequests to the children. Tom's money was to be held in trust until he was twenty-five. I had been given complete control over all Carl's affairs, for as long as was needed. Attached was a list of all his accounts, with passwords.

A smell of burnt engine oil drifted from the site of the crash but otherwise there was silence. Ella approached, followed by two police officers, a man and a woman. She brought another chair, so that they could sit by my side. I saw their eyes scan the pool, the fading borders, the rose garden, the private wood through a gate in the wall.

'My mother is post-operative,' Ella said, her voice clear and firm. 'Please don't tire her with questions. I'll be in the house, if you need me.'

'Mrs Williams,' the female officer spoke first. 'A helicopter has crashed in the field next to your house. I'm sorry to say that we believe...'

'Yes,' I said. 'I know. My husband Carl was the pilot. I'm sure he must be dead.'

'You know?' The male officer spoke, his voice unnaturally high. 'Were you aware of his plan?'

'Of course not,' I said. 'When I saw the company helicopter fly over, I guessed what would happen next. My husband was at the end of his life and the last thing he wanted was a death that was...'

'Going to be painful?'

I shook my head. 'No, not that. Carl could not have borne a death that was ordinary.'

THIRTY-FOUR
DECEMBER 2021

The station was quiet, even on a Sunday morning, three weeks before Christmas. We were coming to the end of the coronavirus epidemic but people still avoided travel on the Underground. I bought my ticket and nodded to the guards at the turnstiles. On the escalator a draught of warm air surged upwards and I recalled the sound of buskers, at first distant, fluting like fairy magic, then louder and louder until their music bounced off the ceramic wall tiles. They will come back.

I measured my journey from the bottom of the escalator by counting posters. Our latest advert promoted the new offices in east London and I paused to look, remembering how Ella had persuaded me to focus on the regeneration opportunities following the Olympic Games, now nine years ago. Dan helped me rescue whatever could be saved from CU.com and we built our solid little property business from what remained. There was nothing to fear from Oliver; like the house and everything else, he disappeared.

I turned left onto the platform and walked along its full length to the tunnel. No one else waited and I shivered, looking around, keen for some company. I studied the Underground map on the wall and read an advert for a children's Christmas party at the Tower of London, wondering if Fran and Jack would allow me to take Helena, my granddaughter. When was it that vending machines selling chocolate were removed from the Underground? It was the kind of dismal, foggy morning where chocolate would have done nicely.

A woman appeared through the entrance and shuffled along the platform towards me swaying like a pendulum, a bag in each hand. She stood close by and I smiled at her beneath my mask, pleased to be with another human being. A gust of hot air smelling of dust and fuel signalled an approaching train. Lights grew in the opposite tunnel and a train juddered towards us, pulling bright, empty carriages. The mice on the tracks scurried away and I thought I'd tell Helena about them when I got to Fran's. Maybe I would make up a new story for her, *The Underground Mice*.

The woman sat opposite me. Her cheeks were glazed with high colour and fine red veins and she wore a man's brown overcoat over a floral summer dress that reached to mid-calf. She placed one bag beside her on each seat so that our feet weren't crushed, and I could see they were full of clothes and shoes. Her grey hair was parted in the middle and pinned back by grips. She studied the gifts I carried, pushing out beyond the handles of my bag, one for Helena and one for the new baby, wrapped in green and gold Christmas paper, with co-ordinating ribbons.

'Visiting family?' she asked, pulling down her mask.

'My daughter's just had a baby, a boy. They already have a little girl.'

She sighed and nodded at the presents. 'Kids have too much of everything these days if you ask me. I had six kids, stillborn twin boys and the other four all grown up now. Don't see much of them. Daughters are what you want, especially as you get older, but you never give up on sons, not if you're a mother.'

I decided to leave my mask in place, since I was visiting a new baby, and tried to make sure my eyes twinkled above the rim. 'No, never,' I agreed. 'I'm so sorry about your babies.'

She shrugged and looked at my left hand. 'No husband then?'

'He died over thirteen years ago. The newspapers said he was the first victim of the financial crash of 2008. It wasn't true.'

'I've had three. The first was an alcoholic, the second gambled, the third died of cancer, five years ago. I'm not good at picking them, am I?' Her shoulders shook with laughter, but she made no sound. Her smile revealed teeth that were white and even.

I still have a tendency to overshare with strangers. 'My husband was a drug addict,' I said. 'He killed himself.'

She nodded. 'You're better off without. Not met anyone else?'

'I have a partner, but we're not married. We've got five adult children and four grandchildren between us.'

We fell silent, absorbed by the rattle of the train, rocking from side to side between stops. Dan's girls had refused any contact with him for five years, but once Lizzie relented, Emma quickly followed. Sarah will always hate me. Dan missed his family so much, there were times when I couldn't bear to see his pain. Tom hated him, more than I thought possible, refusing to stay in the same room as Dan or if forced to remain, mocking everything he said. Tom never settled at the two schools we tried, resenting more than Fran and Ella the loss of the trappings of wealth. Far too often, we didn't know where he was.

My new friend lifted her head from what looked like a doze and asked, 'You live in London or just visiting?'

'Just visiting. We live in Oxford, near my mother-in-law. My son went to live with her once he was sixteen. She home tutored him and he passed enough exams to do a course in health and social care at a local college. He was happily working in care homes but since Covid, he's looked after his grandmother full-time. She has Alzheimer's.'

She nodded and said, 'He sounds like a good lad, the best.'

'He is,' I agreed.

With a nod of her head to left and right, she indicated the empty seats around us. 'I thought you must be a local. Tourists aren't using the Tube now, nor most Londoners. It's only when you get to our age, you don't really care, do you? You've had your life, so you take the risk.'

My vanity was shaken. Are we really of similar age? I'm sixty-two this year but I still feel young. She must see something in me I don't recognise in myself. I am a grandmother, officially elderly, but I've survived cancer and there is still so much to live for. I haven't had my life at all.

'Do you live in London?' I asked, wondering where she could be going, with everything she owned in these bags.

She reached into her roomy handbag and pulled out a bottle of vodka, almost empty. 'Off and on. I travel around. Got a bit of a problem with this, you see. I sleep in hostels or visit my daughters, but they don't want me around for too long. Their husbands are too posh.' She laughed again then sighed, dragging her large hand across her hair. 'Ah, me.'

We travelled on in silence and I imagined her respectable, suburban daughters coping with their drunk of a mother. It would be unfair to boast about my own two daughters, Ella a consultant gynaecologist, and Fran running our business almost single-handedly.

The train ground on, steadily gathering passengers. Her head dropped forward and I guessed she must be sleeping again. At the next station, before I left the train, we touched elbows and wished each other luck. I emerged into daylight and bending my head against the chill wind, searched in my bag for hand sanitiser. Only when confident my hands were clean, I drew my hood over my hair and strode through streets of terraced houses towards the enveloping warmth of my daughter's home.

THE END

ALSO BY ISOBEL ROSS

WRITING AS MORAG EDWARDS

The Jacobite's Wife

The Jacobites' Plight

ACKNOWLEDGEMENTS

As a very early draft, this novel was presented as my dissertation for an MA in Creative Writing at the University of Manchester's Centre for New Writing. I would like to thank the students from my year group, as well as my tutors, for their invaluable contribution in shaping this novel.

Crash has gone through multiple revisions, titles and editorial reviews and has been left in a virtual drawer for years, only to be revived again to face further editing and submissions. I would like to thank the Cheshire Novel Prize for their succinct and focused critique of two early chapters, after which the first chapter was binned, and my friends and colleagues at Leicester Writers' Club for their consistently generous and constructive comments.

I am indebted to my wonderful publisher Bloodhound Books for recognising the worth of *Crash*, in particular Betsy Reavley, Director and Founder, for agreeing to bring this novel to life. The hard work, enthusiasm, and patience of the team at Bloodhound Books has been essential in bringing *Crash* to readers, including Shirley Khan, Editor; Abbie Rutherford, Editor and Proofreader; Tara Lyons, Editorial and Production Manager; and Hannah Deuce, Senior Marketing Manager. A heartfelt thank you to you all.

ABOUT THE AUTHOR

Isobel Ross was born to Scottish parents on a farm in Northumberland, just inside the English border. Although her family made many moves during her childhood, Isobel was educated in Scotland at a co-ed boarding school and St Andrews University. She has lived for most of her adult life in the East Midlands.

Isobel spent the majority of her working years as an educational psychologist but has always written fiction in the corners of her life. She attended many classes, workshops and writing groups to improve her craft and has been a long-term member of Leicester Writers' Club. *Crash* is Isobel's debut novel in the genre of domestic suspense, but she has also written a memoir, *Almost Boys: The Psychology of Co-Ed Boarding in the 1960s*. Isobel Ross writes historical fiction, also published by Bloodhound Books, under the author name Morag Edwards.

A NOTE FROM THE PUBLISHER

Thank you for reading this book. If you enjoyed it please do consider leaving a review on Amazon to help others find it too.

We hate typos. All of our books have been rigorously edited and proofread, but sometimes mistakes do slip through. If you have spotted a typo, please do let us know and we can get it amended within hours.

info@bloodhoundbooks.com